JUN 1 7

Losing
GABRIEL

You'll want to read these inspiring titles by

Lurlene McDaniel

ANGELS IN PINK
Kathleen's Story • Raina's Story • Holly's Story

ONE LAST WISH NOVELS
Mourning Song • A Time to Die • Mother, Help Me Live
Someone Dies, Someone Lives • Sixteen and Dying
Let Him Live • The Legacy: Making Wishes Come True
Please Don't Die • She Died Too Young
All the Days of Her Life • A Season for Goodbye
Reach for Tomorrow

OTHER OMNIBUS EDITIONS
Keep Me in Your Heart: Three Novels
True Love: Three Novels
The End of Forever • Always and Forever
The Angels Trilogy
As Long As We Both Shall Live • Journey of Hope
One Last Wish: Three Novels

OTHER FICTION
Somebody's Baby • Losing Gabriel
The Year of Luminous Love • The Year of Chasing Dreams
Wishes and Dreams (a Year of Luminous Love digital original short story)
Red Heart Tattoo • Reaching Through Time • Heart to Heart • Breathless
Hit and Run • Prey • Briana's Gift • Letting Go of Lisa • The Time Capsule
Garden of Angels • A Rose for Melinda • Telling Christina Goodbye
How Do I Love Thee: Three Stories • To Live Again
Angel of Mercy • Angel of Hope • Starry, Starry Night: Three Holiday Stories
The Girl Death Left Behind • Angels Watching Over Me • Lifted Up by Angels
For Better, For Worse, Forever • Until Angels Close My Eyes
Till Death Do Us Part • I'll Be Seeing You • Saving Jessica
Don't Die, My Love • Too Young to Die
Goodbye Doesn't Mean Forever • Somewhere Between Life and Death
Time to Let Go • Now I Lay Me Down to Sleep
When Happily Ever After Ends • Baby Alicia Is Dying

From every ending comes a new beginning. . . .

Losing GABRIEL

A LOVE STORY

LURLENE McDANIEL

EMBER

Text copyright © 2016 by Lurlene McDaniel
Cover art copyright: front cover photo © 2016 by Shutterstock/JuJik;
back cover photo © 2016 by Shutterstock/Jan Faukner

All rights reserved. Published in the United States by Ember, an imprint of Random House Children's Books, a division of Penguin Random House LLC, New York. Originally published in hardcover in the United States by Delacorte Press, an imprint of Random House Children's Books, New York, in 2016.

Ember and the E colophon are registered trademarks of Penguin Random House LLC.

Visit us on the Web! randomhouseteens.com

Educators and librarians, for a variety of teaching tools,
visit us at RHTeachersLibrarians.com

The Library of Congress has cataloged the hardcover edition of this work as follows:
Names: McDaniel, Lurlene, author.
Title: Losing Gabriel : a love story / Lurlene McDaniel.
Description: New York : Delacorte Press, [2016] | Summary: When baby Gabriel's health takes a turn for the worse, the lives of those involved are forever changed.
Identifiers: LCCN 2015014174 | ISBN 978-0-385-74421-8 (hardcover) |
ISBN 978-0-375-99155-4 (library binding) | ISBN 978-0-385-38399-8 (ebook)
Subjects: LCSH: Nursing students—Juvenile fiction. | Unmarried mothers—Juvenile fiction. | Unmarried fathers—Juvenile fiction. | Premature infants—Juvenile fiction. | Interpersonal relations—Juvenile fiction. | Grief—Juvenile fiction. | CYAC: Nurses—Fiction. | Mother and child—Fiction. | Fathers and sons—Fiction. | Premature babies—Fiction. | Babies—Fiction. | Interpersonal relations—Fiction. | Grief—Fiction. | Love—Fiction.
Classification: LCC PZ7.M4784172 Lo 2016 | DDC 813.54—dc23

ISBN 978-0-385-74422-5 (tr. pbk.)

Printed in the United States of America
10 9 8 7 6 5 4 3 2 1
First Ember Edition 2017

This book is dedicated to Gabriel—

the baby promised through adoption

but never delivered into our family's waiting arms.

I pray that you are well and happy and loved wherever you are.

And yes, another baby boy came to fill our arms and hearts.

ALONG THE ROAD

I walked a mile with Pleasure;

She chattered all the way,

But left me none the wiser

For all she had to say.

I walked a mile with Sorrow

And ne're a word said she;

But oh, the things I learned from her

When Sorrow walked with me!

ROBERT BROWNING HAMILTON (1812–1889)

CONTENTS

PART I   1

PART II   125

PART III   275

PART I

CHAPTER 1

When Alana Kennedy was thirteen, her beautiful cousin, Arie Winslow, tragically died from the leukemia that had stalked her most of her life. Arie was twenty-one, too young to die, but there was nothing her doctors could do to save her. Relatives rallied around Arie, promising to be at her side every minute of her last days to bring whatever comfort they could. Alana—Lani to all—and her mother, Jane, a teacher at Windemere Elementary, were on the schedule twice a week. Lani's sister, Melody, was away at Vanderbilt Law School but kept in constant touch and came home to visit whenever time permitted.

At first Lani balked, not wanting to become part of a vigil on what she called Arie's "death watch." What thirteen-year-old kid would?

"It's what we can do to help," Jane told her. "It's a way to express our love. Please just trust me, honey. You'll be sorry if you check out of coming with me."

So no matter how much it hurt to watch Arie waste away, Lani went. Through the last weeks of her cousin's life, Lani read to her, combed tangles out of her hair, soothed her dry, cracked lips with ice chips and moisturizing salves, and spoon-fed her bites of ice cream that numbed painful mouth sores. Lani was at Arie's bedside on the spring night when Arie's beautiful spirit drifted away, with her loved ones touching and whispering goodbyes.

But *knowing* the inevitable and *witnessing* it were two un-related things for Lani, and she had been inconsolable. She fell into such a depression that her parents grew worried, and when the school year ended, her dad bought her a horse, something she'd wanted since she was a little kid. The palomino, named Oro del Sol, was stabled at Bellmeade, Ciana Beauchamp Mer-cer's farm outside town. Lani rode Oro, groomed him, hugged his golden neck, and wept for the loss of one as lovely as Arie. The horse never seemed to mind her tears, standing patiently until her crying spell was over. And slowly, over those summer days between eighth and ninth grade, Lani felt her heart heal-ing and her sense of loss lessening. And through the experi-ence of helping and losing Arie, Lani found something she had never expected.

She found purpose. She decided that she would become a nurse. Jane had hugged Lani, saying, "Something good often comes out of something bad." Her parents, always supportive, oozed with enthusiasm, just as they had when, at four, Lani had told them she wanted to become a mermaid. Lani thought that discovering she wanted to become a nurse was a poor trade-off for Arie's dying, but she kept it to herself.

She began her senior year three years later in a steamy Au-gust heat wave with a mix of new and former students, many displaced from area schools trashed during a tornado. And although the storm had leveled sections of the town and surrounding farmland, Windemere's old brick school building had escaped the vicious winds unscathed. Go figure.

That August another kind of heat hit Lani smack in her heart, when Dawson Berke transferred in as a senior. He was tall and lean, with a shock of straight dark hair spilling across his forehead and eyes the color of rich dark chocolate. She later learned he'd moved with his father, a physician, from Baltimore, a city far from the lazy, hazy rural world of middle Tennessee. His height made him easy to see in the halls, and his body language made him easy to read. He wore anger like a suit of armor. It was obvious to Lani he didn't want to be there. She'd worn the same defensive armor after Arie's death when nosy friends asked impossibly dumb questions with no answers.

"How are you?" (I'm terrible! How do you expect me to be?) and *"Don't you miss Arie? Her funeral was too sad. I cried for days!"* (Hey, it's not about YOU!) and *"Let's build a memorial for her at school."* (No! Why would I want to look at a memorial of dead flowers and stuffed animals? My cousin's gone forever!)

Lani felt sorry for Dawson, recognizing he'd been ripped from one world and dropped into this one, a world far different from the one he'd left. She'd grown up in Windemere, never traveling farther west than Nashville, nor farther south than Birmingham, and she knew she wouldn't have been happy if it had happened to her.

Lani's gaze somehow found him in the crowded halls like a compass needle locating north. Each time, she quickly turned away, hoping he never caught her staring at him like a doe-eyed calf. Lani might have been a good student, a hard worker full of school spirit and friendly to all, but she wasn't one of the school's elite. *She* would never register on Dawson Berke's radar. The pretty, popular girls would flirt and charm their way through his armor and change his attitude. Lani felt certain that *their* worlds, hers and Dawson's, would never collide.

She was wrong.

CHAPTER 2

Sloan Quentin was destined for greatness. At least, that was what she grew up telling herself. The fact that she was only now seventeen and trapped by circumstance in Windemere, Tennessee, living in a run-down trailer park with a single mother who drank and often "entertained" men, was beyond her control. Her circumstances might be cliché, but she was poised to shed present reality like a snake shed its skin because she held an ace—she was the lead singer in Jarred Tester's Southern rock garage band, and when they performed and she sang . . . well . . . *everyone* listened.

She started her senior year in the dog days of August, when the parched farm fields were being held hostage by lack of rain and the heat was so suffocating she could hardly breathe. She walked from the trailer park's roadside entrance, where the school bus had dropped her, to the trailer where she lived. As she went inside, she expected coolness from the AC unit. Instead, waves of warm, stale stagnant air swamped her. She hit the light switch. Nothing. She blinked in the gloom and realized that the electricity had been turned off. Again.

"Ma!" she shouted. No answer. Sloan swore. *How hard is it to keep the electric bill paid?* But Sloan already knew the answer. Her mother, LaDonna, was "between male friends," and her government subsidy check wouldn't come for another week. LaDonna kept a part-time job in the hair and nail salon, but her earnings and tips went mostly for incidentals, like vodka.

Sloan dug in her backpack for her cell phone and punched in LaDonna's number, knowing that their cells would work because LaDonna always kept the cell service paid. What if a new man tried to reach her? When LaDonna picked up, Sloan blurted, "We don't have any electricity."

"I'm working to fix that."

"It's hot as hell in here!"

"Electric company's giving me a hard time. They want last month's bill paid too. I don't have that kind of money!"

"What about *me, your child*? I'm sweating to death."

"Go outside. Go see a friend."

"How? You have the car!"

"Get off my back! I'm busy."

Sloan bit back a flood of angry words. Swearing at her mother would get her nowhere. Never had. "Don't you get it? I'm hot and stranded." She kept her comeback brief, her tone brittle.

"Customer. Gotta go." LaDonna hung up.

Sloan squeezed her phone hard and screamed in frustration, but with no one to hear her but the trailer walls and a sink full of dirty dishes, what good did it do? Once she turned eighteen in June, she would leave for good with Jarred and the band like they planned. She just had to hang on until then.

Jarred Tester had started the band in the eighth grade with three friends—Bobby Henley playing bass guitar, Hal

Wehrenberg on drums, Calder Wells playing keyboard, and Jarred on lead guitar. Jarred wrote music and did some singing, but it wasn't until he added Sloan, with her take-no-prisoners voice that could hammer a rock song like an air gun or bend a ballad into soft summer smoke, that the band started getting noticed. They played everything from area parties to the county fair, and depending on their audience, Anarchy could shift from classic rock to edgy metal because of Sloan's voice. She also played acoustic guitar, but her voice was her true instrument. And she saw the band as her ticket out.

She called Jarred. "Can you come get me?"

"Now? I'm in the zone, baby, writing new stuff."

"Ma didn't pay the electric bill. I'm dying out here. What if I go hoarse?" He was silent while she stewed. Whenever Jarred wanted togetherness—sex—*nothing* stood in the way. Their almost-three-year hookup was volatile, a roller-coaster ride of hormones and musical chemistry. She had fallen hard for Jarred, never wanting to be like her mother, who lurched from one pathetic loser to another. LaDonna was an embarrassment. Sloan and Jarred were a team. A couple. And the band was her future.

"I got a new song I want to fly past you." Although it wasn't exactly true, she knew it would get his attention. "Come on! Just get me out of here."

He remained silent, obviously thinking it over. "I guess we could go over some things before our Labor Day show."

It wasn't exactly *their* show. The town's picnic, horse show, and softball tourney at the fairgrounds was an annual event. Sloan had no horse and hated softball, but once the sun set, bands and singing groups would take to a platform stage. Most were local, from area churches, "band wannabes," according to

Jarred, but some came from Murfreesboro and Nashville because the picnic brought in big crowds.

"Give me twenty and be waiting out by the road," he said, sounding put out.

She wanted to scream at him but again held back. If she pissed him off, he wouldn't come at all. She hung up feeling like excess baggage, dismissed by her mother, dragged curbside by her boyfriend. Sloan picked up her guitar case, swearing to herself that once she was rich and famous, no one would *ever* tell her what she could and couldn't do!

CHAPTER 3

Dawson Berke was pissed, gut-level angry over the turn his life had taken. This wasn't how his senior year was supposed to be. His father had no right, *no right*, to drag him halfway across the country to this backwater town, taking him from his friends, his girlfriend, his school, his lifelong home in Baltimore.

Sweat poured off his skin as he ran along the gravel shoulder of the rural Tennessee road. He'd already run five miles, and he wasn't the least bit winded, a by-product, he figured, of pent-up fury.

Months before, Dawson had come home from school to the sight of his dad, Franklin, sitting at the kitchen bar. His dad never came home in the middle of the day. Alarmed, Dawson dropped his book bag. "What's up? What's going on?"

Franklin had looked into Dawson's eyes and without preamble said, "I quit the practice today. Told the partners I've taken a new job. Today was my last day."

"*What?* Are you kidding? Why?"

Dr. Franklin Berke was a partner in one of the busiest

pediatric medical offices in the area. Dawson had never known his father when he wasn't helping and healing kids. Over the years, such emergency calls frequently trashed the Berke family's own plans. Perils of being a doctor, one Dawson often resented while growing up. Yet now his dad had called it quits! Turned out he'd only quit in Maryland.

"A former colleague, a doctor, contacted me a few months ago. He's at a small hospital in Tennessee and it's rebuilding. He needs someone to head up their pediatrics department. He thought of me. Maybe you remember that tornado hitting middle Tennessee last year? Blasted the town of Windemere, lots of devastation."

Dawson stood dumbstruck and unable to move under the weight of his father's words. And their implication.

Franklin waved his hand. "No matter. I put our house with a realtor yesterday. I told my friend we'd be there as soon as school's out."

Every word felt like rocks hitting Dawson. Hadn't their lives been enough of a nightmare during the last few years? When he'd been in seventh grade, ovarian cancer had finally claimed his mother, sucking her away after five years of suffering and fruitless treatment. Her funeral on a summer day was scarred across Dawson's memory, but he and his dad had picked up the pieces and carried on. Now he was facing another looming nightmare.

"We? What are you saying? We can't leave! I'll be a senior in the fall."

"I'm sorry, but we have to go, son. I've promised. The opening won't wait."

"B-but— My *senior year*. And what about the track team? They're counting on me!"

"Can't be helped. I'm sorry. Please understand. You'll start at Windemere High in August. It's a decent school. You can go online—"

"I won't go! I'll be out of here next year. You can move then."

"I. *Can't*. Ever since Kathy—"

Dawson watched his father's expression twist with anguish and tears fill his eyes. Was his father going to *cry*? Dawson had never seen the man cry, not even at the funeral. Thirteen-year-old Dawson had cried like a baby, but not his dad. Franklin Berke was a fortress, a walled city. Seeing tears in his dad's eyes made arguments die. A wad of emotion logjammed his throat.

His dad gathered himself and said, "I see her in every corner of this house, in every piece of furniture we picked out together, in every shadow. I can't even sleep in our bed."

Dawson thought back to all the mornings he'd come downstairs and found his father on the sofa in the den. In the month before his mother's death, his dad had slept on a cot in their bedroom beside their bed so she'd be more comfortable and he'd be near if she needed him. Since his mother's death . . . *Too many nights, too many mornings of seeing him on the den's worn sofa,* he now realized. "Y-you never said . . . I never thought . . ."

"I should have told you, been more honest." Franklin cleared his throat. "But you were hurting too. I thought I needed to be strong for you. Well, I can't be strong anymore. I'm falling apart. I can't concentrate on my patients. I need a fresh start. We have to leave."

Dawson panicked. "Wait! I can rent a room from one of my friends. Tad has a ton of space in his house! His sister's in college. You can move and I'll come for Christmas. I know his parents will—"

"No," his dad said quietly. "I need you with me, Daw. You're all that's left of her. All that's left of her and me—of *us*."

"But it's not *fair*."

"Life rarely is. If it was, I'd still have my wife and you'd have your mother."

And that had settled the matter. At least for Dawson's father. No amount of pleading had changed his mind, and as soon as Baltimore's schools let out, Dawson had found himself in Windemere, Tennessee, stranded in Nowhereville, forced into a high school he hated, doomed to finish out his senior year in a place far from the life he'd always known. As if watching his mother die hadn't been hard enough, now he had to "die" from within, stuck in this sucky little redneck town in a part of the country his old friends called a "flyover state."

The only bright spot had been Coach Harrison's eager acceptance of Dawson onto Windemere's track team as a distance runner. Back home, Dawson had shone brightly in area meets. But around here, track wasn't football, so he doubted his track "career" would go anywhere.

Franklin had quickly bought a house to put down roots. The home was a two-story, completely refurbished and modernized in the older but most established part of the town. He bought it outright because real estate was much cheaper in Windemere than in Baltimore, where their former house in an excellent neighborhood had sold for a tidy sum. He quickly turned the basement into a large bedroom/game room for Dawson, who spent three weeks of July back home with Tad's family while the room was under construction. Franklin also bought him a car for his seventeenth birthday. But Dawson

14

saw his dad's generosity for what it was—bribery. He was trying to win Dawson's forgiveness for the move and turn this crap-hole town into instant "home." It wasn't working. He'd never see this place as *home*.

Dawson had been in classes two weeks, and track season wouldn't begin until March, but running kept him from going stir-crazy. After graduation, he would go to the college of his choice. He already had his dad's promise on that. Dawson vowed he would return to the northeast, where he'd start fresh, maybe pick up parts of his old life and friendships. He'd already lost the girl. She'd moved on to another.

Thinking about the girlfriend helped him remember the one girl who had caught his interest at Windemere High. She was pretty, and he often stole covert glances at her in the halls. He should ask Paulie about her. Paulie Richardson was the only guy Dawson had befriended. The dude was stoop shouldered, nerd smart, and largely ignored by others, which suited Dawson. He wanted others to leave him alone, wasn't about to try and fit in with a bunch of backwater kids he didn't want to know, or even *like*.

Paulie lived one street over from Dawson, had two game consoles, two televisions, and a gaming library that rivaled most game stores, along with an endless supply of Pop-Tarts and microwave pizzas. Paulie's parents worked and his grand-mother lived with them, but she never bothered Dawson or Paulie. Franklin worked mind-numbing hours in the new hospital—so much for father-son togetherness. Hanging with Paulie beat going into an empty house every day after school. It also led to dinner invitations that he always accepted because Paulie's grandmother was a great cook and she fixed supper most nights.

Dawson looked at his wrist pedometer. He'd come six miles into the countryside under a flat, heat-hazed blue sky, on a road flanked on both sides by red clay dirt and fields of farmland dry from relentless heat. Hot as hell and about as inviting. *God, I hate this place.* He turned and started back toward his car, which was parked on a turnout that farmers used to turn tractors around. He longed for the smell of the Chesapeake Bay, not too far from his old neighborhood.

Dawson steadied his breathing, concentrated on the sound of his shoes hitting asphalt, and wondered what Paulie's grandma was cooking for supper.

CHAPTER 4

"You want to watch the horse parade?" Paulie pointed toward the rodeo arena.

"Don't like horses unless they're under the hood of my car." Dawson crossed his arms, studying the platform stage at the Windemere Fairgrounds, where crowds were gathering for the Battle of the Bands at the Labor Day picnic. They had arrived midafternoon, eaten free barbeque, and hung around waiting for the music showdown. A softball game was happening in a far field, and a small carnival with rides and games for kids under ten was spilling out happy music in another field.

Dawson watched workers set up mikes, amps, speakers, and lights, and bands started to assemble in the area behind the stage. He was especially interested in Windemere's own Anarchy because posters hyping their performance were splashed on bulletin boards at school and on walls of buildings in the town square. He couldn't care less about a garage band, but the girl? Well, he'd seen her in the school corridors enough to know he wanted to see more of her.

She was dressed in biker-chick black leather, the skintight

pants lined with silver studs that glinted in the lights, and a form-fitting tee with a bright red heart. A black headband held back the tangle of her blond hair. He thought she looked delicious.

Dawson elbowed Paulie. "Tell me all you know about her."

"Sloan Quentin? Belongs to that guy tuning his guitar, Jarred Tester. Why you asking?"

The Jarred guy had long shaggy hair and a toned, muscular body. He wore a black muscle tank, low-slung ragged jeans, and motorcycle boots. One arm sported a straight row of arrowhead tats that traveled downward from the side of his neck to his wrist. Was the guy trying to be badass? Dawson wasn't impressed. "I like her looks. Might want to get personal with her."

Paulie shook his head. "Forget about it. They're joined at the hip. The whole band is just doing time until they graduate. They have a website and a Facebook page. Prowl her there."

Dawson made a mental note to check it out. "Joined at the hip, huh?"

"As well as other body parts. Besides, Sloan ain't your typical down-home girl." Dawson waited for Paulie to explain. "She's different, probably because she doesn't seem to care what other people think. Heard her cuss out a teacher once. We were in fourth grade. Five-day suspension, but what are they gonna do? Everybody grows up together in this town, and we all pass through the system together." He did an imitation of marching in lockstep formation.

"Joys of small-town life." Dawson grimaced. Back home his parents had sent him to public schools because they never wanted him to feel "entitled." Plus, in their area, the public schools were academically sound, racially diverse, and multicultural. He eyed the girl again.

18

Paulie followed his line of sight. "FYI, Sloan really has a set of pipes. She's an awesome singer. Feel free to look, but I wouldn't recommend touching."

"Why, because her boyfriend will kick my ass?"

"Naw, you can probably outrun him."

Dawson laughed. He slapped Paulie's back. "You're a funny guy."

Paulie seemed to bask in Dawson's approval. "Are you sure you don't want to go watch the horses? Pretty girls over there too. Most way more available than Sloan."

"Think I'll just stay here and get a good place near the stage. Looking's free."

Paulie shrugged. "Okay. I'll grab us some popcorn and Cokes. Back in a sec."

Dawson continued to watch Sloan. He had a whole school year in front of him. Maybe it was time to become more social and expand his interests. The small town still sucked, but jazzing up his social life might make his time in it bearable.

⁓

Sloan bounced on the balls of her feet, loosened her arms with a good shake. She was always on edge before she sang, but once the music started, jitters vanished and there was only the music and her immersion in it.

"Shit, that last bunch shouldn't have bothered to show up," Jarred said in Sloan's ear. "A bunch of losers."

"Be nice," Sloan said over her shoulder.

They waited while the other band cleared the stage to halfhearted applause. Sloan was ready to bolt as soon as the MC called them out. She watched the audience edging the platform in a rim of eager faces, many she recognized. The rest of the crowd visually fell off the edges and into the dark, with the upturned stage lights making it impossible to see beyond the fringe. She knew the crowd was big because she'd watched them begin to gather at dusk, jostling for a place close to the stage. The tall lanky dark-haired guy standing on the far right corner of the platform had been watching her all afternoon. The same one who'd been eyeing her at school. He always looked away, never made eye contact, but she knew he was looking. He was a person of interest.

"Crowd's huge," Bobby said, tuning his bass.

The band stood in a clump in the dark at the back of the platform stage, waiting for their call out. "Bigger the better," Jarred said. "Someday we'll fill a Super Bowl stadium. Hey, heard there's a few reps out there. We're going to hit it out of the park tonight. Play for keeps, guys."

Sloan's nerve endings tightened, wondering if the agent talk was true or just hype from Jarred. She wanted to believe it. If they performed well, if they landed an agent, if they got radio play . . . She pulled back from "what-ifs." *One performance at a time.*

Hal trotted onstage waving his sticks and settled behind the drums. Calder jogged to his keyboard. Bobby went next. The MC called, "Now put your hands together for Anarchy!"

The stage lights flashed. Hal began a fast rhythm on his snare. Jarred yelled, "Showtime!" then ran across the stage and started a guitar riff that Bobby joined. The crowd whistled, hooted. The music hit its crescendo and Sloan ran out, grabbed the mike, and hit the words of their opening number from deep in her throat. The crowd erupted. Their noise soaked into her, fueled her, blocked out everything except the driving beat of the music.

She strutted across the stage, dropped to her knees in front of the tall boy, leaned down, and sang straight to him. The crowd went crazy. Then she sprang to her feet, crossed to the other side, and repeated the moves to another stage hugger. Behind her Jarred sent his guitar into a blistering riff and shouted, "Way to go, baby! Pour it on!"

Sloan gave herself to the music. The amps trembled and wiped away all that was wrong about her life. Singing was what she'd been born to do!

Nothing was going to stand in the way of her doing it.

"She sang right to you, man. *To your face!*" Paulie jumped around Dawson like an overeager puppy in the school parking lot the next morning.

Dawson shrugged as if it hadn't mattered and said, "Showbiz. Plus, I was the tallest person at the corner of the stage." But he couldn't deny that he felt like a million bucks on the inside. Hundreds of people in the crowd and it had been him Sloan had singled out, returning time and again during the band's set to flirt openly with him. She had oozed sexiness with her looks and incredible voice.

"You weren't the only person standing there. She had her pick."

"She probably won't even recognize me today."

"So what? Everyone who was there last night *will.*"

Dawson hoped Sloan *would* take notice of him, even if her performance had been all for show. He wanted a shot at the girl. "Let's see if I'm standing in her line of vision at the end of the day."

"What if you are?" Paulie stopped at the threshold of the school's front doors. "You're not going to try and snake her from Jarred, are you?" Dawson gave a noncommittal shrug. "'Cause that would be suicide. He's a mean one, that Mr. Grinch."

Dawson went through the open door knowing all he wanted from Sloan today was an acknowledgment of his existence. He'd come up with a master plan later. Kids nodded and waved to Dawson as if they were friends.

"Told you," Paulie said out of the corner of his mouth. "You're the Man."

Dawson changed the subject. "Hey, you still got the second *War Games?*"

"Yeah."

"After school, then?"

"Great." Paulie beamed. "Grandma's making lasagna tonight."

"She makes damn fine lasagna." Dawson tapped him on the shoulder. "See you later."

Dawson continued down the hall to first period, hoping he'd run into Sloan, perhaps pass her. It didn't happen, and at lunchtime, he learned from one of the guys on his track team that Sloan and Jarred were no-shows for the day. He was disappointed. She was the only thing that had excited him in this pathetic town. A wave of homesickness washed over him. He missed his old friends and familiar classrooms, even teachers at his high school. His dad should have left well enough alone and worked out some way for Dawson to finish in Baltimore. Dawson scooped up his lunch tray and shoved it through the return window. Snagging the girl would be a distraction until he could split for good.

CHAPTER 5

"Come on! Why are you guys dragging? We've got four days to get it together!" Sloan shouted.

The others stopped playing, Jarred and Hal well behind the tempo of Bobby's bass and Calder's keyboard.

"Are you sayin' we suck?" Jarred asked in a slurry voice. "'Cause I don't think so-o-o."

They were practicing in Bobby's garage, the door raised to a show of oaks and maples aflame with autumn color. Coolness nipped the air. They were scheduled to perform during half-time on the football field that coming Friday night for homecoming, but today's rehearsal was a disaster.

Sloan spun, grabbing a fistful of Jarred's sweatshirt. "No, *we're* fine. It's you and Hal who can't keep up. What's wrong with you two, anyway?"

"Just feelin' mellow," Jarred said, drawing the word out in a slow drawl. He bobbed to one side, his eyes half closed. Hal made oinking sounds and Jarred doubled over laughing. Still holding his shirt, Sloan looked him in the face. He was beyond mellow.

He bowed elaborately. "I'm just happy, babe. You got something against being happy?"

"You've been smoking, haven't you? You know how that makes me crazy. What were you *thinking*?" Jarred and weed were never a good match. When he smoked, he was unpredictable; sometimes he turned hateful and harmful. She pushed him, propelling him backward into shelves of sports equipment. A skateboard clattered to the floor.

Jarred scowled. "Aw, come on, baby. It was just a couple of drags. Right, Hal?"

Hal saluted and the two of them melted into giggles.

"A couple of drags" wouldn't have affected Jarred this much. Sloan glared at him. "Why are you doing this? Four days, Jarred. That's all we've got!"

A furrow dug between his eyes as he tried to focus. "Stay off my case. You don't tell me what to do." Jarred pushed the skateboard into her ankle.

She winced when it hit the bone. She turned to Bobby. "Get me out of here."

Bobby put his guitar in its stand. "Yeah, better give it up for today."

"We quit when I say we quit," Jarred said. "I run this band, not you, Sloan. This is my band, not yours."

"We can't practice when you're wasted," she fired back.

"Wasted!" Jarred looked at Hal. "Not even close. Saturday night . . . yeah, we were wasted then." He and Hal snorted laughter.

"Unbelievable." So angry she was shaking, Sloan stalked out to the driveway and slung her guitar onto the backseat of Bobby's parked car. Performing at homecoming was a big deal to her, along with the dance in the gym afterward. She saw this as a way to repeat the buzz following their Labor Day performance. A way to flick the finger at the cliques of snotty girls who looked down on her. Because they did and had ever since grade school.

Bobby came alongside her. "We can do this tomorrow. I'll take control of their stash tonight."

Sloan fought for composure. "We have to nail this, Bobby. Getting this right is important to me. Why does Jarred pull this crap? I mean, weed before a run-through? I always thought we wanted the same thing, but now . . ."

"He doesn't smoke that much. Honest. He's nervous too. We all are. It's not like most jobs, when we're playing for strangers. This is our high school. Everybody we know will be there."

He'd expressed her concerns exactly. This show was different from even Labor Day. Homecoming was the litmus test, and if they bombed . . . Sloan shuddered just thinking about it.

"Come on, I'll take you home."

She was getting into Bobby's car when Jarred charged from the garage and took hold of Sloan's elbow. "Don't get all pissy on me, Sloan. I don't like you jacking me around in front of the guys and telling me what to do. You're my girlfriend, not my warden. I run this group and I make the rules."

His eyes now looked marble hard, the mellow high gone.

Sloan pried his fingers off her elbow. "Well, if you don't stop with the drugs, you're going to meet a real warden one day. We can't perform if you're sky-high. I didn't sign on to your band— or you—to fall on my face!"

"You're a bitch."

She ignored him and opened the car door, and Bobby stepped between them. "Hey, bro, just chill. Don't let my mom come home to find her garage smelling like a joint. She'll call the cops. I know my mom. Come on, man. Have some respect here."

A vein throbbed on the side of Jarred's neck with the tat, making it quiver. He and Sloan had a stare-down. Finally he stepped away. "Take the bitch home. Meet us at the Pizza Shak after you dump her. We'll wrap up here."

Bobby got into the driver's seat, started the engine, and looked over at Sloan. She sat with her hands fisted. "It'll be okay, Sloan. He'll cool down. Come right back to you."

She stared straight ahead, swallowing hard. Her and Jarred's physical fires had cooled. But so had their hours of working on original song lyrics, on tightening verses and melodies, and jamming with everyone to bring something special to a piece. The band played music from other bands for their gigs, but creating original material, getting it noticed, cutting demos, and passing them around was how musicians rose in the ranks. Jarred was music smart, a leader when he put his mind and heart into it. "He's not as serious about the band, not like he used to be," she said. "We need him to be a hundred percent if we're going places after we leave this hole."

"We all want the same thing," Bobby said. "He'll come back around. Wait and see."

They drove to the trailer park without another word.

―♪―

The gym was decorated in a 1980s theme. "Why the flashback?" Lani's friend Kathy Madison asked.

"Zombies, like Michael Jackson's 'Thriller,'" Lani said as they wove their way through the noisy milling throng of kids and toward the side of the gym where the bleachers had been pulled out for seating. The expansive oak floor gleamed in the lights of spinning disco balls hanging from overhead steel rafters. "Since homecoming is so close to Halloween, the committee thought it was a good idea." Lani had been on the committee and had spent the afternoon decorating the gym, barely making it home in time to change for the game and dance.

"Aren't zombies over?" Kathy climbed to the midsection of the bleachers, sat, and looked around the crowded floor. "Where *are* the zombies?"

"It's a surprise."

There was a commotion at the door, followed by a few whoops. No zombies entered, just the Anarchy band. Clusters of people parted to let them through. "They were good tonight." Kathy's eyes followed the band through the doors to the food table, usually forbidden on the lacquered oak floors, set on thick rubber mats. All food had to be eaten while standing on the mats. No exceptions. A ring of chaperones surrounded the area to enforce the rules. "I don't see Jarred."

Neither did Lani. All she saw was Sloan still dressed in black from her performance, her wild blond hair pulled into a ponytail tied with a black leather cord. Watching Sloan slice through the crowd made Lani regret wearing a brown hoodie with the grinning skull outlined in sequins. The outfit that had looked cute in her bedroom mirror now felt childish. Compared to Sloan, she looked like a kid playing dress-up— brown hair, brown eyes, brown clothing. She wasn't pretty, just ordinary, and she came in a plain brown wrapper.

"Sloan really thinks she's hot stuff." Kathy's gaze narrowed hatefully.

"But she is, Kathy." Lani said the words wistfully.

"Not to me." Kathy stared in anticipation as the gym's double doors were thrown open, but Jarred didn't come. "So where *is* Jarred? I'll bet Sloan said something to make him stay away because she hates sharing the spotlight. Look at everyone smiling at her. He's the *true* star of the band, not her."

Kathy's words reinforced Lani's long-held suspicion that Kathy seriously crushed on Jarred and his bad-boy vibe. Lani had never much liked Jarred. In middle school he'd been a notorious bully, especially to skinny, shy Paulie Richardson.

"Control your drool reflex, Kathy. I'm sure he'll show before the zombies do." Lani realized she shouldn't be needling Kathy because she knew what it felt like to carry a hopeless crush, like the one she carried for Dawson Berke. Just then, Lani spied Dawson leaning against a wall, his arms crossed, Paulie at his side. Her heart leaped, then fell with a thud. His gaze was zeroed in on Sloan.

Kathy noticed too, because she said, "Wow! Isn't that the guy she sang to on Labor Day? He looks like a cat ready to pounce. This might be better than the zombies. I'm getting closer to the action." Kathy started down the bleachers.

Lani decided to stay put but couldn't help wondering, *If Jarred doesn't come, what will Dawson do?* Her rational voice answered, *Make a move on Sloan, naturally.* She suddenly felt sad and deflated. Guys were so predictable.

CHAPTER 6

"Where *is* he?" Sloan got into Bobby's face.

"No idea. Said he wanted to get something from the car."

Sloan fidgeted, tugging at the tangled ends of her ponytail. Jarred was supposed to be there. They were a unit, the Anarchy Five. A reporter from the local paper was waiting for them, and Jarred had known about the prearranged interview. Sure, it was small-time, but they needed all the publicity they could get. "Stall the reporter. I'm going to look for him."

"Sloan, let me." Bobby held on to her wrist.

Sloan caught the panicked look on Bobby's face, went hot all over, and twisted from his grasp. "If he's out there smoking . . ." She let the sentence trail, menace in her tone. It felt like a rock had settled in the pit of her stomach. Without another word, she pushed through the crowd and jogged outside.

A full harvest moon lit the cold October night sky. Her breath came out in frosty puffs, making her shiver. She crossed to the packed parking lot and began to systematically tour the lines of cars, angry at herself because the band had arrived early with their equipment in two cars and she hadn't noticed where either had parked. She went up the rows, down the rows, searching for Jarred's old black Mustang, growing more irritated. What good was having a boyfriend who kept letting her down?

Moonlight glinted off tops of cars lightly filmed with frost that sparkled like diamond dust. Sloan's teeth chattered. Someday she'd go live where it was always warm. She was just about to turn back when she saw the Mustang. Windows of cars around Jarred's were clear and see-through. The Mustang's glass was covered with haze from the inside. She'd been right! He was out here getting high and with a reporter waiting in the gym for them. *The ass!* Sloan seized the passenger side door handle and jerked hard. The unlocked door flew open. "What the hell's the matter with you, Jarred?"

The haze wasn't smoke, but instead condensation from human breath. In the backseat Jarred lay panting on top of a girl, both pairs of their jeans shoved down to their ankles, their bare white skin gleaming with sweat. The blast of cold air brought Jarred upright and a scream from the girl. "Hey!" Jarred yelled, groping for his denim waistband and struggling to pull up his pants.

Sloan shot backward, the image of Jarred and the girl seared into her brain. This. Couldn't. Be. Happening. She turned and ran. Felt no cold. Saw no moon, no other cars, only the light pouring out of the gym. From far away she heard Jarred shouting her name; she was afraid she was about to heave. She made it inside. Bobby was standing just inside the door and caught

30

her, held her. "Sloan—" His words died when he looked into her face.

"You knew?"

Bobby's expression was a mask of regret but no denial.

She suddenly felt as if she were suffocating. "How long?"

Bobby said nothing.

"I asked *how long!*"

He shifted his gaze from hers. "A while."

A crowd had gathered in a semicircle behind him. Sloan threw up her hands and backed away from Bobby, the words *Guy Code* tumbling inside her head. "Don't touch me."

Bobby looked stricken. "Hey, please let me—"

Just then Jarred came up behind her, gasping for breath. "Sloan!"

She whirled, checking him from head to toe. "Good to see you got your pants up. How 'bout the girl in the car? She out there waiting for the big finish?"

He glanced at the circle of onlookers; then his eyes darted back to Sloan. "Let me explain."

She launched herself, attacking with fingernails to his face, scraping his cheek until it bled. "I hate you!"

He dodged more blows. The crowd edged closer, cheering on the fight, cell phones whipped out of pockets. "Let's go somewhere. Let's get out of here."

"We are *over!* You hear me? O-V-E-R. And I'm gone from your band too! I don't need you! I don't need any of you!" She threw the words at Bobby, Calder, and Hal, scrunched together behind her. "All of you can go to hell!"

"Sloan, stop it! We can fix this. She's nothing. She means *nothing.*"

She whirled to face Jarred, heard teachers and chaperones burrowing through the crowd, yelling, "Move back! Step aside. Break it up."

If the girl meant nothing, Sloan figured she must be worse than nothing. She made fists and attacked again. He ducked, tried to capture her pummeling fists, but she was too quick for him. *Nothing. Nothing.* The word rang in her ears like a litany. Suddenly she stopped swinging, stepped backward, and with a growl, placed a well-aimed kick hard into his crotch. He doubled over, sank to his knees, gagged, and cradled his junk. "You mean nothing to me!" Sloan shouted, pushed around him and darted into the night, running helter-skelter away from the crowd chanting, "Go! Go! Go!" and the unbelievable pain screaming inside her head and heart.

———

The zombies were anticlimactic. When they came into the gym stiff-legged and howling, people barely took notice. Everyone was still talking about Sloan and Jarred, often hunched together in small clusters over cell phones watching videos of the blowup. Lani felt sorry for the kids who'd gone to the trouble of turning themselves into the undead. Any other night they'd have been a smash hit. Just not this night.

"Bet there's ten videos up already," Kathy said, thumbing furiously through postings on her phone. She glanced up when Lani said nothing. "What? You were here in the bleachers, but I had a front-row seat, and it was awesome. As blowups go," Kathy amended when Lani just kept staring at her.

"I feel sorry for Sloan," Lani finally said. "I mean, he was cheating on her. She caught him at it."

Kathy rolled her eyes. "Well, I feel sorry for Jarred. She took him down in front of everyone! She didn't have to do that. She could have pounced on him in private. I think she did it for the publicity."

"Why would she do that? Who needs that kind of publicity? Her boyfriend is a cheating scumbag."

"I had no idea you and Sloan were so close." Kathy's voice held frost.

"You like Jarred and you like thinking he and Sloan are over," Lani countered. "It's not her making me feel sorry. It's *you* and all the others. Jarred got what he deserved!"

Kathy's face flamed red. "Yeah, I do like him. So what? I think he's cool and sexy and his band doesn't need Sloan Quentin. She's just trailer trash like her mother. My mom says so. Lots of people say so."

Her words stung because Lani had listened to other girls trash-talk Sloan, but she'd never spoken up about it, and she wasn't very proud of it either. A person couldn't help where she came from or what her family members did. "It's Sloan's voice that makes his band popular, you know."

"Tons of good singers in the world," Kathy threw back. "All he has to do is look for another girl singer. There's nothing so special about Sloan." Kathy wiggled her cell phone in Lani's face. "I'm going down to compare videos. *You* can do what you want."

Lani watched Kathy stomp down the metal bleachers and onto the gym floor, where teachers and chaperones were passing from group to group, urging kids to put away their cells and get back to the homecoming celebration. Lani pulled up her knees and rested her chin. She hadn't meant to have a fight with Kathy, but dumping the blowup all on Sloan wasn't fair.

She also revisited what she'd witnessed *after* Sloan had fled the gym. While onlookers were cheering, Lani watched Dawson say something to Paulie, grab his long coat, turn, and jog out into the night.

Like a knight in a medieval story or a childhood fairy tale, he was probably heading off to rescue Sloan Quentin. She had little doubt that he would succeed.

CHAPTER 7

Sloan ran until her burning lungs and a stitch in her side forced her to walk along the shoulder of the road leading away from the high school. Stadium lights had been turned off and there was only moonlight to guide her. *Get away, far away. . . .* She struggled to catch her breath, her throat fiery and raw. The night of her perceived triumph had turned into a night of horror and humiliation. People would definitely be talking about the band tonight. And Sloan Quentin's public meltdown would be topic One. *All Jarred's fault!* She'd known things between them had cooled, but to never have seen his betrayal coming . . . How could she have been so blind, so *stupid* to not have picked up on it?

She wiped away tears and began to feel the night air bite through her long-sleeved tee and skintight leather pants. With no jacket, she was freezing. She couldn't go back, though. How could she *ever* go back? She crossed her arms, shivering as night sounds settled around her. She heard a car come up behind her and the slow crunch of tires on gravel. The car pulled alongside her, and she quickened her pace. The car kept up with her. The passenger-side window glided down. A voice said, "Hey, need a lift?"

She didn't recognize the voice and didn't bother to look. "Get lost."

"Sloan . . . please, I'm a friend. I won't hurt you."

At the moment, she had no friends, but hearing him say her name made her stop. She turned and stooped to see the driver. "Who are you?"

The driver fumbled with the dome light. When it flashed on, she saw a familiar face but couldn't place it.

"Name's Dawson Berke. From school? I was the guy standing at the corner of the platform on Labor Day. You sang to me. Made my day."

Her memory shifted gears. *The guy who looks at me in the halls but never makes eye contact.* Now she recognized him. "What do you want?"

"You look frozen, and my car's warm." He leaned from his driver's seat and lifted the door handle, pushed open the door. "I just want to help."

She hesitated, weighed her options. She knew she couldn't walk all the way back to the trailer park in the cold; she dreaded returning there anyway. She climbed inside, hugging herself. Dawson turned up the car's heater to full blast, letting the car idle on the shoulder of the road. She held her numb hands to the vent. He turned off the dome light. Through the windshield, moonlight flooded the interior. As feeling returned to her hands, she eyed him warily. "Thanks."

Dawson watched her warm herself until her fingers stopped shaking. "What do you say we go get something to eat?"

"Whatever." All she wanted was to get far away from the gym and school.

He pulled onto the road and accelerated. She kept her gaze forward, buckling her seat belt when the car dinged a warning bell insistently.

"Any major food group appeal to you? A favorite place? Doesn't matter to me." He was pretty kicked about being close to Sloan after so many weeks of looking at her from afar. He'd been in the crowd on the sidelines in the gym and had watched the whole scene unfold. As soon as she'd split, he'd gone to his car and caught up to her walking alongside the road.

"Not the Pizza Shak. Anyplace else is okay."

"Couple of places over by the freeway. Chicken, chili, burgers, sandwiches, coffeehouse." He rattled off the fast-food eateries from memory. He knew them all because on the nights his dad was tied up at the hospital or when he didn't stay at Paulie's for supper, he ate at one of the franchises. "I know. Waffles! I like breakfast at night. How about you?"

Dawson's offer of food reminded her that she hadn't eaten before the concert. Performance jitters. "Okay."

The warmth of the car and Dawson's kindness were thawing Sloan from the outside in. She leaned against the headrest and closed her eyes, not wanting to think. Or to feel.

Minutes later, Dawson swung the car into the Waffle Palace parking lot. When they got out of the warm car, he pulled his long coat from the backseat and settled it over her shoulders. Once inside the brightly lit restaurant, he saw there were few customers, so they had their choice of seating. He guided her to a booth in a far back corner. The smell of frying bacon mingled with freshly brewed coffee and warm maple syrup. A waitress gave them a smile and a couple of menus. "Hey, y'all. Coffee?"

Dawson agreed for both of them as they slid into opposite

sides of the booth. Over coffee, they both ordered waffles. Sloan slumped against the faux-leather bench, stealing glances at her rescuer. He wasn't bad-looking, with tousled black hair and eyes so dark they looked black. The cold had given his cheeks a rosy glow. He was tall and lean, not muscular like Jarred— She straightened, irked at herself for making the comparison.

Dawson realized he'd have to do the heavy lifting when it came to conversation. She looked whipped, still pretty, but totally wiped out. He told her she had an amazing singing voice, watched her shrug off his praise. He fumbled for another topic and settled on asking, "You grow up in Windemere?" *Dumb question, Berke!*

"Born and raised. But you're not a local, are you?"

"What gave me away? Be honest."

For the first time, a smile flitted across her mouth. "You talk funny."

That made him smile. Everyone pegged him as an outsider. His accent was definitely not from Tennessee. He told her about moving from Baltimore when his dad took a new job.

The food arrived. She slathered her pecan waffle with butter and syrup and dug in, then looked up to see him watching her. A sideways glance at the window next to the booth, darkened by the night, flashed back her reflection. She looked awful. "Your name's different too. Dawson," she said.

"It was my mother's maiden name—Katherine Dawson. I couldn't be a Kathy, so . . ." He grinned. "How about Sloan? Family name?"

She stiffened. Last thing she wanted to talk about was *her* family. Sloan set down the fork, deciding to get the main issue into the open. "I guess you saw what happened tonight in the gym."

Dawson pushed back into the booth, where a torn spot in the red vinyl snagged at his sweater. "Yes, but it seems like he deserved what you gave him. I mean, if you caught him with another girl doing the deed. Not cool."

She pushed her plate aside. "You got a phone?" He said he did. "Why don't you pull up the videos? I know they've posted by now," she said, sounding edgy and bitter.

It hadn't crossed his mind, but he knew instantly she was likely correct. He took out his phone, went to a video posting site, and launched a video called "Revenge of the girlfriend/Windemere High." He handed her the phone and she watched, the tinny sounds of her yelling loud enough for them both to hear. She winced seeing herself deliver the kick that had put Jarred on his knees. At the same time, she saw "the end" of her and Jarred forever. And her dreams of a future with the band. He'd never forgive her. She fought for composure as she handed Dawson his phone.

It struck him then that when he'd picked her up, she'd had nothing with her—no jacket or purse—and if she was kin to anything female, there was always a purse. "Um . . . did you leave anything at the gym? I could take you back—"

"No." Wild horses couldn't have dragged her back to the gym. She reached into the front pocket of her pants, slid out a lipstick. "Nothing's important." Maybe Bobby would retrieve her phone and purse from Jarred's car. Unless Jarred found her stuff first. He'd destroy it. She had no idea how she would replace her cell phone. Her mother would go ballistic when Sloan told her she'd lost it, and even saying it had been stolen wouldn't save Sloan from LaDonna's tirade. Sloan knew she'd have to replace it herself.

Dawson eyed a clock on the wall, realizing he was pushing against the edge of his one a.m. curfew. He signaled the waitress for the check, and while he paid it, Sloan went to the restroom. Her mirror image was brutal, showing the dark circles of mascara streaked under her eyes. She washed her face, dried off with a scratchy paper towel, smoothed her hair, and retied the leather cord holding it back. She walked with Dawson to the car, and he started the engine and the heater. He turned to her. "Where to? I'll take you home."

His words hit Sloan with glacial gravity. She was supposed to have spent the night with Jarred because his parents had gone to Gatlinburg for the weekend. They'd planned their "sleepover" weeks before. A long night together, in each other's arms. *His cheating arms*, she reminded herself. She couldn't go home either. Her mother was at the trailer with a man Sloan thought was creepy . . . the way he looked at Sloan, like she was candy for the taking. She shivered. Tears welled in her eyes. "I . . . I . . . don't know. . . ." She turned and stared at Dawson, unnerved and panicked. "I . . . I have no place to go tonight."

CHAPTER 8

Dawson turned onto the quiet, narrow street of his neighborhood, lined by old oak and maple trees, in the upscale
older part of Windemere. Most of the leaves had fallen, and
the branches poked into the moonlit sky like dark vampire
fingers. He was taking Sloan home with him, hoping that his
father hadn't been called into the hospital on an emergency
and that once they walked in the door he could make his father understand that Dawson had no other choice.

Dawson had made the decision in the Waffle Palace parking lot when a tearful, trembling Sloan had hesitantly told him
about her plan to spend the night with Jarred, now jettisoned,
and her reluctance to go home because of the man staying
there with her mother. Sloan told him enough to make Dawson realize it was up to him to help her, so he offered her their
upstairs guest room.

During the drive, he tried to assure her she would be safe,
that it would be okay, that he'd take her home as soon as she
was ready to go the next morning, but she had tuned him out,
too tired, too numb to even ask questions. She simply didn't

care. She just wanted to sleep. A bed in this guy's house was as good as any on this particular night.

When the garage door rose, Dawson was relieved to see his dad's car. Dawson drove into the open bay, parked, and came around to open the door for Sloan. His nerves were piano-wire tight, because he honestly didn't know how his dad would react. If he'd been bringing a guy friend home, one who might be drunk or strung out, Franklin would have had no issues with Dawson's judgment . . . but a girl . . .

They went into the kitchen, lit softly by a light above the kitchen sink. "Dad?" he called. "Dad, I'm bringing in a friend."

"In here," Franklin called from the den.

Dawson led Sloan into the wood-paneled room where his dad was sitting in his recliner, a book across his lap, his reading glasses shoved atop his head, the television, mounted on the wall, glowing with images but muted. "You're kind of push-ing your curfew, Daw," Franklin said lightly. But when he saw Sloan, he rose from the recliner. "What's this?"

Dawson did the introductions. Sloan shifted from foot to foot, her gaze darting around the room like a cornered cat's before landing on Franklin Berke's face. "Pleased to meet you, sir," she said.

Dawson guided Sloan to the worn leather sofa beside the recliner and spread an afghan on her lap. "Just cozy up here while I talk to my dad in the kitchen."

Sloan needed no urging. She sank into the cushions, pulled the afghan up to her chin, and clutched it tightly with both hands.

In the kitchen, Franklin braced his hands on the gran-ite countertop and skewered Dawson with a look. "Explain. What's going on, Daw?"

The good thing about having a doctor for a father meant that the man was an excellent crisis manager. He was a big-picture kind of man. He listened, stayed calm, only reacted when he grasped the scope of a situation. Dawson knew exactly how to talk to his father. *Present facts first. Be impartial. Don't argue. Know when to stop talking.* Driving home, he'd silently rehearsed his story and now offered up the pieces—ugly public fight with her boyfriend at the gym, stranded, fearful of going home because of the alcoholic man who was bedded down with her mother. He quickly finished with "So I brought her here because I thought it was the safest thing to do."

Franklin stared at Dawson until Dawson thought his dad's eyeballs would fall out. Finally Franklin said, "She needs to call her mother, let her know where she is."

Dawson's spirits buoyed. "It's really late, Dad." Dawson knew that Sloan had already told her mother she would be out all night, but he didn't think telling Franklin this would help his cause. "And truth is, her mother doesn't really care. That's why I brought her with me."

"Her mother doesn't *care* where her daughter is spending the night?"

"It's complicated. Her mom . . . well, she drinks. Sloan's on her own a lot."

"And she has no other friends she can stay with? No *girl-friends?*"

"If there had been any other way . . . Please believe me. We're it for tonight." Dawson used the corporate "we," having heard his dad use it when he wanted to pull reluctant listeners into his frame of mind.

Franklin pressed his thumbs into his eyes wearily. "How old is Sloan?"

Dawson didn't know for sure, but he understood what his dad was asking. *Is she underage?* "Not sure. She's a senior like me."

"I can't risk my reputation—"

"Dad! One night. I live in the basement. She'll be up in the guest room."

"I live upstairs too."

Dawson hadn't factored that in when he'd formed his rescue plan. "You can have the sofa in my room," Dawson offered quickly. "Just for tonight."

Franklin fell silent, placed his palms flat on the counter. Eventually he nodded, but his expression was as hard as the granite under his hands. "I'm unhappy about this, Dawson. Real unhappy."

Dawson blew out the breath he'd been holding, knowing he'd won the battle. "I know. And I'm sorry to dump this on you, but . . . thanks. I . . . I mean it."

Franklin rolled his shoulders. "I'll go up and get the guest room ready. You stay with Sloan until I call you. And, Dawson? Two things: you'll sleep on that god-awful sofa tonight, and don't ever pull a stunt like this again."

Lani came into the kitchen to find her dad, Randy, sitting at the counter, waiting up for her and thumbing through messages on his cell. He looked up and smiled. "Hey. How was homecoming?"

"Fine. The zombies were awesome." She crossed to the fridge, got a soda, and returned to take a stool next to him. No use going into details. "And thanks for lending me your car." She put his car keys on the counter. "Mom in bed?"

"I'm the night owl, remember?"

She took a long drink from the soda, knowing she was more like her mom, an early riser. She loved riding Oro in the early morning and watching the dark gray-blue of a night sky turn gold with the sun's rise.

"Lani, something came across my desk yesterday. A reporter brought in a news story you might be interested in reading." Randy searched his phone's emails.

When her dad was fresh out of college with a degree in journalism and newly married, he had passed on better jobs in bigger cities in order to raise his family in Windemere because he liked the laid-back lifestyle. The small local paper that hired him spotlighted mostly "soft" news, focusing on local sports, interviews, farm reports, every imaginable community event—engagements, weddings, births, anniversaries, obituaries—a true repository of small-town rural life. He often joked, *"We're full of news no other paper is likely to print."* These days the paper was struggling to survive in the digital world.

"What kind of story?"

"The new hospital is sponsoring a start-up program called Step-Prep to train health care workers, especially nurses."

Lani was instantly interested. "Go on."

"The program will work hand in hand with Middle Tennessee State University. Reporter said the volunteer aspect is called Helping Hands, aimed at sixteen- to eighteen-year-olds. Personally I think it's just a way to get free labor." He winked. "But if you stick with it and enroll at the college in the school of nursing, you'll work with a mentor, get hands-on experience and some money." He grinned. "In three years you'll graduate as an RN able to step into a full-time job."

"Seriously?" She was already planning to go to nearby MTSU in Murfreesboro and live at home. "Being a nurse is my dream job."

"What about your job at Bellmeade?"

Ciana had hired Lani to muck out stalls and exercise horses for owners who couldn't or didn't have time to do it themselves. The part-time job came with a reduced boarding fee for Oro and allowed Lani to pay for a portion of his feed bill, which always escalated in the winter. Coupled with earnings from babysitting, she was able to shoulder most of the costs for her horse. "Never giving it up. Oro's my best friend." She quickly realized that after her fight with Kathy, the horse might be her *only* friend.

"Time crunch, Wonder Girl. You still have your senior year to finish."

She waved away his words. "Are you kidding? I can do both. What do I have to do to get into the program?"

He tapped a text into his cell. "I'm sending you the info. Apparently there'll be a general meeting in December at the hospital with the program starting in January."

She heard the message hit her phone, opened it, and skimmed it quickly. But it was the last part of the article that grabbed her interest the most. It read in part: ". . . *seminar given by the program's creator, and head of pediatrics, Dr. Franklin Berke.*"

Her dad stood and stretched. "My mattress is calling."

"I'll turn out the lights," she told him, which she did, but then sat back on the counter stool thinking about what had happened at homecoming and how it had made her feel to see

Dawson run after Sloan—hopeless. She sighed, switched gears, remembering instead how she'd felt when she was thirteen and the desire to become a nurse first surfaced. Four years later, she had the opportunity to explore that dream. In the soft ambient light of the kitchen, Lani raised the soda can high and whispered, "To you, Cousin Arie."

CHAPTER 9

By November, the homecoming blowup was ancient history. To no one's surprise, Jarred never returned to Windemere High, dropping out not because (rumor had it) of *the Scene*, but because he was flunking every subject. Bobby Henley told others that Jarred had moved to Nashville and gotten a job and that the band was now defunct.

As for Dawson and Sloan, they were a couple. A twosome. Paired off. Joined at the hip. Together. Obvious to all who saw them in the halls holding hands and rubbing shoulders. "Isn't that just like Sloan?" Kathy sniped to Lani. "She kicked Jarred to the curb like dog doo and wormed her way into another 'lucky guy's' life."

After their fight in the gym, Lani kept her thoughts to herself around Kathy. Saying nasty things about Sloan wouldn't change things, nor would it make Lani feel better about the "Dawson and Sloan together forever" scene.

"Did you know Dawson's dad is a doctor?" Kathy said, pausing at the water fountain.

"I've heard."

"She thinks she's so freakin' hot. But she isn't. Won't take this Dawson guy long to figure it out. Anyway"—Kathy sniffed—"Jarred had a way cooler car. I could hear him coming from blocks away. Dawson's car sounds like a windup toy."

Lani bent, took a drink from the fountain. She and Kathy had been friends since second grade, but now Kathy had turned into someone Lani wasn't liking very much. She thought again of the hospital's volunteer program and the upcoming seminar and saw a future beyond high school. She was going into that future, away from this one, to a place where more mattered than a guy's wheels.

——❧——

For the first time since being forced to move to Tennessee, Dawson was flying high. With the band and Jarred out of the picture, Sloan was his. The one casualty was Paulie. Paulie told him, "It's okay. I get it. Girl comes first," but Paulie's look of rejection belied his upbeat tone. Dawson was sorry about it, but there was no going back to lone-wolf status for him.

Sloan was unlike any girl he'd ever dated, or even known. She was able to come and go as she pleased—no parent dumping curfews on her like Franklin did on him. She went all out on anything she did and left him breathless and off balance with her sense of daring. His days started and stopped with wanting to be with her. He picked her up for school, brought her home, hung with her before, after, in the halls, at lunch. He did weekend chores swiftly so they could be together. She loved driving his car very fast on the rural back roads with all the windows down no matter the weather.

"Speeding ticket's on you!" he shouted whenever she jammed down the accelerator.

"Cop will have to catch me first!"

Somehow they got lucky, never got a ticket, never had an accident. Not that they would have survived one at the speeds Sloan liked to drive.

They studied together, always at his house. Franklin never let him slack off on schoolwork, insisting grades and test scores mattered more than girlfriends. Dawson wanted to go to college. Sloan did not. She wanted to break out, become a singer. She wanted fame. So if Sloan didn't crack the books with Dawson, she hunkered down with headphones or brought her guitar and retreated into a private world he didn't enter. *Let her sing.*

For Sloan, Dawson took her away from her despised real-life world. He had money to spend, and he was willing to go and do things Jarred never could afford. If she wanted to see a certain movie, Dawson took her. Grab a bite? *"Where to?"* Bowling, paint ball, laser tag—Dawson went for it. He bought her little gifts, made her happy. But the most surprising part to her was that he didn't ask for anything in return. Like sex. Not at all like Jarred, who had pushed her for sex anytime they were alone. Dawson held her, kissed her, tasted her, touched her body, but always pulled back. The only thing she missed from the days before Dawson was singing in the band and the adrenaline high that performing for an audience brought with it. Dawson Berke couldn't give her *that.*

One afternoon, Dawson brought her home from school so she could grab a change of clothes, and LaDonna drove up. Sloan's stomach knotted, but she was trapped and knew there was nothing she could do about having Dawson meet her mother, something she'd been avoiding. She only hoped LaDonna was sober.

"I'm sick. Got a killer headache. Had to leave work and everything," LaDonna said, eyeing Dawson when they walked out of the trailer.

"We're just leaving." Sloan took Dawson's hand and pulled him toward his car, parked on the gravel and dead weeds in front of their trailer with its flecking green paint. The November day had turned blustery, the sky gray, as if smudged by a dirty pencil eraser. A plastic bag had blown onto a light pole, wrapped around as if holding on for dear life. Music from the open window of a nearby trailer floated on the wind.

Dawson slowed, offering a smile and a wave. "Hi. I'm Dawson Berke. Sloan and I go to school together."

"My, you're a tall one." Sloan's mother batted her eyelashes. Dawson took a step back. He didn't know what he'd expected, but LaDonna was *no* version of her daughter. The woman was short, plump, with a doughy-looking face and bleached hair that looked fried. Hadn't Sloan said she worked in a beauty salon?

Resigned to introductions, Sloan let go of his hand. "My mother, LaDonna Quentin."

LaDonna said, "Never seen you with Sloan before." She smiled, showing deep dimples that prettied her up. "Sloan never brings her friends around. I'm forever asking her to, but does she listen to me? You friends with Jarred?"

"I don't really know the guy," Dawson said, thinking it odd that he and Sloan had been together since October and Sloan had never mentioned her breakup with Jarred.

Sloan ground her teeth. *Why would I bring friends to this dump?* As if LaDonna even *cared* who she hung with or what

51

she did as long as Sloan didn't hang around when LaDonna had a new man. "Dawson and I have to go."

LaDonna turned on her daughter. "Well, I wouldn't want to hold you up. Never mind that my head's splitting wide open and you could fix me some supper later."

Dawson gave Sloan a questioning glance. He knew her father wasn't around, so he wondered if she'd return to the trailer and help LaDonna.

Sloan said, "Gee Ma, nothing to fix but peanut butter and jelly. But no bread, though. Guess you left it off your grocery list."

LaDonna flashed Sloan a hateful look. "Go on, then. I'll take care of myself."

After a couple of drinks . . . Sloan was familiar with La-Donna's habits. She'd seen the pattern all her life . . . leave work, come home, have a drink, go bar hopping. Today was Friday, after all. "Come on," she said to Dawson.

"You'll have to come visit," LaDonna called to their backs. "When I feel better."

"Sure," Dawson said, doubting it would happen. The rancor between the two women was tangible. He and his dad could get into some tangles, but they both got over it, went on with life. He basically *liked* his dad, while Sloan seemed to want nothing to do with her own mother.

Once in his car, Sloan sat ramrod straight, staring out the windshield. Dawson could see and feel her animosity and wondered why it was so entrenched, but he was unsure if he should ask about it or forget about it. He started the engine and drove along the pockmarked asphalt that passed for a road through the park. He reached over and took Sloan's hand. "You okay?"

"Good as I can be with *her* for a mother."

"She said she was sick."

"In more ways than you know."

"Want to talk about it?"

"Nothing to talk about. We just stay out of each other's way." She looked over at Dawson, wanting to forget the encounter. "Think we could stop for a burger and fries? I'm starving."

"Yeah, missed you in the cafeteria."

"Got busy, had to skip lunch." In truth, she'd had no money to buy food in the cafeteria and hadn't signed up on the freebie list at the beginning of the week. The condescending air of the cafeteria lady had put Sloan off too, so she'd gone without.

"If that's what you want."

Sloan flashed him a smile. "How about buying me a chocolate shake. This big." She used her hands to measure from her lap to the top of the car, making him laugh. She leaned across the console and kissed his cheek. "I'm lucky to have someone like you."

His heart swelled. She was like a little girl sometimes, with quicksilver moods that flashed from sulky to sunny, from sexy to innocent. She could let go with a stream of swearing to rival guys in the locker room or curl up in his arms like a kitten. She fascinated him. Not only because she was hot—so hot she made his blood sizzle—but also because she was an enigma, a puzzle he wanted to solve.

Before turning onto the main road, he grinned at her. "A chocolate shake for a kiss. Fair trade."

Sloan rewarded him with a nibble on his earlobe that sent shivers through him and a kiss that seared his mouth. She broke the kiss and laughed deep in her throat. He shoved the car into gear and peeled out, laying rubber away from the trailer park entrance.

CHAPTER 10

Sloan spent every free minute at Dawson's house during the holiday break. One night the three of them decorated a fresh evergreen tree that Franklin centered in the front window of the living room, where it could be seen by everyone walking or driving past. Holiday music played through the whole-house audio speakers, and a fire crackled in the room's brick fireplace, mixing the smoky scent of burning wood with the woodsy smell of the evergreen. They drank warm apple cider, munched on cookies, and wrapped the tree with endless strands of twinkle lights, yards of garlands, and an amazing assortment of colorful decorations.

The evening was like one out of a storybook, far different from the Christmases of Sloan's childhood, when Santa Claus was gift delivery from a social service organization or charity church group. Her mother knew how to work the system, so Sloan always got presents, but rarely what she wanted. "You just act grateful no matter what," La Donna would tell her. The gifts were plentiful before Sloan aged out of cuteness. As she grew, the presents morphed from pretty dolls, toys, games, and puzzles to clothes that never quite fit.

"Hey, here's an ornament I made for Mom in first grade." Dawson held up a circle with his school photo glued inside it. Gold paint flaked onto the rug.

Sloan studied the image of the dark-haired boy with the gap-toothed smile. "You haven't changed a bit."

"I'm taller." He grinned and dipped in for a kiss.

"These were Kathy's favorites." Franklin opened an old egg carton, where gorgeous crystal snowflakes nestled in white tissue paper. Almost reverently he took each one out and looped their cords around the highest branches, and Sloan swore she saw his eyes glisten with a sheen of moisture.

After Franklin went upstairs, she cuddled with Dawson in front of the fire under an old quilt. He kissed her, savoring the taste of apple and cinnamon on her breath. "So tell me, Sloan Quentin, if you could have anything for Christmas, what would you want?" He'd already bought her gifts, using up three weeks' allowance. She was worth it.

"I want to *be* someone."

He was expecting a flirty comeback like she usually gave when he teased with her, so her answer baffled him. He rose up on an elbow to search her face and saw that she was serious. Whoa. "You *are* someone. You're my girl."

She regretted her answer. Somebody like Dawson, who had the best things in life, would never understand the hunger inside her, how it drove her, and she had no words to explain it to him. So she smiled and darted him a kiss. "Then how about the Crown Jewels?"

He saw her gaze flit away, and he knew she had shut him out.

She had little money and stressed over what to buy Dawson for Christmas but finally hit on an idea. She called Bobby, and during a long, cold afternoon in his garage, she recorded a mix of ballads and folk tunes, with Bobby on guitar. He downloaded the recordings to his laptop and took it home to balance the vocals and add layers of additional chords. Days later he appeared at the trailer park with a CD that had her photo pressed onto the front and handed it to her.

She hugged him. "Bobby! Thanks sooo much!"

"You sound great on it."

"Couldn't have done it without you."

"Made me miss our band."

"Me too," she confessed. "But I don't miss the drama with Jarred." Cold seeped through the old trailer walls. "You ever hear from him?" She didn't know why she asked—maybe because creating the CD reminded her of how much she loved performing.

"Not for a while. I know he's hanging with some musicians in Nashville, playing some weekend jams, nothing big. He's always been good on the guitar."

The talk of making music made her miss it even more. "And he's probably high," Sloan added.

"Never sure about old Jarred, but he loves music. Kicked us into gear in middle school and made us into a band." Bobby threw her a glance. "You look happy."

She shrugged. "True story."

Bobby offered a wistful smile. "Dawson's a lucky guy."

Sloan shifted, suddenly self-conscious. "I like him. He's normal, and he's nice to me."

Bobby nodded, his expression one of acceptance. He opened the trailer door backhanded and stepped out and down. "Well I should run. Have a good Christmas, Sloan."

"You too." She watched him walk to his car. "And thanks again." She closed the door, leaned against it, ever aware that Bobby cared for her. She'd never given him any encouragement. He was a nice guy, but she felt only sisterly toward him. No chemistry. Zilch. Sloan quickly wrapped the CD, then called Dawson to come pick her up.

The seminar in the hospital's new auditorium about the Step-Prep program was so well attended that Lani was afraid she wouldn't make the cut. But most of the attendees turned out to be people already enrolled at MTSU, taking nursing and medical classes. Dr. Berke gave a welcome speech, outlined the basics, then turned over the podium to the head of nursing, Mrs. Trammell, who outlined the interview process, the immunization and health record requirements, the upcoming January training sessions, the mandatory service of up to fifteen hours a week during the volunteer phase, and the shadowing by a mentor during expected twelve-hour shifts throughout the program. Once completing the internship hours and classroom credits, the person would earn a diploma and be on an inside track for a job. None of the requirements made Lani want to back out. She wanted to be an RN. All that stood in her way was filling out the paperwork and acing her interview. Her heart squeezed in anticipation, her stomach churned with apprehension. *Go big or go home.* Wasn't that what athletes said?

As it turned out, Lani was only one of four high school

students from the county to sign up for the 100 percent volunteer part of the new program. With such a small group, she felt better about being accepted. She quickly wrote her name on the "Call for Interview" list.

She hurried to the parking lot, where tall mercury light poles were wrapped with red and white foil to resemble giant candy canes. The temperature was dropping and a cold wind promising snow flurries made her teeth chatter as she ducked into her mom's car. She backed out of the parking space, in a hurry to get home. Her sister, Melody, was coming in for holiday break from Vanderbilt. There was a tree to decorate, cookies to bake, gifts to wrap. Christmas! Her favorite time of year. Tonight she and Mel would sit on her bed, drink hot chocolate, and talk *forever*.

~~~

"How's it going?" Franklin asked.

Dawson was spending a morning of his holiday break hunched over a pile of paperwork on the floor of the den. "Look, another acceptance letter." He waved the piece of paper. He'd been filling out paperwork and submitting applications for months to different colleges and universities, all in the northeast.

"That's five, yes?"

"What can I say? Everybody wants me."

Franklin laughed. "I'll keep that in mind when I'm writing tuition checks. Thinking of any special major?"

"Probably business." His high school aptitude test scores showed he had organizational, social, and leadership skills, scoring in the top five percent in math and in something designated as "high moral character." Big hurrah.

"Not medicine, like your old man? Country needs doctors."

Dawson didn't want to live his father's life. He'd seen medicine from both sides, from dark and light. Sometimes it fixed people. Or not. It hadn't fixed his mother. Plus the profession was all-consuming. He wanted a simpler way to make money, and earning a business degree seemed smart to him. "Can't be a doctor. I'd have to learn to play golf."

Franklin burst out laughing. "Reason enough. My golf game stinks. No time to perfect it." Then he grew serious. "Daw, the move here hasn't been all bad, has it? You've seemed pretty content lately."

Having Sloan in his life had settled him and given him something to look forward to each day. "Still not in love with this place, but yeah, things are better."

Franklin nodded, glancing at the paperwork on the floor. "What about Sloan? The two of you spend a lot of time together. She have college plans?"

The question dinged an alarm bell in Dawson's head. He leaned back on his elbows. "She's a terrific singer, has a really great voice. College isn't for everyone, you know. Why you asking?" Sloan's talk of a singing career was ever in Dawson's head. He knew how badly she wanted it, but for him, letting go of her once they graduated wouldn't be easy.

"I just . . . well, I don't want her to change *your* plans about college. Sometimes feelings for a girl can do that."

"Dad, I wouldn't be doing all this paperwork if I wasn't going to college." The look of relief on his dad's face didn't get past Dawson.

"Lots of girls on a college campus."

"And I plan to meet them." The words were more false than true. Sloan would be a hard act to follow for any girl who came along.

"I'll miss you when you leave."

Franklin's nostalgic expression made Dawson uncomfortable because in spite of their head-butting over the past year, he would miss his father too—he just didn't want to say so. "You're not going all *girly* on me, are you, Dad?"

Franklin feigned horror. "Wouldn't dream of it. Simply a statement of fact. I've had you hanging around with me for almost eighteen years, you know. There's going to be a hole when you go away."

"Don't rent my room. I'll come back to visit."

Franklin crouched, grinned. *"Mi casa es su casa."*

"Dad, your accent sucks."

Winter sunlight spilled across the floor from the windows. Dawson began to straighten up the papers and file folders on the floor. "I think I'll go for a run. Want to go with me? I'll run sloooow," Dawson said. "Course, if you're too old . . ."

"Old! Me? Let me get my gear. Game on!"

Together they rose from the floor laughing, bumping, and jostling one another to get out the doorway first.

CHAPTER 11

Sloan and Dawson were curled up together on the sofa in Dawson's basement on New Year's Eve, watching a horror movie. Gore dripped in living color on the big-screen TV. They had strung Christmas lights together around door frames, with bulbs that blinked in syncopation with music from his iPhone dock. His basement was a safe haven, away from the trailer and a life she hated.

Sloan wasn't in the mood for the movie. She wanted to watch the megastar singers and bands performing for the New Year's Eve party in Times Square. She imagined herself onstage in Times Square. Head trip!

He grinned, stroking her hair. "Popcorn?" He tossed popped kernels into his mouth from the bowl on the coffee table.

"Not now." She cozied into Dawson's side like a burrowing kitten. She heard Franklin moving around upstairs. "Your dad going to watch the ball drop with us?"

"Probably." Dawson didn't sound happy about it.

Sloan liked Franklin—he was nice to her—but she never felt truly alone with Dawson because his father constantly hovered in the background. She had no memories of her father, knew nothing about him except from LaDonna's vile descriptions of him, and of how he'd walked out on them. Yet Franklin often reminded her of a too strict teacher: *Do this, don't do that. Don't be late. Have you studied? Where are you going?* Franklin's house rules were so numerous, Sloan didn't know how Dawson kept track.

"Let's dump the movie, figure something else to do before Franklin crashes our party."

Her kiss shot shivers through Dawson. "You're making me crazy." *No exaggeration.*

For weeks she'd taken to teasing him with her hands and mouth and tongue, running her hands under his shirt and waistband of his jeans, stroking his skin, turning it fiery, but darting away when he grabbed for her, laughing and wagging a finger and saying, "Uh-uh." And for weeks he'd been wound tighter than a string on her guitar. He kept control, but just barely.

Sloan loved the game of keeping him on edge, of pushing, retreating, challenging his willpower and her power over him, something she found intoxicating, compelling. Feeling in control was a high she liked, one she'd rarely known. So far he'd always backed off.

Now, in the soft light of the room, she ran her hand beneath his shirt and across the flat plane of his abs, edged slowly downward under the waistband of his jeans. She heard his breath catch. With unexpected lightning speed, she snatched the TV remote from his hand and clicked over to a station promising a ripping good New Year's Eve party.

"Hey! No fair!" Dawson yelped, outmaneuvered. They

wrestled for control of the remote, Sloan squealing and laughing, him tickling her mercilessly.

"Mine, mine, mine!" Dodging his hands, laughing, she fought to keep the remote.

"Mine!" he countered, rolling her backward on the sofa and pinning her hands above her head. He pried the remote from her fingers, flipped it back to the movie.

"Excuse me!" Franklin's voice from the basement stairs sobered them both, made them sit upright and twist their clothing back into place.

Dawson went hot, then angry. How long had Franklin been watching them? "So are we making too much noise? Neighbors complain?" Sloan scooted to the far end of the sofa.

Franklin came over, shot Dawson a warning look about his attitude. Realizing that his dad was wearing his winter coat, Dawson slouched. "Hospital called and EMTs just brought a family of four into triage. Pretty bad wreck with a semi. I need to check out the two kids, and if a surgeon's called in, I'll stay and keep an eye on them."

The scenario was familiar to Dawson: Hospital calls. Dad leaves. An accident with injuries. He ditched his hostile mood. "Okay."

Franklin wrapped the new plaid scarf Dawson had bought him for Christmas around his neck and tucked the ends into his coat. "You two be okay here alone?"

"Sure." Dawson saw that his dad was in a hurry to leave. He glanced at Sloan and she nodded, wide-eyed.

"There's a deli tray upstairs. Help yourselves. And, Daw, when you drive Sloan home tonight, be careful. Lot of drunk loonies out on the roads." Franklin turned, but halfway up the stairs, stooped and said, "Hey, you two . . . Happy New Year. Sorry we can't celebrate it together."

Sloan returned his sentiment. Dawson mumbled his. When the kitchen door shut, every creak and whisper of the house was magnified. A scream from the horror movie made them both jump, then burst out laughing. Sloan politely reached for the remote. "I'm really over this movie."

"Me too." He gave over the remote and she surfed the channels, until she settled on one featuring the bands she most liked. During a commercial break, he said, "Time to raid the deli tray."

Sloan followed him upstairs. Dawson dragged the tray from the fridge heaped with deli meat, cheeses, sliced veggies, and dip. "Yikes! Who was your dad expecting? The whole neighborhood?"

Dawson grabbed condiments and a bag of deli buns and set all beside the tray. "What? There's barely enough to share."

She rolled her eyes. "Maybe I can take home a doggie bag." She said it in jest, but it was in part a request. LaDonna was out for an all-nighter, and Sloan had no idea when she'd drag herself home the next day. As usual, there wasn't much to eat at the trailer.

Oblivious, Dawson slathered mustard on the top half of a bun. Sloan bumped him hard with her hip, making him drop the bun facedown on the countertop. "Hey!"

"Butterfingers," she chided, grabbing her plate and a bag of chips and hurrying down into the basement.

He found her curled up on the sofa, munching her sandwich. He gave her a wicked grin and wiggled a soda can. "You forgot your drink. I brought it, but there'll be a price for handing it over."

She gave him a smug look. "I have a drink." She fished under the sofa and lifted up a bottle of champagne. "Unlike you, I'm willing to share for free."

"Whoa, girl. Where'd you get that?"

"State secret." She'd lifted it from a convenience store days before when the clerk was busy and not watching, but she wasn't about to tell him that.

Dawson took the bottle, wrapped in black foil and stamped with gold letters. He'd had beer and wine at parties with his friend Tad, but he'd never tasted champagne. Once Franklin had allowed him a sip of bourbon that had burned his mouth and made his eyes water. "Firewater," Franklin had joked. "I'd rather you try it with me than at some party." Dawson never confessed he'd already tried it at age thirteen at Tad's house. Now he gave Sloan a conspiratorial grin. "You like this stuff?"

"Never had it before. Thought we should drink some together. For New Year's Eve." She wanted to taste the stuff and had hoped Dawson's dad wouldn't mind if they all sipped it together to welcome the New Year. But now Franklin was gone.

"I'll get some glasses."

"Hurry. The ball drops in fifteen."

He returned with glasses and set them on the coffee table. "When did you sneak it inside?"

"When you weren't looking, silly."

He worked the cork up, and when it popped out, the liquid erupted into a cascade that gushed down the bottle's sides and onto the floor. They laughed while Sloan sopped up the overflow with an afghan from the sofa.

Dawson poured two glasses full of the golden liquid that roiled with tiny bubbles. He gulped it. She tasted it. He scrunched his face. "I think you're supposed to sip it," Sloan said.

They each drank a second glass full. "Taste grows on you," Dawson said.

"Makes me want to giggle," Sloan said, giggling.

He poured them each another glass as the TV started playing "Auld Lang Syne."

"Uh-oh, here it comes! Watch." She pointed at the screen as an enormous crystal ball began its descent from a lofty tower and the crowds in Times Square hundreds of miles away from Windemere shouted out a countdown from ten to one. When the ball came to rest, and the brilliantly lit number of the New Year flashed on the screen, and confetti blanketed the TV people, Sloan set down her empty glass, set aside Dawson's glass, and dove into his arms. Her head was spinning, and when his hot and hungry mouth met hers, she made up her mind as to how she wanted to complete their celebration.

Sloan pushed up his sweatshirt. His dark eyes bore into her blue ones. "What . . . ?"

She tugged off her sweater and bra. His gaze roamed her body with a look more intoxicating than the champagne. "You make me happy, Dawson." She lifted his hand, pressed a kiss into the palm, placed it against her breast, and watched goose bumps rise across his bare skin.

He couldn't stop staring at her. She was so beautiful. . . . His head swam and heat spread through his body, hot fingers of need. "You make me happy too. I—I love you, Sloan." He'd never said that to a girl, but it was true. He loved her.

She threw back her head, smiled, and looked back down at him. "So then let's be happier together." She kissed him, lowering her body onto his. Skin pressed against skin. Breath mingled with breath.

On the wall, the TV announcer told the viewing audience good night and Happy New Year. Dawson fumbled to find the remote, and when he did, the screen went dark and the room went quiet, bathed only in the colors of Christmas past.

CHAPTER 12

"You have a true affinity for this place, don't you?"

Lani was busy gathering vials of blood specimen results in the lab for delivery to various departments. She smiled at Cassie's question. "I'm a medical junkie. I've wanted to be a nurse for years, so it never seems like work to me. I love it here."

In the three months Lani had been a volunteer, she had learned every nook and cranny of the hospital, from the ER to the surgery rooms, from the chemo center to the newborn nursery and pediatrics, along with the floors of patient rooms and central staff centers on each floor. The ICU, radiology, imaging, labs, the gift shop, and staffing rooms where she had her own locker were as familiar to her as the rooms in the house she'd grown up in.

"Years?" Cassie, a third-year student and Lani's friend at the hospital, offered a wry smile. "What are you . . . all of seventeen?"

"I'm an old soul, trapped in a teen's body. I know what I want. How 'bout you? Why are you here?"

"I took care of my mama for years before she died. I knew I could do this . . . take care of sick people. All I needed was the classroom credits and I could have a career. What's your story?"

"I caught the nursing bug the summer my cousin died. She had cancer and spent days in bed, too sick to get up. I liked making her comfortable." Even now, the memory of that thirteenth summer brought tears to her eyes. "Before she . . . left us, she told me how much it had meant to her to have me around when most girls my age were off having fun."

"Well, you're good at it," Cassie added quickly. "Plus the floor nurses really like you—some of them are real crabs too. Some even ask for you to work with them. A huge compliment, you know."

"My secret is chocolate. I bring in bags of it and stuff it in the nursing station drawers. A person can make a ton of friends with free chocolate."

Lani grinned and Cassie laughed. "I've wondered how the stuff keeps magically appearing. Keep up the good work."

Lani picked up her lab deliveries and hurried out the door. She couldn't wait until May and graduation so she could spend even more time in the hospital. She had cut back on her hours at Bellmeade but had promised Ciana she'd teach a riding class in the coming summer. At school, her senior class was counting down the final days too. Many had already signed letters of intent to different colleges. Kathy would go to University of Florida: "And par-ty!" she'd said with a whoop. Three football players had signed with University of Tennessee at Knoxville. Others had plans to join the military, go to community colleges and tech schools, but Paulie had won the college lottery with a full ride to MIT in Boston. "Genius trumps us all," Lani told Kathy.

"Nerd. How about Dawson? Heard where he might be going?"

Kathy took pleasure in needling Lani about her crush, which she'd been unable to hide from Kathy's X-ray vision. Lani shrugged it off. "Doesn't matter. I'm sure it won't be MTSU."

"Wonder what Sloan will do? They're always hanging on each other. Bet you couldn't slide a butter knife between them."

"No idea." Lani didn't want to talk about either Dawson or Sloan, although Kathy's observation was true.

"Maybe she'll follow him to college."

Refusing to rise to Kathy's bait but seething inside, Lani smiled sweetly. "Maybe she will. Whatever. I just hope he'll be happy wherever he goes, even if Sloan tags along."

Kathy offered a derisive snort, signaling she didn't believe Lani's sentiment for one second.

Lani kept walking.

Sloan took the test three times and failed it three times. She stood in the cramped bathroom of the trailer, staring at the stick and its plus sign. *Yes*, it silently announced, *you are pregnant*. Her knees went weak as the irrefutable truth slammed into her. Her menstrual period, gone missing for ten weeks, wasn't going to show up in March. She gagged and retched into the toilet. Dry heaves now. Because she was pregnant, or because she was scared? Both reasons were interlocked and inseparable.

All the time she'd been with Jarred, she'd taken the pill, but once they fell apart, she forgot about taking it. Why bother? The side effects of the anti-pregnancy drug were annoying.

The pill made her breasts sore. Not to mention the bloating! But once she and Dawson had started having sex, she'd gone right back on it. She hadn't missed a dose. Now her breasts throbbed, she was throwing up, and the pregnancy tests were all positive.

She braced her palms against the wall over the toilet, fighting the urge to heave again. Her knees trembled. Her head ached.

LaDonna pounded on the flimsy door. "Hey, hurry up in there! I got an appointment. What's taking you so long?"

Fear seized Sloan by the throat. How would her mother take the news? She shuddered just thinking about it. "Hold up! I'm getting in the shower . . . running late."

"Well, move your ass!"

Sloan turned on the water, hoping to drown out LaDonna, and realized she'd never make the school bus. She felt awful. "I think I have some kind of stomach flu. Don't think I'll make it to school today," she called from under the stream of hot water.

"Then get out of the shower and go to bed. I'm in a hurry!"

Sloan pulled herself out of the stream, did a haphazard dry-off, and wrapped the towel around her. She opened the door, and the steam rushed out.

LaDonna stood glaring. "You look like crap. Don't give me no flu."

Not contagious, Ma. Sloan stepped around her and crossed to her tiny bedroom, barely big enough to contain the pulled down wall bed, dropped facedown onto her rumpled sheets. She thought of the school gossip, of all the hateful things the kids would say about her. They'd talked about her before, but singing in the band had allowed much of the talk to roll off her. Now she had nothing. Fear and nausea clawed through her insides. She moaned. She didn't want to be pregnant . . . didn't want to be a mother. She wanted this growth out of her, wanted it gone. Sobs welled up. She struggled to swallow them down, lost the fight, and smothered her face into the bedding, shoulders heaving uncontrollably.

She sent Dawson a text about being sick, and he called her at lunchtime. "How you doing?"

"Still hanging over my toilet," she told him. Morning sickness was all-day sickness for her.

"Want me to come by after school, check on you?"

"No." The single word was terse, said without invitation for discussion.

She told him the same thing when he called after school, that night, and the next morning.

Rebuffed, he couldn't figure out why she was acting this way. How sick was she? "You need a doctor? My dad—"

"No! I'll be fine."

"I'll ditch classes, bring you one of those chocolate shakes you like," he offered at lunchtime on the third afternoon.

She didn't want him to come because she didn't want to face him. She couldn't even think of how to tell him. He'd most likely dump her anyway. "You don't have to keep tabs on me, Dawson. I don't need you hanging all over me, you know. I'm sick. I'll get well."

Her words hurt. Something had happened to make her shut him out. *Maybe her mother* . . . LaDonna was unpredictable. No telling what she'd done to Sloan. "Um . . . okay . . . call me if—" He heard her click off, and not wanting to look stupid standing in the hall, he said, "Bye," to dead air. He shoved the cell into his backpack and went to class, where he sat brooding through the lecture.

Maybe he'd done or said something that had ticked her off. But no matter how hard he searched his memory, he couldn't figure out *what*. Now she'd all but blown him off. *What the hell!* He got mad. *If that's the way she wants it* . . . Maybe they needed a break from each other. He didn't like the idea, but her moodiness was wearing thin with him. Two could play the same game. He decided to give her space. Lots of it.

CHAPTER 13

Sloan spent four days nursing her "stomach flu," while crying, confused, miserable, and afraid. There were clinics where she could go to terminate her pregnancy, and she visited several sites online that explained the procedure and what to expect, recovery times, and legalities. Since she was in an early stage of pregnancy, the process seemed simple and quick. No muss, no fuss. Yet she was terrified of the whole idea. Terrified also of having a baby. She felt caught in a spider's web of indecision, stuck and immobilized, torn between two choices and not wanting to participate in either.

Her mother kept insisting Sloan get up and go to school. Sloan told her, "On Monday. Flu can take about a week to get over, you know."

LaDonna eyed her. "You sure that's all that's wrong with you?"

Sloan trembled, holding LaDonna's prying eyes. "I told you I have the flu. I'm getting better. That's it."

But as soon as LaDonna left, Sloan threw up.

Dawson spent five tortured days worrying about Sloan, not

74

calling or texting, revisiting her curt replies in his head simply to keep him angry and away from her. He wasn't going to beg for her company! When she was still AWOL on Saturday, he gave up and drove to the trailer park. LaDonna's car was gone. A relief. He parked, walked up, and knocked on the door.

Sloan had seen him drive up, knew she had to tell him. Her torturous week had led her to the place of realizing it was his problem too. She'd need his help getting to the clinic to end what had happened to her. She went to the door and opened it, and at the sight of him looking worried and so tall and strong, she launched herself into his arms and broke down crying. He caught her, staggered, pushed them both back inside the trailer. "Baby! What's wrong? Did your mother—"

"I'm pregnant, Dawson! And I don't know what to do."

The words rolled over him like an avalanche, flattening him, squeezing the breath from his lungs. Sloan clung to him, crying out of control. He held her close, shaking like a leaf in a windstorm, finally pulling away, guiding them both to the couch because he wasn't sure his legs could support him any longer. The table was piled with used tissue, evidence of tears long wept. "Are you . . . I mean—"

"I'm sure." Her voice was hoarse with tears.

He said, "But we were careful." He had used protection, and she'd said she was on the pill. He had joked, "Double insurance." So very, very careful. *Except once.* New Year's Eve. Months before. One time. Only once. Their first time. Feeling sick, he closed his eyes. The night had been magical. Lying in each other's arms, feeling her skin on his, their bodies limp with completion, satisfaction. Loving her in every way. Back to now. "What . . ." He stopped, started again. "Have you told your mother?"

"No." Sloan's face had a greenish tinge.

"When will you—"

"Not till I have to." What was happening to Sloan was exactly what had happened to LaDonna as a teenager. Once when her mother had been drunk, she'd blubbered out a story of how the man called her "stupid" for getting knocked up and walked away. Sloan cringed, thinking of LaDonna's coming scorn.

"What do you want to do? If you want to get married . . ." He threw out the first thing that popped into his head.

"No. No way. I don't want to be married. I want to be a singer!" The words were determined and fierce. "Maybe I can get rid of it. At some clinic. Maybe your dad can . . . you know . . . help." She broke down again.

Get rid of it. Her words felt like a slap. Get rid of it as if it were a hangnail. No harm, no foul. Problem solved. "I . . . I don't know, Sloan. . . . I need time to think."

"Don't you get it? I don't want it inside me. I don't want a baby! I have plans."

The words were venomous, but they hit him like cold, sharp stones. "Can we . . . well, you know, talk about it? Not right now," he hastily added. "But later. Tomorrow or the next day. After I . . . I talk to Dad."

She sagged and tears filled her eyes. "I feel sick."

"It's okay. You should rest." All he wanted to do was bolt.

She swiped her eyes, hunched over, then looked up into his face. Her blue eyes, red rimmed and raw from crying, pleaded for a solution. She turned into a scared little girl. "You won't leave me alone?"

"Course not." In truth, he wanted to run and not look back.

"You want to go someplace? Out to eat, or something?" He was treading water, trying not to drown.

She shook her head. "I want to go to sleep. For maybe a year."

He led her to her room. The bed, almost wall to wall in the small space, was a pile of wadded sheets and blankets. Clothing was heaped on the floor in one corner, stuffed partly into a closet. The air smelled stale. He straightened the bedding a bit, helped her settle, pulled the bedsheet to her chin.

She clung to his hand. "Stay. Until I fall asleep, okay?"

He eased onto the bed and held her hand until he felt her fingers loosen. When he was certain she was asleep, he rose on cramped legs, shakily left the trailer, and got into his car. The sun was setting and the sky was blood-red. An omen? He sat until the red faded to pink, then pale indigo. He forced the key into the ignition and backed out of the weed-strewn space. He only had one place to go. One person to help them both.

Dawson drove home aimlessly, taking back roads, killing time, holding off the inevitable for as long as he could. The March sky was ink black by the time he came home and parked in the garage next to Franklin's car. Inside, the house was silent. Dawson walked to the back of the house, to the den, and found his father stretched out on the sofa sleeping, his glasses shoved on top of his forehead, a medical journal open across his chest, warm lamplight from the pole lamp above the sofa pooling on him. Dawson leaned against the doorjamb, staring at the peaceful picture, printing the image into his brain. The last picture from the world he used to know. Once he woke Franklin, once he talked to him, the old order would pass away. Not with tornado winds, but with words from his mouth.

Dawson took deep breaths, as if readying his body for a marathon. He sat in the club chair at the arm of the sofa and gently shook his dad awake. Franklin came up quickly. Doctors could do that, wake instantly. When he saw Dawson, he grinned sheepishly, stretched. "Must have dozed off. Long day."

Dawson locked gazes with his father.

"Hey," Franklin said, sitting upright, reading the look and letting the journal slide to the floor, where it made a *whap* sound. "What's up?"

Dawson blew out a breath, forcing away the knot of emotion clogging his throat. "Dad. We have to talk." He took a second to gather himself, knowing his next words could never be taken back, so he said them slowly, solemnly, so that Franklin would know it was the absolute truth. No jacking around. "Sloan's pregnant."

CHAPTER 14

S loan couldn't stop crying. She huddled beside Dawson on the sofa in the Berkes' den, the shadows of the late afternoon leaking through the window like dark fingers. They were facing Franklin, who had dragged over a desk chair to sit directly in front of them, his face grim.

Sloan's heart hammered, the I-don't-give-a-damn front she'd wanted to display completely vanquished. She was scared and trapped, a life out of her control. Dawson had talked her into this face to face, telling her over and over that his father would help them. So she'd come.

"Sloan, I know you're scared. I know you don't know what to do. This is why we're here . . . so we can figure this out together." Franklin's voice was calm and soothing.

His doctor-to-panicked-patient voice, Dawson thought, a far cry from the fury Franklin had heaped on Dawson. Shock. Disbelief. Disgust. *Disappointment*—a parent's great weapon turned on a child he once cherished. "How could this happen? We had 'the talk' when you were a kid. You *knew* about protection! If you decided to have sex, it was your responsibility to be safe. This didn't have to happen. It *shouldn't* have happened!"

He'd let his father rant and pace. Dawson had no defense, not even *"I got caught up. One time. Just once."* He absorbed the angry words knowing he'd screwed up and deserved Franklin's rage.

Franklin's final blow came when he'd spun and said, "What about your future? College? All those plans we've made? This changes everything, Dawson. Everything! And what about Sloan? What are the two of you going to do?"

For two days their house had been a war zone, a hot war now turned cold, with Sloan and him facing a firing squad of indecision. Dawson sat with his fists clenched against his thighs, his jaw rigid. And now here all of them sat. Deciding.

Franklin offered Sloan another tissue. "Have you told your mother?"

Sloan shook her head.

"She should know."

"Why? If I get rid of it, she doesn't ever have to know."

"Is that what you and Dawson want to do?"

Sloan sidled a glance at Dawson. "Well, I don't want to have a baby. But . . . but the other thing . . ." *The other thing . . .* "It's simple, isn't it? It just gets sucked away, doesn't it?"

Dawson leaped to his feet, angry at her. "Listen to yourself, Sloan! You're talking to my father about his *grandchild*!"

Sloan drew back. *Franklin's grandchild.* Until this moment, she hadn't thought of the baby as a person. Nor had she thought that what was growing inside of her belonged to all of them. "I—I'm sorry . . . I didn't mean—"

Franklin took her hands in his but looked up at his son. "That's enough, Daw. It's a reasonable question." Still holding

80

her hands, he said to Sloan, "There are clinics for the procedure, but you do have other choices. That's why we're here exploring them."

She felt him squeeze her hands reassuringly. "I know . . . it's just that . . ." She broke off, unable to put her turmoil into words.

"Dawson told me you are unsure about getting married."

She refused to make eye contact with Dawson. "I . . . I . . . well, I mean, not really . . . I want . . . just want to leave Windemere. And to sing—" She felt like a cornered animal, desperate to say the right thing but unsure of what that was.

"Dawson played that Christmas CD you made for him. I was impressed. You are a good singer." He smiled to reassure her. Sloan calmed. Franklin motioned Dawson back onto the sofa with a glare and a nod. When Dawson sat, Franklin asked, "I've heard what Sloan is considering. So now tell me, son, what do *you* want to do? You're the baby's father. You have a say in this, you know. I want to hear from both of you."

Dawson felt hot and squirmy. Over the long days, he'd thought about little else. His head had filled with regret and resentment, but now the look of fear and expectation on Sloan's face turned toward him blanketed his anger. *This is my baby too. My baby. Mine.* The den was warm and smelled of leather and old books, and the lamp, set on a timer, blinked on, spilling soft light across the Persian rug at their feet. He thought of their old house in Baltimore, so far away, and of his mother, her arms around him from her bedside, her whispered "I love you" in his ear. He took deep breaths, blew them out. "I . . . I don't want the baby to die."

Sloan trembled, but Franklin's hands felt firm and warm, grounding her.

"Why?" Franklin asked, never taking his eyes off Dawson's face.

The clear answer came immediately, bringing a film of tears to his eyes, and it took a few moments to make his voice cooperate. "Because . . . because what if it's a little girl? And what if she looks like Mom?"

Franklin shut his eyes as Dawson's words spilled over him.

Sloan glanced between them, knowing that her feelings, needs, and wants weren't part of this equation. This baby wasn't even about her at the moment. She'd known that Dawson's mother had died of cancer, but she'd not fully grasped the gulf of emotion, the cord of family that bound these two men together. This baby was the main event. It was a link that bridged time, knotted together the past and the present. She heard a rush of blood to her ears, like a wind vibrating through her. She, Sloan Quentin, was the conduit to maintain the connection. They needed her, the girl no one had ever needed. "Please tell me what to do."

Dawson realized an abortion seemed the simplest solution. It meant he could go to college as he'd planned. He could leave this town for good, shelve this chapter in his life and move on. But the what-ifs . . . haunted him. "I want to keep our baby," Dawson said, his voice barely audible. "Please . . ."

"What about me?" Sloan's head was spinning as she grappled with being pregnant and giving birth. "How—"

"We'll take care of you," Franklin said, interrupting her flights of panic. "You can live here with us if you want to. We'll cover all your prenatal care, medical bills, and delivery costs. You can graduate in May. After the baby's born, we'll take total responsibility for her care. And we'll take care of you too, until you decide what you want to do." He threw Dawson a look that warned him to keep silent.

Dawson sat stock-still with the enormity of his own words and of his father's offer sinking in. He and Franklin both wanted the baby to be born, meaning he would be a father at eighteen. Franklin had known all along what Dawson would choose. Dawson wanted to resent how his dad had steered the direction of the choice, how he'd made up Sloan's mind for her without her ever suspecting. But he couldn't.

To Sloan the offer felt like a lifeline. With Franklin and Dawson beside her, she could get through the next few months. Nine months to have a baby, close to four months already gone. She'd hidden it so far at school. Maybe she could hide it until graduation. Maybe not. What she understood was that she would be cared for, cared about. She'd be safe. And when it was over . . . ? She couldn't think about that part right now. "Will . . . will you go with me to talk to my mother?"

"Absolutely," Franklin said. "We'll face this together. All of us. You won't be alone, I promise."

―――

Her mother was out on the Saturday afternoon Franklin and Dawson came to move Sloan into the Berkes' house. At first LaDonna had thrown a fit, threatening a lawsuit because Sloan was only seventeen, but once Franklin told her he was going to cover expenses for the baby, plus give LaDonna "a little extra money each month until the baby was born to ease her separation experience," she had accepted the plan as "the best thing."

Dawson had been surprised by LaDonna's quick capitulation

to give up a grandchild. On the drive home after that first meeting, Franklin's only comment was, "That woman is a real piece of work."

Sloan couldn't wait to leave the trailer. After years of LaDonna's alcohol-fueled tantrums and spiteful tirades of how Sloan had ruined her life, she was glad to be moving. Once she turned eighteen, there would be no more social service perks for her mother anyway, so escaping now was all the more agreeable. Giving birth to the baby seemed a fair trade-off to her.

She met Dawson and Franklin at the trailer's door. "I'm packed."

Dawson reached for the lone roller suitcase and battered case that held her guitar. "Got it."

Franklin stared at the two pieces. "This is all?"

"All I want to take," she said with a shrug. "Can't fit into any of my clothes anyway, so I'm just taking a few of my favorites for after the baby's born."

"We'll buy you new clothes," Franklin told her. "Before and after," he added quickly.

She warmed to that offer quickly, but once they arrived at the house, Franklin put her stuff in the upstairs guest room. She had been given the status of a visitor, a girl just passing through, without a passport—no pressure over getting married. They ate supper from takeout cartons at the kitchen table, but it wasn't like times she'd eaten there in the past. This meal was subdued and awkward with few words spoken and long stretches of silence. Sloan's stomach was queasy and her mind numb. She was a stranger in a strange land, placed there by circumstance, not because she belonged. Before he went up to bed, Franklin said, "I'll arrange an appointment with one of our ob-gyns tomorrow, get you on prenatal vitamins. If I get called out in the middle of the night, I'll try not to wake you going down the hall."

Later that night when they were alone, Dawson asked, "Want to watch TV downstairs with me?"

"No. I'm just going to bed."

He fidgeted, went to the refrigerator, and copped a soda. At the top of the basement stairs, he said, "I'm glad you're here."

The words sounded hollow to her, but she forced a smile. "Me too."

Later during the night, she woke, shaking all over from fear and loneliness. Quietly, she bundled up in the quilt from the bed and stole down the stairs and into Dawson's basement room. As silently as possible, she got into bed beside him.

He was awake and felt her body's pressure on the mattress. He told himself he should say something to her. But he didn't. So they lay beside one another in the dark, without speaking and without touching.

CHAPTER 15

Lani was one of the first to know about Sloan and Dawson. When she went into the ob-gyn clinic at the hospital to pick up vials of blood work for the lab, she saw them sitting in the waiting area, a chair width apart. Each was concentrating on their cell phones, and although she passed right in front of them, they never looked up, never noticed her. The receptionist buzzed her into the patient-doctor area. Lani hurried to the staff room where the samples waited and where she stood for a moment catching her breath, waiting for her heartbeat to slow and stomach to settle.

One of the OB nurses, Patsy, breezed through the doorway of the all-white room. "Hey, Lani. Full house today. Rooms are packed with mamas-to-be. Whoa! You okay? You look pale as a ghost."

"Guess I didn't eat enough breakfast this morning," Lani lied, and forced a smile.

"Low blood sugar will get you every time. Sit down. I'll bring you some juice from our fridge in back." The woman didn't wait for an answer, just left.

Lani eased into a straight-back chair and took deep breaths, trying to wrap her head around what she'd seen. And how much it hurt. She wanted to shrug it off, be indifferent, wanted to act as "a trained professional" in real-world lingo. She'd never had a chance with Dawson in the first place. He had belonged to Sloan Quentin for months. So why did seeing him in that waiting room hurt so much? Her answer—because now there was no more pretending, no more scripting of a kiss for herself that would never come. The door of wishful thinking slammed in her face.

Patsy returned and handed her a juice box. "This will hike up your blood sugar quickly. Go to the cafeteria and grab some food, though. If you don't, your glucose level will fall again."

Lani poked the little straw into the top of the box with trembling fingers. She took a swig. "Um . . . I saw someone sitting out in the waiting room. Looked like a guy from my high school."

Patsy glanced over her shoulder and leaned closer. "Dr. Berke's son and his girlfriend. Sad story. They're just kids. The girl's several months along and hasn't had any prenatal care. Doc Berke asked Dr. Ortiz to handle the pregnancy because teens are in the high-risk category and high risk is his specialty." With every word, Lani felt her heart tumbling like rocks down a chute. "Ortiz likes the daddies to come to as many of the appointments as possible so he can hear exactly what's going on during the pregnancy. It helps a father bond with the baby that's coming."

"Makes sense." Lani could hardly speak. The juice tasted sickly sweet.

Patsy caught Lani's eye. "You won't say anything, will you? I mean, it's important to respect their privacy."

Lani nodded. "I won't say anything."

"I figured you wouldn't." Patsy flashed a big grin. "You feeling better yet?"

Lani got to her feet. "Much," she lied again. "Well, better get the blood samples over to the lab before they send out a hunting dog for me." She picked up the sealed bag of vials. "Thanks for the juice."

"See you next time."

Lani went out to the waiting room, saw that Sloan and Dawson were gone, and surmised that they'd been called back and put into a small exam room. She hurried down the hall, remembering homecoming night and images of Sloan dressed in black leather, singing into a mike, looking like every guy's wet dream. Good thing the band had broken up already because Sloan would be trading her guitar for a baby sling. Lani knew she wouldn't say anything at school but also knew the news would get around. This kind of news always did.

"Guess what?" In the middle of the next week, while Lani was standing at her locker, Kathy came alongside zinging like a buzz saw. Lani froze, knowing in her gut what was coming next. Kathy blurted, "Sloan's pregnant. And Dawson's the daddy!"

Lani kept focus on her combination lock. "Where'd you hear that?"

"It's all over school. A few of the cheerleaders heard Sloan in the bathroom this morning in one of the stalls, and when she walked out, they could tell she'd been hanging facedown in the toilet."

"Maybe she has the flu." Lani spun the dial and tugged, but the lock held; she'd missed a number and started over.

88

"Nope. She's moved into Dawson's house. Marylyn saw them on Saturday going up on the porch with her suitcase. Anyway, today just confirms it. Moving in. Tossing her cookies this morning. No flu, Lani. Sloan's all preggie. Couldn't happen to a more deserving slut, eh?"

Lani wanted to slap the glee off Kathy's face. "*Really?* Is that the *only* topic of the day?"

Kathy cut her eyes. "I know it's all about Dawson for you, but babies are so preventable. I'll bet she wanted it to happen . . . maybe even planned it."

Lani saw no reason for Kathy to torture her. She knew how Lani felt toward Dawson, and Lani knew for a fact that Kathy not only had no boyfriend, but she also hadn't even had a boy kiss her since seventh grade. Lani conquered her lock. "Well, I'm sorry it happened and *very* sorry people haven't got anything else to talk about, especially *you*." Lani gathered her books, shut her locker, and scuttled down the hall, knowing that she'd just cut some kind of cord between herself and Kathy. Most likely irreparable.

~~~

Sloan ignored the gossip and stares as best she could. Let them talk! She'd faced them down for years, and she'd do it again. There were laws in place allowing pregnant teens to finish school and with graduation so close, the administration and teachers ignored her "condition." She hid her growing abdomen under baggy shirts and pants with expandable waists. *Ugly clothes.*

For his part, Dawson stayed by her side, walked her through the halls with his arm slung around her shoulders, even asked her if she'd like to do prom night. "If you want to go—"

"And wear what? Do they make preggie prom dresses? Do I want to be stared at all night long by girls wearing size twos? Get caught by roaming photo-trolls for a spot in our yearbook? I'm not the sentimental type, Dawson. Prom doesn't mean shit to me."

So while their classmates dressed in beautiful gowns and tuxes and rode in rented limos to the prom held in the ballroom of the local Holiday Inn, Sloan and Dawson went to a midnight showing of a blood-and-guts action flick.

In the dark, nobody saw what you looked like.

On the first weekend of May, Melody graduated from Vanderbilt Law School with honors, in an early morning ceremony held outdoors on the lawn of Curry Field. Heralded by the sound of a trumpet, the law graduates, dressed in black gowns and wearing black caps with purple tassels, followed a line of distinguished robed professors in a pomp and circumstance processional. When Mel crossed the stage to accept her diploma, her parents cheered and Lani imagined herself receiving her nursing degree in a ceremony at MTSU. She was already over high school, mentally comparing it to a cadaver. Her future, her dreams, lay beyond the walk in two weeks in her high school cap and gown. In three years she'd be an RN.

Once the diploma ceremony concluded, a noon reception serving strawberries and champagne was held on the lush lawn of the Vandy library. The crystal-clear day glowed with sunlight and the scent of magnolias floated in the air. Randy put his arms around Melody's and Lani's waists, while Jane took endless digital pictures. Then Jane traded places with him and took more pictures. Mel gathered her family, held up her cell, and took several selfies. Lani groaned. "Enough already! My face hurts from smiling!"

"Life event!" Randy held a finger high. "Must be thoroughly documented!"

"We're so proud of you both." Jane hugged her girls, and Randy set out on another round of in-the-moment preservation.

The family went to the Capitol Grille inside the stately Hermitage Hotel, a building rich with tradition and Southern charm, graced by an elegant lobby of arched ceilings, thick rich carpets, damask and velvet fabrics on sofas and chairs, and huge urns of fresh flowers placed on tables and credenzas. As soon as they ordered their food, Melody tapped her water glass lightly with the edge of her knife. All eyes at the table turned to her.

She cleared her throat. "I have an announcement! I have a job. A real job in a law office." She held them in suspense for a few beats, then leaned forward and said, "And it's right there in Windemere. I'm moving back home."

CHAPTER 16

For a moment no one spoke; then everyone spoke at once. Landing a job right out of law school wasn't always easy for new grads. Mel interned two of her three summers while in law school with a firm in Nashville, but a job in her hometown? "*Seriously?*" Randy asked above the others' voices. "That's terrific!"

Over the holidays, Melody had confided in Lani about the interview and how much she wanted the job. Lani had been surprised because she'd thought Mel would have gone with some big firm far away from Windemere. But Melody had told her, "I'm just like Dad . . . not a fan of big-city life. I want to come home." Once she became an RN, Lani would take a job at any children's hospital offering her one. Until then she would live at home, forfeiting the "going away for college" experience of many of her classmates.

"Of course, it's contingent on my passing the bar exam in July."

"Piece of cake," Randy said.

"Not true, Dad. The exam's hard and lasts two days. People choke."

Jane reached over and clasped Melody's hand. "Don't keep us in suspense. Where in Windemere will you be working?"

"You remember Mr. Boatwright in that old Victorian house off Main Street?"

"Of course. He's been in practice for, what, a hundred years?"

"Very funny, Dad. He's a very trusted attorney with a big practice."

"Tax and real estate, if I recall."

"And plenty of insurance lawsuits after the tornado. My turf." Melody, looking wolfish, rubbed her palms together. "Many people in town have held policies for decades, but when they wanted to rebuild, their insurers began holding back on the payouts. It's not right. People deserve better. They need an advocate." Melody's impassioned plea turned heads at a nearby table.

"I hear these stories every day at the paper. . . . Some are pretty sad. The wheels of justice grind slowly. Can you speed them up?"

"Going to try."

"You getting your name on Boatwright's shingle?"

"In gold script."

Randy grinned. "I like knowing my girl is taking up a cause to help people. Nice going, kitten." He used her childhood nickname, and Melody did an eye roll.

Lani giggled. Mel was "kitten." She was "cupcake." She swore she'd never dump a nickname on a child. Too embarrassing in mixed company once a girl started wearing lipstick and shaving her legs.

The waiter arrived with their food, and conversation slowed while he set the plates around the table—steaks, fish, roasted chicken.

"You moving back to your old room?" Randy bit into a fried mushroom.

"No." Melody said the word gently, glancing between her parents. "I'll have my own apartment near the office. You know that old redbrick two-story house on Magnolia Street? Completely redone after the tornado. I've already signed a lease."

"You don't have to pay rent." Jane looked aghast. "It's free to live at home. We can fix up your room, change the paint, new bedding . . . whatever."

"I'll be getting a paycheck, Mom. I want my own space. But thank you for the offer."

While the waiter poured a round of fresh water from a glass pitcher, Lani watched the play of emotions on her parents' faces. Her sister was wrapping up her childhood, closing out the chapters, making her own choices. The return to the town was not a return to the past, but to her future. So no matter how much Mom fixed up Mel's childhood room, her sister would never live in it again. Lani wished she were on the same road instead of just beginning the journey.

Franklin took Dawson and Sloan out to dinner and invited LaDonna to join them after the high school graduation ceremony on Saturday afternoon. Windemere had a couple of better eateries, both high-end chain establishments near the mall by the interstate. He chose the steak house. Once seated at the table, Sloan felt nauseated by the smell of the sizzling meats from a surrounding table, but she was determined to make it through the meal.

LaDonna had dressed in her best outfit, a black skirt and low-cut red top. Her hair was newly bleached and had been poufed professionally at the salon. "Wasn't that just lovely? My sweet little girl all graduated."

Sloan took a long sip of water to keep from gagging. When had she ever been LaDonna's "sweet little girl"?

"You must be so proud too, Franklin. Oh my . . . I *can* call you Franklin, can't I? I mean, since we're all going to be family soon."

Dawson glanced at his father, wondering why he'd invited Sloan's mother to this meal. When Franklin had met with her after Sloan had moved in to their house, she'd acted belligerent and contentious. Until Franklin had mentioned money, and then LaDonna's whole demeanor had changed. And now here she was eating a meal with them, all chummy and chatty. He saw that Sloan wasn't happy about it either.

"Of course you can call me Franklin. Graduation is a big deal, twelve years of schooling, done. We should all celebrate it together."

Dawson thought he and Sloan should be at a blowout grad party, celebrating. Instead his life was upside down. Inside out. Free-falling into . . . *what*?

A waiter appeared asking for drink orders. Franklin went for ice tea and Dawson and Sloan went with colas. Sloan saw her mother teeter on the edge of ordering alcohol but retreat to ice tea. A relief because LaDonna drinking wouldn't be a good thing.

Feeling as if she were going to jump out of her skin, Sloan excused herself and hurried to the restroom. She slipped into a stall and rested her forehead on the cold metal door, telling herself to get a grip, that the meal wouldn't last forever. But when she came out of the stall, LaDonna was waiting for her at the sink, her eyes glinting like marbles. "You've been avoiding me ever since you moved over to the boy's house, and I want to talk to you in private."

Sloan's stomach knotted. "This isn't a good time. How about next week?"

"Now is a good time."

Resigned, trapped, Sloan turned on the water. "What?"

"I just want to remind you that that baby inside you is a gold mine. Play your cards right, and we can make out real good with that doctor and his son."

Sloan backed away from the sink, where LaDonna was crowding her. "What do you mean, a 'gold mine'?"

"Don't act dense, girl. That man, Franklin, he wants this grandchild. Bad."

"What are you saying? That you don't?"

LaDonna drummed her fingertips on the countertop, ignoring the question. "His boy don't seem as happy about it, but *hell*, why didn't you tell me sooner? I'm your mama! At first I couldn't figure why you'd dragged those two with you when you first told me."

"They wanted to be with me when I told you." Not the exact truth, but close enough in Sloan's mind. "To explain how they would take care of me. I like that, Ma. Being taken care of."

"If that's a way of spitting on me, save it! *No* reason at all for you to have this baby if you don't want to. Why didn't you just take your ass to one of them clinics? You could have had it taken care of like *that*." She snapped her fingers to make her point. "You didn't even have to tell the boy he was going to be a daddy."

As if the day's events—the boring ceremony, the endless speeches from magna-this and magna-cum-that, of being seated alphabetically rows away from Dawson, of wanting to run screaming out of the auditorium—hadn't been hard enough. Now she was cornered by LaDonna and being verbally flogged. "But I *did* tell him."

LaDonna's eyes narrowed, and she poked Sloan in the abdomen. "Well I'm not stupid, girl. I got to thinking, Why? Why would you *choose* to have this baby? Babies are a lot of trouble, you know. And expense. And then the wheels in my head started to turn. And I realized you had a plan."

LaDonna's voice was soft and slithery. Sloan backed against the cool tile of the wall. "A plan? What are you talking about?"

"You want to have that baby because you know Franklin will pay money to keep it in his life." LaDonna looked triumphant.

"What are you saying? I didn't have a plan. All I wanted was to get out of this place, go somewhere else." Her mother's conclusion washed over her like muddy water. True, she hadn't wanted the baby at first, but after learning what it meant to Franklin and Dawson, things had changed.

"Just what the world needs. Another unwed teen mother!" *Catty.*

"Dawson wants to *marry* me."

"Well, girlie, your daddy said he'd marry me too when I told him I was PG. So I had you, and six months later he was gone. Like the wind. Just walked out the door and left me with a squalling baby and not a dime. I had nothing!"

LaDonna had said he'd walked out when she told him she

was pregnant, but now Sloan heard another truth leaking through the fabric of the story: *I would have aborted you if I'd known he would leave.* Her mother had never wanted her! She rushed to the sink and retched.

LaDonna ripped paper towels from the dispenser, wet them, and pressed the wad to Sloan's mouth. She patted her on the back.

Sloan shuddered, not from nausea but from her mother's touch. She had just learned that she had been a tool, a way to make the man who'd contributed half her DNA to stay. The gamble had lost. He'd left them both.

"There, there . . . I do recall that terrible feeling of wanting to puke when I was pregnant with you. I thought I would throw up my toenails some days. I was over six months along with you before it passed. But it does pass, I promise." Her tone had changed to a cooing, which was worse than being yelled at.

LaDonna turned Sloan's face toward hers, wiped a mascara smear from her cheek. She smoothed Sloan's hair. "My, you look a fright, but that's okay. Creates sympathy." She peered into Sloan's eyes. "I'm right, aren't I? You let yourself get knocked up by a doctor's son because you understood what you'd gotten hold of." LaDonna, seeming completely sure she'd drawn the right conclusions, smiled as if congratulating herself.

"What would that be, Mama? What do I get?"

"An eighteen-year meal ticket if you handle it right. Those men will do anything to keep that baby near them. So here's what I'm thinking. You have this baby, and you bring it back to the trailer. We'll take care of it together. And they'll give us money to raise it up for a real long time." She flashed a smile. "That sound like a good idea, honey?"

Sloan's insides turned cold and solid as ice.

LaDonna patted her again. "Now let's put on our smiley faces and go have a big old dinner that Franklin's just itching to pay for. It's graduation day." She beamed a smile, grabbed the door handle, and stood back so that Sloan could pass in front of her.

"Little tummy episode," LaDonna said once they sat down at the table, her hand on Sloan's elbow. "You know how delicate a mama-to-be is at this stage."

Franklin gave Sloan a concerned look, and Sloan offered a weak but hesitant smile to assure him she was all right, although it wasn't true. When the waiter returned, she ordered a salad, unsure she could keep it down. She felt battered and bruised. Under the table, she felt Dawson grope for her hand; he captured it and held on until her icy fingertips warmed from his touch.

CHAPTER 17

When he was a kid, Dawson had owned a furry brown and white hamster he named Earl. Earl's lifestyle commitment was to live in a cage where he slept, ate, burrowed into fresh sawdust changed every week, and exercised like a demon on a hamster wheel most of the night. Now all these years later, Dawson knew what it was like to live like Earl. Except that Earl probably didn't think much about his life, while Dawson Berke dwelled constantly on his own life and what it had become—mind-numbing, pathetic, lonely. *Lucky clueless Earl.*

The first thing he'd done after Sloan moved in was to open the file folder with his college letters of acceptance, brochures, forms, and applications and stuff each one into his dad's paper shredder. He didn't want to be reminded of what he wouldn't have come September. Plans deferred due to unforeseen circumstances.

After graduation, Dawson took a job with a lawn service and came home every day hot, sweaty, and covered with grass clippings. He hated the job, not because of the hard, sweaty work but because he felt trapped, hammered in place, and without options. Months before, he'd had plans for college. He'd had choices. Now he was on the hamster wheel, spinning and spinning and going nowhere.

Franklin had told him that after the baby was born, they could live with him so that Dawson could save up money, maybe get his own place. He also said he'd pay Dawson's tuition at MTSU community college. Dawson knew his dad was attempting to help, but no way could he think about his impending fatherhood plus classes, studying, and holding down a job. In truth, not much *was* helping him during this long hot summer of Sloan's pregnancy. Gone was the fun they once had together. She was moody and temperamental, but the good news was that they rarely argued. That would have required talking to each other. He kept reminding himself that he *loved* this girl—didn't he? Still he was unhappy, angry, and scared. And yet watching her belly expand, feeling the baby kick when he lay beside her in bed, was a head trip.

The baby, seen only in sonograms, had a human shape in shades of gray. Once, the image caught the fetus sucking its thumb. They also learned it was a boy. All the little guy had to do was gain more weight, turn his head downward into the birth canal, and be born in mid-September. All Dawson had to do was figure out how to take care of his . . . what? Family?

He wished he could talk to his mother. Would she be heartbroken over what was happening? Would she like Sloan? Would she still love *him*? Endless unanswerable questions. Another hamster wheel.

Sloan was sharing the guest room with a crib and a changing table. Dawson and Franklin had painted the walls pale blue, set up a dark wood crib, and draped a blue baby blanket over the railing. She usually slept in the room's double bed but would sometimes venture down to Dawson's bed and the comfort of his arms. Most of the time, she felt bewildered and disconnected, unable to get her head around the idea that a living human being would emerge from her body and that she would instantly turn into a mother.

She rarely left the house. She had no car. She spent hours writing music, playing her guitar, remembering how great the world looked from a stage with a view of an audience clapping and shouting her name. Life wasn't turning out the way she'd planned. Dawson said he loved her many times. She wanted to love him. But her head wouldn't stop filling with memories of the things she had always wanted. Her bright spot was separation from her mother.

LaDonna came around occasionally, usually during her noon lunch hour if she was in town working. Not wanting to listen to LaDonna's plans about Sloan and the baby moving in with her, Sloan never answered the door before two o'clock. She was stacking clothes from the dryer one July morning after Dawson and Franklin had gone for the day when the doorbell started to chime and wouldn't quit. This early, she figured it wasn't LaDonna. She went to the door and threw it open to a flood of sunlight and to Jarred Tester standing on the porch.

Stunned, she backpedaled, looking for shadows to cover her. When she found her voice, she said, "Go away."

"Can we talk?"

A rush of heat flushed through her. "Go. Away."

"Please, Sloan. Just let me talk to you. I'll leave as soon as

I do." Boldly he tried the screen door handle. It wasn't locked. She pushed back, but he pushed it open, reached in, and caught her wrist. "We can sit on the porch. In plain sight. I haven't come to scare you." His voice was soft, non-threatening. He tugged her gently into the sunlight. "I just want to talk."

She was powerless against the pull of him and followed him to the wicker chairs at the far end of the porch. He turned and took both her hands in his, his eyes assessing her, widening as he took in her expanded belly. She felt humiliated. "Please leave." She couldn't stop staring at him. He looked different now, more polished, and slimmer, with an expensive haircut and clothes that fit his toned, muscled body perfectly.

"Not till I say what I want to say." Jarred gentled her into a chair and then took the one across from her, a small wicker table between them. He didn't let go of her hand. "You look—"

"I know what I look like, so forget any lies you're going to tell." She snatched her hand from his, angry because he'd stirred up feelings and memories she didn't want. "Why are you here? To gloat? I'm not sorry about homecoming, Jarred. Not one bit!"

"Not asking you to be sorry about it." He offered a conciliatory smile. "That was all on me and I deserved it. But that was then. This is now. New day. Fresh start."

Her gaze tracked the arrow tips down his neck that disappeared under the collar of his shirt and reemerged from under the sleeve. Easier than looking into his eyes. "How'd you find me?"

"Stopped by the trailer last night and your mom told me. Drove here and parked down the street last night." He gestured with his head and she spied his Mustang sitting along the curb.

"Last night?"

"Slept in the backseat. I cleaned up at a gas station around six this morning and waited for the house to clear so we could talk."

She remembered the last time she'd looked into the Mustang's backseat. Feeling angry all over again, she pushed against the rising tide. "So what did my 'mommy' have to say?" She could only imagine how LaDonna must have dissed her to him.

"She was drinking, so I got an earful." He waved his hand to blow off whatever LaDonna had told him. "But she kept saying she's looking forward to you moving back with the baby when it's born. That true?"

"I'm not."

"You married to this Dawson?" She shook her head. "Planning to?"

"Don't know." She lifted her chin. "He *wants* to marry me." Jarred went quiet. A butterfly settled on a bush next to the porch railing. A bird chirped. Heat built. Sloan fingered the hem of the oversized tee she wore. "So why did you come and sleep all night in your car just so you can talk to me alone?"

Jarred leaned forward. The wicker creaked. "I'm putting the band back together. Bobby and Hal are on board. Calder's headed off to college, but that's all right. I have a new keyboard man in Nashville named Josiah. He's older and he's good, better than Calder. His dad's some big-deal hedge fund guru and richer than God. They have an estate *and* Sy has a recording studio on-site. Very sweet . . . you wouldn't believe the equipment." Jarred's eyes shone as he described the state-of-the-art sound-mixing boards, amps, mikes, and top-of-the-line everything. "But Sy's parents don't live there. They've got a place in New York, so Sy's got the Nashville house to himself. Been living there myself for three months."

She closed her eyes, pictured the former band, felt tears behind her eyelids. "Sounds like you landed on your feet with this Josiah."

Jarred planted a hand on her knee, and warmth seeped through her skin. "Look, we won't be some cobbled-together garage bangers. We'll have a new sound, a new look. We have a place to live and one hundred percent access to Sy's studio. We'll pull our music together, cut a demo, shop it around. I'm talking a business deal between us, nothing more." He made a circle in the air. "This will be my band, but we'll all be partners. This is legit, Sloan. I want this music thing real bad."

Me too. "So you're starting over. I'm happy for you."

He rested his arms on the chair and leaned back, studying her. "When I first got to Nashville, I worked my ass off, barely scraped by at first. Slept in my car for a while. Lots of odd jobs and a fill-in as a session artist for other bands. That's how I met Sy. We clicked artistically."

"And the drugs?"

He waved his hand as if shooing a fly. "Nothing, I swear. Sy doesn't touch the stuff, so neither do I. Music business comes first. Always."

"And what do you want from me?"

"I want you to sign on, Sloan. You're the best singer I've ever heard. We were good together . . . the writing, the way we were on the same wavelength." He didn't mention everything else they once had together, but she couldn't forget it. Jarred continued. "Everything I've been writing was with you in mind on vocals. There are people out there who still remember Anarchy. We were damn good. And you know it."

She knew it, all right. And, oh God, how she wanted it. A kick from inside her belly cruelly flung her back to earth.

She flattened her palm on her protruding abdomen. "I'm not exactly in singing shape, Jarred. I can hardly breathe, much less sing."

"When's it supposed to be born?"

"September."

A smile lit his face. "No prob. Hal's coming next month, but Bobby can't come until after Labor Day. We'll wait for you." He let the offer dangle, then added, "If you marry this Dawson, he's welcome to come too. Lots of bands have families and hit the road with them."

Sloan couldn't see that happening. Dawson would never go for it. Just her and the baby . . . ? Torn between past and present, she went silent, her mind churning with feelings and fears.

Jarred stood, looking down at her. "I know I've thrown a lot at you. You don't have to decide this minute. Just think about what I've said, okay?" He reached into his shirt pocket and handed her a business card. "This is how to reach me." She studied the card—the bold black lettering, the line drawing of a guitar—and nodded. He walked to the porch's top step. "After that baby's born, once you know what you want to do, call me either way. I won't look for another singer until I hear from you. But don't wait too long, Sloan. We've got to get this moving."

Sloan sat on the porch long after Jarred drove away in his Mustang, which shone with new black paint, chrome hubcaps, and booming subwoofers, proof that he did have some money. From down the street she heard a dog bark at the mailman coming up the sidewalk of the quaint neighborhood. While she watched the postal guy's progress, she reminded herself of two truths: Jarred knew her weaknesses, her sweet spots. With

Dawson she had security and comfort. Life wasn't perfect between them, but she trusted him.

Yet that evening when Dawson came home, stinking of sweat and grass clippings, she said nothing about her morning visitor.

CHAPTER 18

S loan went into labor seven weeks before her due date. The pain started in her back, woke her from sleep. It hit in waves and made her yelp. She woke Dawson, who ran upstairs and woke Franklin. "I hurt," she said through clenched teeth when Franklin came to her bedside. "Bad! I hurt bad. Make it stop!"

Franklin took her hand. She held his in a death grip. "Let's run you into the hospital for a quick check."

"Isn't it too soon for the baby?" Dawson asked over his father's shoulder. "I mean, the doctor said September."

"Let's get her looked over. Just to be sure."

Confident. Assured. His father, Dr. Berke, a rock. Dawson helped Sloan to the car.

The nurse on the maternity ward confirmed that Sloan was in labor, called her doctor, and whisked her into a room. Dawson stood blinking in the brightly lit hallway, feeling lost and powerless. Suddenly Dr. Ortiz rushed down the hallway from the elevator, gave him a wave, and disappeared into the birthing room. Franklin appeared wearing hospital green from head to toe.

"What's happening? Why are you in scrubs?"

"Because we can't stop her contractions and because I'll be his pediatrician. You want to come in? You're the father. You're allowed."

Dawson felt paralyzed. They'd gone to a few birthing classes. He'd seen the videos, but now the world was in upheaval, and he couldn't grab hold of anything solid inside himself. "Just . . . help her."

"Do you want to call her mother?"

Dawson shook his head. "Sloan doesn't want her here. She told me so months ago."

Franklin vanished into the room.

Minutes later, Dawson heard voices through the closed door. Doctor talk, hectic scramblings, no baby's cry. His heart went stone cold.

—⁂—

Sloan was asleep, the soft night-light over the bed spilling on her face, the rest of the room in deep shadows. Dawson stood over her, a knot of emotion stuck in his throat. He reached down and smoothed her forehead. "You did good."

An hour before, Franklin had come out of the birthing room, swept the green cap off his head, and offered a tight smile. "There's a complication."

Dawson fought his gag reflex. "What's wrong?"

Franklin put his hand on Dawson's shoulder. "He's little . . . four pounds. And his lungs need some time to mature. He's on oxygen and we need to fatten him up. Sloan's just fine, sleeping. She's being taken to a room."

"What do you mean . . . about . . . his lungs?" Dawson's thoughts swirled around the baby.

"Just not ready to breathe on their own, not uncommon in preemies."

"But he's okay. He'll be okay . . . won't he?"

"He's in the NICU and he's *my* patient now." Franklin rested his hand on Dawson's shoulder. "He's getting the best care possible. Just not ready to take on the world yet." Franklin ventured a smile. "He's got your black hair. A full head. Just like you had when you were born. I wish your mother . . ." Franklin pressed his thumbs into his closed eyes. "Sorry. Just tired."

Dawson could only nod. How many times in his life had he wished for the same thing?

Franklin offered a wry grin, wiping away the sadness of loss. He squeezed Dawson's shoulder, shaking it like a dog with a toy. "And I'm a grandfather. What do you know!"

"Well, congratulations, old man. He's related to me too, you know." Dawson banked down his fears and returned his father's smile.

Franklin flung his arm around Dawson's neck and hauled him into a fatherly neck-lock. "Right back at you." They stood grinning stupidly at each other in the hallway, feelings buoyed by each other's pleasure. "You want to see him?"

Dawson had to gown up and wear a mask before going into the neonatal unit. His enthusiasm sobered with every precaution Franklin made him take. The unit was small and its interior dimly lit. Dawson counted seven incubators, but only three held babies. Machines hovered like sentries around each clear plastic shell, emitting beeps and hisses that attested to the work they were doing—sustaining life.

A neonatal nurse, also wearing a gown and mask, greeted them and gestured toward a unit near a wall. Franklin led the way. Dawson followed, but when he looked inside, what he saw so overwhelmed him that he almost turned and ran.

"I know it looks scary, but Dad says he's really doing okay."

It was the morning after the delivery, and this was Sloan's first look at her son. *Her* son was not the chubby perfect newborns in the photos in the birthing books. Her baby lay splayed out, a tube down his throat with tape holding it in position, the other end attached to a machine that breathed for him. There were wires taped to his chest to monitor his heartbeat, and IVs between his toes to hydrate and feed him. He was rail thin, with gauze pads over his eyes, and so small he all but disappeared under all the medical attachments and warming light. Sloan recoiled.

"Dad says it's temporary," Dawson assured her. "Breathing problems are common in preemies. But his lungs will grow stronger. He just needs time."

Sloan heard Dawson's words, but staring down into the incubator pushed against what he was saying and what her eyes were seeing. The newborn's chest rose rapidly, like the beating heart of a bird; his tiny fists were balled, fists so small that they hardly seemed real, doll's hands, maybe clenched in protest to what was happening to his body. She felt queasy, but she couldn't turn away, so mesmerizing was the sight of the baby in the bubble. How could this being who looked more alien than human have possibly come out of her body?

Dawson slipped his arm around Sloan to comfort and assure her. "I know how you feel. I felt the same way the first time I saw him. But his heart's strong. He just needs to fatten up. We . . . uh . . . we can touch him through those armholes with gloves."

She looked from the portals in the plastic incubator to the nearby box of gloves.

"Dad says it's good to touch him, that babies need to be touched. He needs to know we're here. Want to?"

Stroke the baby like she would a sick puppy? Sloan trembled. "I want to go back to my bed."

Dawson felt a letdown. He'd hoped that seeing the baby would encourage Sloan, comfort her and make her feel connected. "All right. We'll come back later." He led her out of the unit, eased her into the mandatory wheelchair, untied her mask, and pushed her down the hall to the elevator. In her room, he helped her into bed. "I know he isn't . . ." He stopped, started again. "But the main thing is he's going to be all right. Dad wouldn't tell us that if it weren't true."

She wouldn't meet Dawson's eyes. Across the room, a new vase of blue-tinged flowers had appeared on her dresser with a helium balloon proclaiming *"It's a BOY!"* The vases and flowers were from hospital staffers. None from anyone she knew.

Dawson took her hand. "How are you feeling?"

She hurt inside and out. "I'm sad. For him." But she was sad for herself too. Sorry she hadn't been able to keep him inside of her long enough so that he was whole and perfect. "I wanted him out so much," she whispered. "All summer. I just wanted it to be over. Maybe . . . I shouldn't have—"

"Wishing him out didn't make him come early. Doesn't work that way. He's little, but he'll get great medical care. And so will you. Dad says once your OB clears you, I can take you back to the house."

"And the baby?"

"The baby stays until he gets cleared to leave. Maybe a few weeks. Or less." He struggled to find something uplifting to talk about to her, flashed on an idea. "Hey, you know, Dad says we should give him a name so we can fill out his birth certificate. You have any preference?"

Her mind blanked. She shrugged. Most of the men in her life had been of the "pass through" variety. Their names and faces blurred in her memory. She chewed on her bottom lip. "You want to name him after you? Or your dad?"

He shook his head. "Not really." Silence stretched. Dawson took a deep breath, knowing this was going to be up to him. "I was kind of thinking . . . of maybe . . . Gabriel, after my great-grandfather. What do you think of naming him Gabriel?"

She thought it was as good a name as any. "Sure. That's fine."

But Dawson could tell she wasn't enthused. "Okay, then how about Gabriel Franklin Berke."

"That's fine." She dropped his hand and rolled onto her side. "I want to sleep now. Really tired." Sleep meant oblivion, a way for her to deal with what could not be changed.

Dawson eased into a bedside chair feeling wrung out, lonely, lost. He stayed until he was certain that she slept.

113

CHAPTER 19

Lani arrived in the nursing administrative offices, her heart pounding and her mind racing. Why had she been called in? Had she done something wrong? A volunteer didn't get called into Mrs. Trammell's office on a whim. Lani wracked her brain, mentally recounting her previous week on the job. *Running blood samples to lab, sponge-bathing an elderly woman in a bed, subbing in the gift shop midday three times, wheeling patients to and from radiology . . .* All routine. Tasks she'd done many times over. She paused at the outer door, chewed on a fingernail, took a deep breath, pasted on a smile, and walked inside.

"Hi, Lani," the receptionist said. "Go right in. Mrs. Trammell's expecting you."

Lani's knees went rubbery, but she entered the inner sanctum, where the head of nursing smiled and motioned her to sit in a chair in front of her desk. "You're not in trouble," were Mrs. Trammell's first words. "In fact, I called you in because of your excellent work and exemplary attitude. In short, you play well with others. Every staff person who's come in contact with you thinks you're going to be a wonderful nurse."

The praise blindsided Lani because her thoughts had never gone in this direction. "I love my work," she said, despite her adrenaline overload.

"It's obvious." The woman rifled papers on her desk, looked up, flashed a quick smile. "And you'll begin courses at MTSU soon?"

"Yes. In a couple of weeks." She'd made out her class schedule, adjusted her hours at Bellmeade so as to not conflict with her volunteer hours. "But I don't mind working more hours if you need me."

Mrs. Trammell smiled. "Good. Maybe we will. Truth is, we're shorthanded, so I'm thinking of asking you to be a snuggler. What would you think about that?"

And an hour later, Lani found herself gowned and gloved in the dimly lit preemies unit with Delilah, the RN on duty, walking between incubators and the machines keeping alive babies born too soon. Delilah spoke softly. "Snuggling's a primo job, and a simple one. Usually volunteer grandmothers do it, most are retired nurses from the community, but a couple of them are on vacation and one's out sick, so we thought we might train some of our current volunteers. And your name came up."

"I plan to go into pediatrics."

"Well, this is a good place to start. Simply put, snugglers hold, feed, and rock babies." She gestured with her chin toward a grouping of wooden rocking chairs clustered in a corner. "Of course, you'll glove and gown, but the job's pretty simple. Some of these preemies will be here a long time, and they need to be held and cuddled. Human contact—very important. Incubators are a nice place to sleep, but nothing replaces loving arms. Parents and families normally do this, but sometimes circumstances come along . . ." She paused beside two incubators holding very frail-looking infants. "These two are crack babies, and their birth mothers walked out right after delivery."

Lani watched as the babies twitched and trembled from drug withdrawal. The sight of them, knowing they were abandoned, helpless and addicted, took the wind out of her. "What will happen to them?"

"Health and Human Services will take them over once they're healthy enough to leave. Sometimes the mothers get clean and claim them, but not always."

Delilah moved on, halted beside another incubator. "This little guy's closest to being released if he has no further setbacks."

Lani read the name card . . . *Berke, Gabriel* . . . and her heart did a stutter step. The baby wore a pale blue cotton knit cap with black hair peeking from under the cap's edges. A cannula in his tiny nose delivered oxygen. "He's doing better?"

"Oxygen only now because he's off his feeding tube, and we're teaching him to suckle from a bottle."

"Teaching him?" Lani thought babies were born able to nurse.

"His sucking reflex must be retrained. Which is where snugglers come in. His father shows up before and after work each day to feed him, and Dr. Berke stops in often, but a preemie can take a long time getting only a few ounces down. He needs six ounces about every three hours." Delilah unwrapped Gabriel's blanket, wound round him like a cocoon, and flicked the bottoms of his feet. "Hey, little boy, wake up. Time to eat."

The baby's face puckered as if in protest, but his eyes remained closed. Delilah brought one of the chairs closer, gestured to Lani. "Sit." When Lani did, the nurse placed him in her arms careful that the oxygen line was unobstructed.

Lani had held several babies on the peds floor, but none this small. She was scared but didn't want to show it.

Delilah took a bottle from her pocket and pulled the covering off the smallest nipple Lani had ever seen. "Your job is to make sure he drinks all of this formula. When he drifts off, flick the bottoms of his feet to keep him awake. It's important to help him get through every feeding."

Lani teased the nipple between Gabriel's tiny lips, but he turned his head and pushed his fists into the blanket.

"He's fighting you, but don't give up. Snuggle him close. Let him feel your warmth. That's right. Good. He's calming." From another part of the room, a baby began to cry. "Whoops. Duty calls. Catch my eye when the bottle's empty and I'll come and put him back in his nest." Delilah started to walk away.

"What about his mother? Doesn't she come to rock and feed him?"

"She did for a while. Not so much anymore."

Lani gazed at Gabriel's sweet face. *Dawson's child . . .* She cuddled him so that his ear lay pressed against the left side of her chest, where he stilled, relaxed, drew in the formula to the steady rhythmic sound he'd heard every moment he'd been growing in the womb, the beat of a human heart. *Her* heart.

Sloan rattled around the house, drifting through rooms like a ghost. Gabriel had spent five days on a ventilator that had coated his lungs with a surfactant that all healthy lungs

117

needed to aid breathing. Yet he remained in NICU on oxygen twelve days after being born. "Failure to thrive," Franklin had told her and Dawson. "But he's learning how to take a bottle and is starting to put on weight. A good sign." Dawson spent every minute of his free time at the hospital with Gabe. She did not.

Sloan thought back to when she'd gloved up and first touched the baby. Through the glove's thin membrane, Gabriel's skin felt warm and incredibly smooth. Franklin had told her, "You can hold him and rock him. That's why we have rocking chairs. It's important that he's held. To bond . . . you understand?"

"How about it?" Dawson had given her a hopeful look. "He's light as a feather."

"Tomorrow."

The allure of Jarred's plan to put the band together never ceased replaying inside her head. Especially at night when darkness ruled. She'd slept in the guest room every night since giving birth. "To recover," she told Dawson, but also to think, to worry, and to wonder about the future and its possibilities. Dawson had broached marriage to her once more, but her heart grabbed and her palms got sweaty when he pressed her. "Still thinking about it."

In the daylight, her thoughts dwelled on Gabriel, on his coming home. Franklin had promised a helper, a licensed RN, until Sloan felt better able to cope with caring for him. But once the nurse left, what then? *Motherhood.* The very word terrified Sloan. Texts from LaDonna, who'd somehow learned about the early birth were disturbing, insistent that Sloan and the baby return to the trailer once his hospital stay was over.

"I'm the grandmother. I got rights!" was what she texted or shouted if Sloan answered her cell.

Sloan wondered if that was true. What kind of rights did her mother have? *Could* she make demands and *would* her demands be upheld by the law? She knew LaDonna had fought for and won her "rights" before. The memories were fuzzy, but Sloan knew that a lawyer had been involved and then bigger welfare checks had started coming. LaDonna had celebrated her legal victory with a whoop. Sloan cringed. There was no way in hell she could be a part of letting LaDonna get her hands on that baby.

Now alone in the house, Sloan couldn't turn off her thoughts or her fears. She stared out the oversized kitchen window, at the morning sunlight filtering through the limp leaves of a dogwood tree. She watched a sparrow perch on a branch, but when it caught sight of her through the glass, the brown bird stretched its wings and flitted away. She envied it. *How simple. Spread your wings and fly.* And in that instant, she made up her mind about what to do.

Sloan hurried upstairs, found her purse, fished Jarred's card from its hiding place in her wallet, and dialed his number. He answered on the second ring.

"Sloan! How are you? What's up?"

"Baby's delivered. He came early."

Long pause. "Do you want me to come get you?"

"Yes. Now. I'm alone . . . you should come right away."

He stuttered a bit, said something over his shoulder, then, "I'm on my way."

Knowing she had about fifty minutes until Jarred arrived, Sloan grabbed her roller bag from the closet and started packing. Leaving most of the maternity clothes in the closet and dresser drawers, she packed the things she'd brought with her months before and only kept a few of the baby-mama pieces until she could get into hers again.

When she finished, she looked around the room, her gaze flitting from the cozy unmade bed to the sunlit window, and knew that she was leaving a safe haven for the unknown. Franklin and Dawson had kept the bargain they'd made with her, of paying her medical bills and meeting her day-to-day needs. Her conscience pricked and she glanced around for a piece of paper, thinking she should leave a note. What could she possibly say? She blew out a lungful of air, reminded herself that she'd kept her end of the bargain too . . . she'd had the baby. She left no note. Dawson would figure it out.

Sloan fidgeted for the fifty minutes it took Jarred to arrive, chewing her bottom lip, pacing, staring out the front window. When his car pulled into the driveway, she gave the house, her home for months, one last look. It had been a refuge, a safe haven, but she couldn't dwell on it. The baby was better off with Dawson and Franklin. They would know how to handle LaDonna. Staying in Windemere, being a wife and mother, was more than she could handle, and LaDonna would never go away as long as Sloan was in the picture.

She descended from the porch. Jarred tossed her things into the backseat, settled her in the front. Once on the Interstate speeding to Nashville, he said, "I'm glad you decided to do this. You won't be sorry."

Riding with him in his car after so many months felt awkward. She wasn't sure of her feelings for him anymore. He was edgy, volatile, and not exactly trustworthy, but he excited her, and always had. Music was the thing that bound them. Feeling like a fleeing prisoner, she said, "I want to sing. This is best for all of us."

Jarred reached over and cupped her hand in his. "We're going to be a huge hit, Sloan. I got big plans for the band. I'm changing the name—did I tell you?" He hadn't. "Yeah . . . Loose Change. Lots of opportunity for us in Nashville." He gave her a sideways glance. "Um . . . is it going to take long for . . . you to, you know, get your body back in shape?"

She shot him the finger.

He grinned. "Don't get me wrong, Sloan. You're still pretty . . . like always. I'm just thinking about the way you used to look onstage. The fans loved your look. Me too."

She leaned into the headrest. "Don't worry, I'll be ready when the band is."

"Sure. Right. We've just got a lot of work ahead of us. The good part is that you're on board. You won't believe where you'll be living. I mean, Sy's house is one of those uber-modern places—" He stopped because Sloan wasn't listening, but instead was staring out the side window. "Hey." He squeezed her hand. "No matter what happened between us before, I never forgot what we once had. You still my girl?"

She was a hundred miles away from that high school girl he'd once known. "I'm my own girl, Jarred." She rolled down the window and let the hot wind whip her hair into tangles.

Jarred turned on the radio, blasting the volume until she felt the bass vibrate through the car's seat. He started singing to the song as the car hit eighty.

CHAPTER 20

"She's gone." Dawson stood in the doorway of his father's hospital office, hands braced on either side of the door frame.

Franklin, stuffing papers in his briefcase, looked up, startled. "Who's gone?"

"Sloan. She just up and left."

His eyes widened. "Are you sure?"

"Hell yes, I'm sure! She promised me she would come with me tonight to see Gabriel, but she's run away." He'd come home to shower, pick up Sloan, and return to the hospital, but he'd felt the emptiness, the echo of silence the minute he stepped through the doorway. Bounding upstairs, he called her name. No answer. He threw open her bedroom door, saw the closet door opened wide, several hangers stripped of clothing, and the dustless places on her dresser where her cosmetics had lain. The missing guitar case was the final confirmation. At first Dawson had stood, gripping the doorknob, his gaze skimming the room, taking it all in, absorbing the truth, unwilling to truly believe it. Reporting it to Franklin only made him angrier. "She's *gone*."

"Maybe her mother—"

"She hates LaDonna. She'd never go there."

"Any idea where she might have gone? How she left without a car of her own?"

"I don't know and I don't *care*." He balled his fists.

Franklin flattened his palms on his desk. "I don't know what to tell you. I'm sorry, son."

"Why would she do that? Run away?" His anger morphed into bewilderment. "Okay . . . maybe I'm no prize, but Gabriel . . . he's just a baby. What mother leaves her *baby?*"

"A scared one." Franklin shook his head. "Maybe she'll return after some time thinking things out."

"You don't know Sloan. She won't be back, and I won't go looking for her. She doesn't want us. I don't want her!"

From the corridor, a voice from the PA requested some doctor to come to the third floor. Franklin straightened items on his desk, then looked to Dawson still in the doorway. "Question is, what are you going to do?"

"What kind of a question is that? I won't run away. I'm not a quitter like Sloan."

Franklin hunched, staring down at the mahogany surface. "It won't be easy—raising a baby on your own." He looked up. "We'll talk tonight, at home. Go on to the NICU now."

Dawson needed no encouragement. He spun on his heel and walked away.

At the neonatal unit, he gowned up, went inside, and let the nurse lift the baby out of the plastic shell and slip the blue blanketed bundle into his arms, careful to not disturb the cannula delivering oxygen. Dawson settled into the rocking chair just as he'd done every day, twice a day, waiting for Gabe to improve. He thought to all the times Sloan had declined to come to the hospital with him. In hindsight, it had been an announcement of her intentions. She had never meant to stay. The only two women he had loved had left him. Cancer had taken his beloved mother. A painful but valid exit. The other? She had deserted him. Bile rose in his throat. Like himself, Gabriel was motherless. *Not fair.*

He peered down at the sleeping baby, not much bigger than a football. Picking up the bottle of formula the nurse had set beside the incubator, he rubbed the nipple across Gabe's lips. This time the baby took it without encouragement, a good sign. The little guy was growing stronger, and with health would soon come release from the hospital, and Dawson would take him home. Alone. His heart lurched. How could he do this, raise a child, by himself? Suddenly the nursery walls were closing in and he couldn't breathe. He'd sometimes felt this way before an important race, but this was no cross-country match. This was a lifetime event.

Gabe's knit hat slipped back and the soft down of black hair fanned out. The boy's eyes popped open and stared up at Dawson without blinking. Dawson exhaled, calmed his jitters, and forced himself to settle. He offered a half smile and, in a Darth Vader voice, said, "Gabriel, I am your father." The baby yawned, closed his eyes. A wave of protectiveness for the infant surged from some deep inner core. He put Gabriel on his shoulder, patted his back, and was rewarded with a tiny burp. "I won't leave you, Gabriel Berke. I swear to God." Then he began to rock, as much to soothe himself as his newborn son.

PART II

CHAPTER 21

Lani never much cared for the month of February. The days were often damp with light snow or freezing rain, skies were gray and bleak, the land brown and lifeless, and when the sun shone, its light looked faded and watery. February may be the shortest month of the year, but to her, it was the most dismal. Except for this February. She was on her way to an interview for a job she wanted with all her heart. She certainly needed the job, but her wanting of it transcended her need of it.

As she drove slowly down the tree-lined street in the older, most picturesque section of Windemere, the moneyed section of stately old homes dating back to the late 1800s, her mind returned to the night before and her fight with her boyfriend, Ben Claussen. Sitting in Ben's car in front of the apartment she shared with her sister, Melody, the car still toasty warm from the heater and the hot breaths of tongue-tangled kisses, she'd told him about her interview. Ben had recoiled. "A job interview! You *have* a job. Dammit, Lani! We hardly see each other now."

"But this will be a caregiver job, Ben. It's perfect for me."

She'd put off telling him until the last minute because she knew he'd want to try and argue her out of it.

"Classes, your hospital duty, your current job, your horse, oh, and then Ben." He ticked off his grievances. "I'm last in line, Lani. *Last.* You're first for me."

"That's not fair. I told you when we first met how it was going to be. I'm not just on idle here. I want a nursing career." She was finishing up her second year of nursing credits at MTSU, and Ben, an engineering student, was completing his third year. He had a full scholarship and mostly worked for spending money. He'd been a lifeguard at the community pool the previous summer, where they'd met, and they had been dating ever since. Ben was charming, funny, good-looking, and crazy about her. She liked Ben—she did. It was fun having a boyfriend, but Ben wanted every minute of her free time and all of her attention—more of either than she had to give. She also realized other girls would be standing in line for him, but she could only give what she had to give to being a couple.

"This interview thing sucks, Lani."

"You know I have to work this summer, and it needs to be a better job than the one I have now."

"News flash—it's only February."

"My boss at the hospital asked me to interview for the job. What was I supposed to say?" She tried to placate Ben. "It's just an interview. No guarantees I'll even get a job offer."

"You'll get it," Ben grumbled. "And I'll stand in the back of your line."

Now driving down the street watching house numbers go past, she ignored the prick from her conscience about her other reason for wanting the interview. She turned off the engine in front of a large redbrick two-story house fronted by a

128

porch with dark wicker furniture and an expansive plate-glass picture window. She thought the place charming, even in colorless February.

Lani took deep breaths to calm her racing heart. *Professional,* she told herself. Most of all, she had to look and act professional. She gathered her things, went up the three steps to the brightly painted front door, and rang the bell. Moments later, the door opened and she looked into the dark eyes and surprised expression on the face of Dawson Berke.

Dawson felt a momentary shock seeing this woman on his doorstep. His father had failed to mention she was closer to Dawson's age than either Franklin's or Paulie Richardson's grandmother. All Franklin had told him was "I'm sending someone over for you to interview. She's sharp, dedicated, and conscientious. Please consider her. We need help with Gabe, and she's qualified."

Lani smiled brightly, held out her hand. "I'm Alana Kennedy, but everyone calls me Lani." She had wondered if he would hold even a glimmer of a memory of her from their high school days, realized quickly he did not, and felt a momentary letdown. *Why should he when he'd been with Sloan?*

He shook her hand awkwardly, remembering her purpose for coming, his lack of interviewing skills, and Gabe's need of a daytime caregiver. "Come in. Please."

She followed him through the small foyer and into a formal living room where the furniture had been shoved against the walls, clearing the center of the hardwood floor for a child's racetrack for motorized Matchbox cars. "My son's." Dawson gestured at the setup. "His playroom's in the basement, but we play race cars here because there's plenty of space. Maybe we should go to the den." She followed him into a room of comfy

129

well-used furniture. A lone Persian area rug in hues of reds and purples covered a portion of the bare wood floors.

He motioned for her to have a seat on the sofa and took the leather chair near it. "Dad said that you're studying to become a nurse and that you might be interested in a caregiver job."

"Yes, to both. I'll finish my second year in May, but I've been in the hospital Step-Prep program since Dr. Berke started it. A volunteer at first, but now a very serious student in the three-year nursing program. I want to go into pediatrics when I graduate, but for now the program keeps me in the hospital and gives me clinical experience." She didn't want to oversell herself, but after seeing his initial reaction to her had decided she might have to persuade him she was right for the job.

"You impressed Dad with your work ethic, as he calls it. Dad's dedicated to his job too."

She smiled and shrugged. "I'm doing what I love. Makes a difference as to why I do it."

"Gabe's only had one caregiver besides me and Dad since I brought him home from the hospital . . . Mrs. Richardson . . . but she wanted to retire and move to Florida. She left at Christmas. Gabe misses her. We all do." Paulie's grandmother had been the perfect helper when Gabe had been a baby, but once he'd turned two on his last birthday, she'd had trouble keeping up with him. "My work schedule will pick up soon, so we need someone here at the house with him."

"I can work full-time once classes end."

Dawson eased back into the chair, studying the brown-haired, brown-eyed girl. She was pretty, not beautiful, but she had an effervescent smile and her enthusiasm sparkled. "So, um, tell me more about yourself."

Lani laced her fingers together to keep them from betraying

her nervousness. "I was born and raised here. I live with my sister now in one of those renovated apartment buildings over on Magnolia Street."

Mentally he mapped the distance. "Not so far." It meant she could get to the house quickly if necessary.

"My sister Melody's a lawyer over on Main. Works for Mr. Boatwright in that converted Victorian that's painted in shades of green."

"I've seen it. You come from a family of lawyers and doctors?"

"A teacher and a journalist." She flashed a smile, took a measured breath, and decided to put the unsettling part of history on the table. "Full disclosure. You and I were in the same senior class."

He straightened, and his heart kicked up a beat. "Ah. So you must know my story . . . my whole story."

Feeling the specter of Sloan Quentin hovering in the room, Lani picked her way around the thorny past, saying, "Small-town-itis. In Windemere, if anyone sneezes, someone blesses him two streets over."

That made Dawson laugh and it pleased her. "Anyway, after graduation, I worked in the hospital along with some part-time jobs. Currently hold one out at Bellmeade horse stables and the other serving food at the Waffle Palace. Imagine the daily excitement—'Maple syrup, or blueberry, sir?'" She mimicked her waitress voice.

He grinned at that too.

"Everyone has a story, but since graduation, all of us have moved on. And so I remember when Gabe was born . . . in fact, I fed him and rocked him while he was still in the NIC unit."

Dawson startled. "You did?"

131

"It was part of my job," she quickly added. "But it was my pleasure too. We're called snugglers. I still volunteer if the unit's shorthanded."

Again, her smile softened him.

"Gabe was three weeks old before I could bring him home."

"I remember when he left the unit. We all cheered. Every time a preemie goes home, it's a victory." She glanced around the room, at the gas fireplace with glowing logs, at the framed photos and family pictures on walls and perched in bookcases. There was a large montage of Gabe at maybe six months and another with Dr. Berke, Dawson, and Gabe hovering around a cake with a single glowing candle. "Is Gabe here?"

"He's taking a nap. That's why I asked you to come right after lunch. I wanted to talk to you before he meets you." Dawson glanced at the mantel clock. "He'll be up soon, but you should know he's shy around strangers. Don't be too put off if he hides from you."

Lani brightened. "But I'm no stranger. Gabe and I are already friends."

Another revelation Dawson was unprepared to hear. Since Christmas and Mrs. Richardson's departure, Dawson and Franklin traded off days of staying home with Gabe. Dawson worked three days a week and weekends at Hastings Construction and took evening classes at MTSU toward his business degree, but with the building season coming on, he needed to work longer hours. Franklin took Gabe to the hospital with him two days a week—where he had staff to help him with his grandson. "My father didn't mention that Gabe already knows you."

"Oh! I thought he did." She thought she may have fumbled the interview because Dawson seemed totally surprised by the admission. "Dr. Berke asks me to watch Gabe when he brings him to his office for the day—that is, if I'm in the hospital." What she didn't add was that she made time to be with Gabe, letting Dr. Berke know she would be available on the days Gabe came with him.

"You're full of surprises."

Dawson's tone didn't sound as friendly. Lani's stomach clenched. Why hadn't Dr. Berke told Dawson more about her before she'd come? "I . . . I think that's why your dad asked me to interview. Because Gabe already knows me."

"And because of his condition," Dawson added, feeling manipulated. This wasn't really an impartial interview at all. His father had handpicked this girl, this Lani, to care for Gabe. She was a gung-ho nursing student, focused on pediatrics, personable, kind, friendly, already familiar with Gabriel's medical circumstances, in need of a good-paying job—and apparently a favorite of her boss, Gabe's grandfather. What Franklin *really* wanted was Dawson's seal of approval on the girl. Why hadn't Franklin simply hired her himself instead of going through the pretense of Dawson giving her an interview? He cleared his throat. "I . . . um . . . have a couple of other interviews." His conscience twinged with the lie, but he was irked by his father's subterfuge.

"Oh, of course! No problem." She shot to her feet.

Dawson stood too, and started to speak, when the clatter of Gabe coming down the stairs calling, "Daddy! Daaaddy. Find me, Daddy," broke the awkward silence.

133

CHAPTER 22

"I'm in the den, Gabe."

Seconds later, the child raced into the room, arms wide open. He saw the woman and froze.

Lani immediately stepped forward, crouched, and smiled. "Hey, Gabe. It's me! Lani."

The boy looked confused, but then his eyes brightened and he ran forward and threw himself into Lani's arms. She was knocked backward but held him, laughing. "You're so strong."

Gabe looked up at his dad, all smiles. "It's Lani."

His son's exuberance surprised Dawson. "I guess you *do* know each other."

"We color together. He loves to color and he's good at it."

Gabe's face beamed with her words. "Color now!" He whirled and zipped through the doorway.

"Gabe! Later!" Dawson called, but the boy was gone.

"I . . . I don't mind." Lani rose from her crouched position. "I'm happy to stay with him for a little while, if . . . if that's okay."

Dawson didn't want Gabe disappointed, but he was still

stewing. "All right. Color until I get his snack ready in the kitchen." He turned for the doorway. "Look, Lani . . . I don't mean to be difficult, but I worry about him, his health and all. I'm sure you're competent with kids."

She wanted this job more than to just curry favor with Dr. Berke. Gabe had stolen her heart and she wanted to care for him. "I understand your special concern for Gabe . . . and his asthma."

Dawson turned back toward Lani, reminding himself he shouldn't take out his irritation with Franklin on this girl. Since birth, Gabe's lungs had been his weak spot, and his asthma most likely a lasting effect of the premature birth. "Look, I'm not playing the overprotective parent role with you. It's just that I'm still dealing with his diagnosis too. It's been less than a year, and he's been to the ER twice and hospitalized both times. We don't know all his triggers, not until one sneaks up on him and he's wheezing, can't catch his breath, and turning blue."

Naturally Lani knew it, but held off saying anything.

Dawson gestured around the room. "That's why, except for this rug—pure silk and cleaned often—all the floors are bare hardwood, all curtains replaced with blinds. The house has a HEPA air purifier too, because we already know certain inhalants can bring on an attack. Mold and dust mites for sure." Dawson tried to express the difficulty of protecting Gabe from a world full of potential hazards. Here at home, his son was relatively safe, but outside these walls, he was always vulnerable.

"But I also want him to have a normal kid's life. He can't live in a bubble. And when spring comes and everything starts blooming . . ." He shook his head. "Who knows? Sure hope pollen won't be a problem, because my little guy loves to be outside. He's undergoing some allergy testing, and so far his triggers are inhalants. I just want him to be safe."

She looked into Dawson's dark eyes, and her heart filled with compassion. "I know how to take care of a child with asthma. I help with all the asthmatic children when they're checked onto the peds floor. I give breathing treatments, play with them, and cuddle with them when they miss their families. I do what I can to make their lives better until they're well and can go home. I can handle an emergency if one comes up." She opened her purse and extracted a bronchial inhaler. "I carry this with me every day because I like being prepared."

Gabe raced back into the room, rattling a plastic box of crayons and holding a coloring book. Lani knelt so that he could spread out on the floor. "Dinosaurs? We're coloring dinosaurs. I'm so surprised."

Gabe giggled at her tease. "Green ones with brown spots." Gabe had a habit of dropping his r's that always made Lani smile. He spread open the book to two clean pages and stretched out on his belly.

Lani stretched out beside him and rifled through the box of mostly broken crayons. From the doorway, Dawson watched, still feeling manipulated by his father but knowing he couldn't be an idiot either. He couldn't arbitrarily reject this Lani simply because his dad was calling the shots.

"So how did the big interview go?"

It was the first question Melody asked when Lani stepped into the apartment's shoe box–sized kitchen the two of them had painted bright apple green. "Not sure." She settled at the scarred old café table tucked in a corner of the room near a window. "It was going fine until Dawson found out his father had sort of rigged the interview in my favor."

"Why should that bother him? I'd think he'd be thrilled to have someone preselect candidates for a caregiver job with an asthmatic child. You're the one I'm thinking about. Honestly, if you get the job, the possible liabilities—"

"Stop with the lawyer talk, Mel. I want this job. I *need* this job." Lani had touted the caregiver job possibility to her sister before the interview but hadn't confessed her high school crush on the interviewer. *Water under the bridge of life.*

Melody stirred a pot of chili on the stove, and its rich peppery aroma filled the room. "You doing something with Ben tonight? Mom and Dad are going to Skype us around seven."

"No. He's got a research paper due, so I'm home." Lani remembered the day their dad had come home and said the local paper was shutting down and he'd lost his job. *"Digital takeover of print. Farmers all have smartphones. No one reads the farm reports in the paper these days. They just call them up on the Web."* He'd said the words cheerily, but the family had known he was devastated. After an eight-month hunt for another job, he'd taken over the reins of a small biweekly paper in Kenai, Alaska. Jane had retired at the end of that school year, and they'd moved. They called often, raving about the wilderness landscape, or the midnight sun's glow, and even the long dark winters. "Cozy. Always a fire warming us and elk in the front yard to entertain us." Lani and Mel had flown out to visit them twice since they'd settled.

Their house had been rented to a newly married Winslow cousin and her husband, who made the mortgage payments, freeing Lani and Mel of responsibilities for the place. Mel's job paid the bulk of the sisters' current living expenses. Lani's jobs barely covered insurance and gas on her mother's old car that she'd inherited from their move to Alaska. Her parents still covered her college tuition, but all extras came from her earnings.

"So the job will pay well?" Mel tasted the chili.

Dr. Berke had hinted that it would. "Way more than I earn now," Lani ventured, but knowing she'd take it whatever the salary.

"No day care available?"

"Too risky given Gabe's asthma."

"And no mother."

"I told you she left when he was still in the hospital."

Mel shook her head. "Sad."

"Raising Gabriel is a family effort for Dr. Berke and his son. I want to help. It'll look good on my résumé too."

"And you're the only one qualified? Seems strange."

"Thanks for the vote of confidence."

"That's not what I mean. Surely there are registered nurses or other health care workers qualified to take the job."

"But Dr. Berke asked me to interview. I want this job, Mel." She frayed the paper napkin at her place setting, remembering the unenthusiastic expression on Dawson's face. And even if she was hired, Ben wouldn't be pleased. "Dawson said he had others to interview, so I doubt I'll get it."

Melody stepped away from the stove, put her arm around her sister. "Hey. No moping. If you don't get the job, and you're over slinging waffles, you can always sell your horse."

Lani ignored Mel's suggestion. "Not happening. I may have to eat hay with him, but I'm not giving up Oro."

Melody grinned. "Just checking out your priorities. Now make a salad so we can eat this bodacious chili I've fixed."

Dawson was waiting in the kitchen when Franklin came in from the garage.

"Hi. Had a late emergency. Gabe in bed?"

"Sound asleep."

Franklin eased his briefcase onto the granite countertop, as if sensing the tension in the air. "Everything all right?" He rolled his shoulders and faced his son. "How'd the interview go?"

"You mean the one you blindsided me with? I felt sorry for the girl. She was as clueless as me about the setup."

"Not fair. I sent you an excellent candidate for Gabe's care. Didn't you like her?"

"Yes, I liked her."

"Then what's the problem?"

Dawson struggled to find words to express his frustration. Living with his father gave him and Gabe a home, at little expense. Plus Franklin paid for Dawson's night classes at MTSU, so he could work all day. Franklin's generosity made it easy for Dawson to save money, and Dawson was grateful, but he felt stagnant and saw nothing changing for him. He wanted to be out on his own. He wanted more for himself and Gabe than living in Windemere still tied to his father. He wasn't sure yet what more was. He only knew he wanted it. But he had no other choice right now. Unable to articulate his feelings, Dawson asked the only question he could come up with. "Why did you choose this girl, a student nurse?"

Franklin sighed wearily. "Yes, I have RNs working with me at the hospital, but frankly, I need every one of them on the floors. It isn't easy keeping personnel at small rural medical facilities, you know. That's one reason I came up with the Step-Prep program. Tying a job to college credits gives me more loyal personnel. I can spare Lani because she's a student and not full-time. She's conscientious, Gabe already likes her, and she needs a job. I thought it would be a good fit."

"But she's *my* age. And still in school. She's not going to stay in the job after summer's over."

"Son, I love Gabe very much, and Lani's one of my brightest and best. She can handle an emergency. I trust her. But if you want to interview others, do so. Gabe's your son, and you have the final say for him. Now I'm going to wash up, come down, and find something to eat." Franklin picked up his briefcase and walked out of the kitchen.

Dawson stood for a long time staring into the space his father had left behind. Much as he hated to admit it, his father was right. Lani, a girl from high school he didn't even remember, a girl Gabe already knew and trusted, was perfect for the job.

Resigned, he reached into his pocket, pulled out his cell, made the call, and offered her the job.

CHAPTER 23

"Stop! Sloan, you're murdering my song. You sound like a screeching cat! Way off-key!" Jarred slung his guitar off his shoulder, keeping a stranglehold on the instrument's neck.

Sloan whirled on him. Truth was, Sloan had perfect pitch and everyone in the studio knew it. "Hey, it's my song too! We wrote it together, so don't play the ownership card on me. We've gone through this part a hundred times and my throat's raw. What's wrong with the last five takes?"

"Lots of takes mean lots of choices when we start mixing."

"So when do we stop?"

"When we get it right," Jarred fired back. "When you sound like I want you to sound on the lyrics."

"Oh—it's all *my* fault? You were late on the start-up. Bobby and Hal were easily three beats behind, and Sy"—she threw a glance to the keyboard man—"well, he was the only one keeping up with me." She was kind to Josiah because this was, after all, *his* studio, *his* property, and *his* goodwill. Besides, he would do the final mixing.

Sy acknowledged her comment with a wink. The others

in the studio went silent. At his perch behind his drums, Hal flipped his sticks end over end, caught them expertly. Bobby hugged the long neck of his bass guitar, stared up at the ceiling. Josiah eased into a nearby chair, all waiting for the latest blowup between Sloan and Jarred to subside.

"You don't drive this song, Sloan. I do. My band. My rules."

"We're a team, a band, all for one, or have you forgotten that part?"

"We're *not* equals, Sloan. No way. No how."

After spending half the night struggling to perfect the song and sucking caffeine and nicotine, Sloan knew she had to either walk away or bash Jarred over the head. "You're an ass. And this band's going nowhere!" She stalked out of the studio and into the shocking brightness of an April day. They'd hit the studio at midnight; now the sun was almost overhead. She needed sleep.

She headed toward the house of stark white concrete rising into the blue sky off a manicured lawn, intent on climbing the stairs to the bedroom she shared with Jarred. She passed flower beds exploding with hot pink azalea bushes and rows of yellow daffodils. She made it to the bricked patio surrounding the pool of sparkling turquoise water when Bobby caught up to her.

"Hey! Stop. Wait!" He put his hand on the patio door just as she was about to slide it open.

"I'm not going back, so don't try and drag me. I hate Jarred!"

"We're all taking a break." Bobby took her hand. "Let's sit."

"Bobby, not now!" She snatched her hand from his, not a bit surprised he'd been the one to come after her. Bobby was the negotiator, the one who soothed and calmed the band's volatile mix of creative personalities. Every band had one.

The surprise would have been if Jarred had run after her. "I'm whipped . . . not in the mood."

"Just hear me out." He settled her on one of the numerous lounge chairs spread across the deck, dragged another closer so he sat facing her. "It's not you, and you know it. He's having trouble booking tour venues for the summer. Not small-time stuff like last summer, but something bigger, better."

"We all want something bigger. It's been over *two* effin' years, Bobby! We have a CD, we have some people who love us, but that's it. No local airtime, no labels looking at us, no agents calling. Why is that, Bobby?" She didn't expect an answer, but she wanted to vent. "I know about his booking problems. He's always bitching about it. But I'm asking why does he have to handle everything himself—the money, the schedule, the songs we sing, the way we sing them?" She ticked off Jarred's perceived offenses on her fingers. Everyone in the band had day jobs—except Sy, who didn't need one. The jobs were low paying but with flexible hours to accommodate their bookings, and they gave chunks of every paycheck to Jarred, who deposited the monies into a special account that paid all the band's expenses. "Why can't we score a real agent? One who can help us? But no! Jarred has to handle *everything*! He makes me crazy!"

"It's Jarred's way. He likes to run the show, and we all agreed to let him two years ago, remember?"

She blamed herself for agreeing to what was supposed to have been the democratic rule Jarred had promised back in Windemere but now had turned into a dictatorship. She had been an absolute emotional mess when Jarred first brought her to Nashville. The guys had treated her with kid gloves, no one asking about or even mentioning the baby she'd left

143

behind. Perhaps Jarred had told them not to say anything. It didn't matter. She didn't want to talk about any of it anyway—couldn't talk about it, really.

At first, working to come up with a new sound for the band had been therapeutic, an emotional balm for the desolation she'd felt. She used to think of the baby every day . . . *tiny Gabriel,* with tubes and IVs and full-time nursing care. Had he gone home with Dawson and Franklin? Had he even lived? But she had burned her bridge when she'd left, so she forced herself to stop thinking about him. An act of will that grew easier over time. In some ways it was as if Dawson and Gabriel had never happened to her. But now, after over two years of effort, she felt the band was chasing a dream they'd never catch.

"I'm just sick of the bars, the bubble-gum teen parties, the bar mitzvahs, the country clubs, and stage-sharing with bands not half as good as we are. We need help! Why can't Jarred see that?"

Bobby rubbed his eyes, red from lack of sleep and cigarette smoke. "Everybody pays their dues. You know there aren't any overnight sensations in this biz, Sloan."

She'd heard the refrain a hundred times, and in the beginning, when they'd all first gathered in Sy's palatial house, Sloan thought she'd caught the brass ring. She'd never seen a place like it, a soaring contemporary styled house of stacked white cubes with a glass wall facing a pool and colorful gardens. But these days she felt more like a prisoner locked in a never-ending cycle of running after her dreams but getting nowhere.

And yet she owed the band her loyalty. Her voice, the voice that was supposed to carry the band into their future, felt flat, stripped and raw. Sloan looked to the side of the yard that held Big Blue. "Wonder if it will ever move again."

Bobby followed her gaze and grinned at the old school bus they had all converted into their band's tour bus. Painted neon blue and complete with sleeping quarters and space for all their gear, the Big Blue Beast made quite a statement rolling along the highway from gig to gig. The band's name glowed in big yellow letters on each side, along with cover photos of their lone CD, sold at every venue. The words *Road Hog* were painted bright red across the rear door. "Sure it will. Can't keep a bus that awesome locked in the yard like a dog." Bobby lifted her chin, peered into her eyes. "We'll get through this dry spell, Sloan. We're good and you know it. We just need a break. The right person to hear us. Some DJ to pick our CD from the slush pile and put it on the air. And it *will* happen for us. Just a matter of time."

Bobby's pep talk did little to buoy her spirits, but her anger was out of juice. She leaned back into the lounger, closed her eyes, and let the bright warm light of the sun wash over her. "So you're saying that I should just 'Keep calm and carry on'?"

"Can't hurt. Might help."

She raised an eyelid in time to see the patio doors slide open and a froth of giggling girls surge outside, heading for the pool. Sloan swore and pulled up from the chair. "The bubble heads are here. I'm gone." The troop of females were leftovers from Saturday night's party. Sloan disliked them, long-legged twits who hung around flirting and drinking and popping into anyone's bed they could cozy into. Certainly not one of them had any clout or connections. They were users and takers.

Bobby lumbered up from his lounge but didn't take his eyes off the bikini-clad troop of pretty women. Guys were coming across the lawn toward the house, not only the band, but also several others who, once she and Bobby left, must have driven the back access road leading to the studio. More groupies . . . *spongers*, to Sloan. The girls waved and shouted for them to hurry. A couple of guys ran toward the pool, ripping off their shirts and executing cannonballs into the cold water. Girls shrieked and scattered. One called out, "Hey, Jarred! Want to swim to the bottom with me?"

Sloan shot her a threatening look, and the girl slunk to a lounger and stretched out on her stomach, turning her face away from Sloan's glare.

Jarred walked to Sloan, slid his arm around her waist, and nuzzled her ear, as if nothing had happened between them. "You're the best-looking one here, babe."

She wanted to hammer him but instead said, "Creative differences. It happens." The words tasted sour in her mouth, but backing down was her best choice with these female vultures waiting to scoop him up.

"We good?"

Her smile was tight. "Always," she said, and together they went inside the house and up the stairs to the bedroom.

CHAPTER 24

L ani finished at MTSU with a 4.0 grade point average. She worked Saturdays at Bellmeade, exercising horses, mucking stalls, and doing chores for Ciana. Weekdays she took care of Gabriel from seven in the morning until either Dr. Berke or Dawson arrived home, typically between five and six. She squeezed dates with Ben into Saturday nights and Sunday afternoons. Lani felt guilty over dialing back their together time, but she couldn't help it. Her work came first, and dating was a luxury, not a necessity in her life.

Dr. Berke allowed her to claim the job as part of her credits toward her clinical requirements in the Step-Prep program. "It's my program," he told her. "So I make the rules." The whole situation was a win-win for her, but she couldn't make Ben understand.

As spring burst into blooming trees, flowers, and grasses, and the pollen count climbed into the three and four digits, Lani became super vigilant about Gabe's asthma. She kept an app on her cell that she checked often, keeping him inside when the pollen count was predicted to be at its worst but taking him to a nearby park when the count was lower or when the air had been washed clean by a rain shower. Dawson had been right about how Gabe loved being outdoors. It was the first thing he asked about every morning, the last at night. "Park?"

"Maybe tomorrow, Gabe," she would tell him.

At the park, Gabe ran to the swings, butt-slings held up by thick chains. He refused the child safety swings that locked him in securely, crying if she tried to put him in one. "Gabe not baby!" So Lani taught him how to wrap his small hands around the chains and pushed him gently, always standing behind him, ready to grab him if he went too high or started to slip off.

"Gabe fly!"

"Like Superman," Lani would tell him.

If Dr. Berke had an emergency or if Dawson got stuck on a job site, Lani stayed and tucked Gabe in for the night. Dr. Berke paid her overtime, but she'd have done it for free. She adored Gabriel, found him bright, inquisitive, and sweet natured, quick to catch on, eager to please. The toddler owned her heart.

If Dawson came home midday, usually because of being rained out on a job site, she stayed to watch him and Gabe roll around on the playroom floor like exuberant puppies, giggling and laughing, tickling and wrestling (or as Gabe said, "wesling"). Or sometimes instead of leaving at the end of her workday, she joined the two of them under the basketball net mounted on a pole at the top of the driveway. Dawson would hand her the ball and she'd dart around Dawson holding Gabe on his shoulders and take a shot. Or Dawson would hand the ball to Gabe, hold him high enough for the boy to touch the rim, and Gabe would shove it through and shout, "I win!" and Dawson and Lani would do a little victory dance to celebrate.

More often she hung around on purpose, all the while telling herself she shouldn't and that she needed to leave. But she didn't, sometimes staying for an impromptu dinner with the three of them. Old feelings, ones she had buried back in high school, struggled to the surface. Dawson—the boy she'd crushed on, now in her life every day. *You have a boyfriend; you have Ben*, she told herself. It was neither professional nor wise to think of Dawson any other way. And yet . . . *and* . . . *yet*.

At first Melody said nothing when Lani came in after long evenings at the Berkes'. But one night Melody gave Lani her stern lawyer expression and said, "Don't let them take advantage of you."

"What are you talking about? Do you think any nurse walks out at quitting time when she's caring for a special patient?"

"You're a babysitter, Lani."

Lani's back stiffened, and she glared at Melody. "I've spent a lot of time working at the hospital, learning how to be a nurse. Gabe's not an ordinary child. He has a condition that can take him down in the blink of an eye. I'm his caregiver, his nurse when he needs me to be. I'm not just a babysitter."

Melody held up her hands in surrender. "Sorry, no insult intended." After a moment, she asked, "What about Ben? How's he taking all this, all your busyness?"

Lani sighed. "Actually, he's unhappy about it. I've tried to explain how much the job means to me, and my career, but—" She shrugged. Ben shared an apartment with three other guys in Murfreesboro, a good thirty-minute drive to Windemere. One of his roommates always seemed to be hanging around

149

the place, so he and Lani were rarely alone there, and he didn't like that either. He'd returned to his summer lifeguard job, and intent on laying a guilt trip on her, he hired on at a local restaurant three evenings a week, telling her, "To take up the slack in my boring nights."

Lani smiled at her sister. "But I'm happy, Mel. Really happy."

Melody tipped her head to one side, giving Lani a searching look. "How will you ever return to your old life of classes and hospital work when summer ends and Dr. Berke hires a new caregiver?"

And in that flash of reality, Lani's happiness factor crashed. *How indeed?*

Dawson moved upward from the edge of the roof while driving nails with expert hammer blows into overlapping shingle tabs. Laying asphalt roofing tiles was hot, back-aching, mind-numbing work, but he was good at it, and after two years on the job he'd landed weeks after bringing Gabe home from the hospital, he was getting good pay to do it. He figured he'd make it to the base of the chimney of the new construction house in about two hours. Together with the other men, he was part of a team, and the sound of their hammers was a symphony of progress. The roof would be shingled by quitting time. The hammers stopped for lunch and water breaks only.

When the call for water went out, Dawson tucked his hammer into his utility belt and rested his back on the brick chimney. The spot offered some shade, along with an amazing view of the Bellmeade farm. The main house had been completed a year before, a modern take on a Victorian rebuilt from the ground up after a tornado had blown it to smithereens. Another smaller ranch-style house, several yards from the main one, was also brand-new. The one his construction team worked today would be finished in a couple of months.

Dawson chugged from his gallon water jug and then leaned it against the chimney. From his vantage point, he could see an oval exercise track, a checkerboard of fields and pastures in the distance, plus stables and corrals where horses were penned. On the track, a man rode a big black horse, and even from this distance Dawson saw that both were fighting to control the pace.

Control. Circumstances—unforeseen and life-altering—certainly had taken control of Dawson's life. He remembered how rough it had been at first to care for Gabe, how he'd sometimes sit up all night walking the colicky baby, and later there was the asthmatic wheezing. He learned diapering and feeding skills, and as Gabe grew, he'd learned patience and tenderness. He'd also learned to cook, at least mac and cheese and hot dogs and even one green veggie—peas, he thought with a wry smile.

Being a teen father hadn't come with a playbook, and without his dad's helping hand, he couldn't have managed. The bridge between them now was Gabriel, the boy with a runaway mother. Dawson retreated from thoughts of Sloan, except to wonder what, or how much, he'd tell Gabe about her, knowing one day Gabe *would* ask. *Everybody has a mother.*

Dawson took another long drink, partly to quench his thirst, partly to wash away the taste of Sloan's memory. Right now, he and Gabe had Lani, and Dawson knew he'd done the right thing by hiring her. She was cheerful, caring, and competent—a perfect fit for both of them. He didn't worry about Gabe with Lani in charge. Problem was, he was beginning to experience feelings for Lani that went beyond gratitude. When they played basketball with Gabe and their hands touched, he wanted to hold hers longer. Or when they spoke face to face, he'd watch her lips and wonder what she'd taste like.

Dawson took a deep breath and shook his head to clear out thoughts he didn't need to be having. Maybe Lani was simply a temptation because he'd been too long without a girl. These days his life focused on Gabe, work, school—and besides, where could he go to meet any women in this tiny town?

Around him, Dawson heard the other men stirring. Water break was over. One of the men called out, "Hey, Berke! Boss wants you on the ground."

Dawson quickly descended the ladder and found the crew chief waiting at the bottom and holding out a cell phone. "What's up?"

"People are trying to track you down. You didn't answer your phone, so they called our head office and they called me."

The crew was discouraged from taking personal calls while on the clock, so Dawson kept his cell on vibrate and hadn't felt it go off as he'd worked. Dawson's stomach tightened. *Gabe!* He took the phone. "This is Dawson Berke."

A man's voice said, "I'm Dr. Lopez, attending physician in the ER. Your father's had a myocardial infarction—a heart attack," he clarified. "You need to come to the hospital right away."

CHAPTER 25

D awson bounded off the elevator on the cardiac floor and jogged to the nurses' station. A nurse looked up, offering a kind smile. "Hi, Dawson."

While personnel and staff knew who he was, he knew few of them. "My dad. They said he was up here in the ICU."

"Yes. They brought him up thirty minutes ago."

"Can you take me to him?" Dawson had come straight from the construction site and he wasn't exactly clean and fit for the ICU. He didn't care. Tight bands constricted his chest, his mouth was dry, and his hands, usually rock steady with a hammer and nails, were shaking.

"Dr. Lopez is with him. I'll let him know you're here." The nurse went down the hall and through double doors that sealed off the cardiac intensive care unit from the remainder of the floor. Posters hung in a straight line on pale blue painted walls with rules about "Ticker Care." How different this floor was from the pediatric floor with its sunny yellow walls and images of giraffes nibbling on trees, elephants peeking over tall grass, a lion with a goofy grin.

Dawson paced. When the doors swung open again, a dark-haired man in scrubs came toward him. "I'm Tomas Lopez, your father's heart specialist."

"How is he? I mean, he's okay, isn't he? What happened?"

Dr. Lopez started to explain. "He's stable at the moment, but in guarded condition. We have more tests to run, but I suspect it's more than one blockage in his arteries. His heart's not in good shape to start with."

"It isn't?"

"Probably from his years of coronary heart disease."

Dawson reeled. "Heart disease! What heart disease?"

Lopez sighed. "He's been under my care for a few years for heart issues. First at Vanderbilt, now here."

"Years!" Dawson couldn't believe what he was hearing. How could his dad have kept this from him? And why would he? "But he does everything *right*. He doesn't smoke; he eats smart, jogs. He . . . he's never said a word to me about this."

"I'm sorry to be dumping this on you in the middle of a crisis. So far his heart issues have been controlled with meds and lifestyle, but now the muscle is damaged," Lopez answered.

"Can I . . . I want to see him. I *have* to see him."

"You can, but he's sedated and won't know you're there."

"Don't care. He's my *dad*."

Dr. Lopez weighed Dawson's words, offered a terse nod, and led the way through the double doors and into a large room ringed with beds, each surrounded by beeping machines. *Constant vigilance.* Dawson tasted bile when Lopez halted beside the bed that held Franklin. His dad wore an oxygen mask, and IV lines ran into his arms. Electronic lead wires attached to a machine were taped to his leg and chest. Blood pressure readings stood out in bold blue numbers on another machine. Emotion clogged Dawson's throat. Franklin, who had looked so vital just that morning, kissing Gabe's tousled hair, waving goodbye to Lani and Dawson, telling them "Have a good day," now looked dwarfed against the white sheets, and very ill. Sucking in a breath, Dawson scrubbed his palms on his pants. "Can I touch him?"

Dr. Lopez handed Dawson some antibacterial lotion and a paper towel. "Do this first." The doctor patted Dawson's shoulder, a sympathetic expression on his craggy face. "Really sorry, son."

"Where was he when it happened?"

"Walking down the hall, reading a patient's chart. He collapsed. We got to him instantly and were able to get meds into him fast, the best preventative for more damage. We had to defib—"

"His heart stopped?" Dawson's knees almost buckled.

"He came back quickly. If a person's going to have a heart attack, no better place than right here in the hospital."

Standing in the cool and darkened unit, with no way to distinguish day and night, Dawson was upended. He felt useless. "I . . . I want to be here when he wakes up."

"He's heavily sedated. No need for you to wait around now. We'll be running tests and then make a decision about what we'll do. Go home, see your family, and come tomorrow. We'll call you if there's any change."

Gabe. His son's image bloomed in Dawson's mind. He didn't argue with Lopez, only nodded and left the unit and the floor. In the lobby, he sent a text message to Lani.

Coming home early. Need to talk.

Lani fidgeted in the Berke kitchen, polishing and re-polishing the granite countertops, eyeing the clock and the minute hand that seemed to be glued in place. Dawson's cryptic message had unnerved her. Whatever was driving him home early wasn't part of the norm. Her nerves tingled. Whatever it was, it couldn't be good news. Gabe was safe upstairs taking a nap, so she had control of that much. When she heard Dawson's car pull into the garage, she resisted the urge to throw open the door and ask, "What's wrong? What's happened?"

When he came into the kitchen, the look on his face let her know her concern was well founded. Dawson braced his hands on the counter and told her about his father's condition. She may still be a student, but she knew the nature of heart attacks and of their crippling effects. "How can I help?"

"Can you stay with Gabe? He won't miss Pops right away. He's used to Dad not being here for periods of time—you know, those days Dad gets stuck at the hospital—so he may not ask for him at first, but sooner or later he will."

Her heart went out to the family. "Of course I'll stay . . . all night if you need me to. I can sleep on the sofa." Gabe had a nanny cam in his room and several monitors so that she could look in on him from anywhere in the house.

"You may have to. Right now I'm going to clean up and go back to the hospital."

"I'll be here as long as you need me."

"Thanks." His dark eyes clung to hers. "He'll be all right, won't he? I mean, from what you know as a nurse."

She didn't want to mislead him, pretend a knowledge she didn't yet have, so she chose her words carefully. "Every case is different, but I know that Dr. Lopez is very good. Your father lured him here from Vanderbilt with a Chief of Cardiology carrot." She gave Dawson an encouraging smile. "It was the talk of the hospital, because Dr. Lopez can go anywhere he chooses, but he came to our little world . . . a big coup for Windemere. Your dad's in good hands."

Her words were reassuring. He trusted Lani, was grateful for her. Dawson reached for his wallet and tossed money onto the counter. "Take Gabe for a Happy Meal for dinner. He'll like that. I'll text you when I know something."

"I'll be right here."

But Dawson had headed out of the kitchen before she finished the sentence, his thoughts back in the cardiac unit, on his father, and on his mind-blowing fear of losing him.

CHAPTER 26

The party was impromptu, word sent out via social media on a sultry Nashville night to celebrate a small country AM radio station playing two songs from the Loose Change CD. Hal heard the songs first, and then Bobby while driving to work. Sloan had yet to hear either of the songs on the air, although she kept Jarred's car radio glued to the station.

The party was also an excuse to have a crowd gathered when Jarred made a midnight announcement—a game changer for their band. Sloan weaved her way through the partygoers, or as she liked to think of them, the moochers. In fairness, some of them were true supporters, having "discovered" the band months before, but most of the people were there for the booze and the joints.

She brushed past one stoner, who grabbed her butt. She slapped away his hand, snarled, "Touch me again and I'll break your finger," and continued to the staircase. She looked up and saw that Jarred and the others were waiting on the second-floor catwalk leading to the seven-bedroom wing of the house.

She had once asked Josiah why he let strangers inside such

a fine house to party when he knew they would trash it. "It pisses off my father," he'd replied. "Dad wants me to go into finance like him. Investment banking . . . juggling money, stocks, investments." He said the words as if they were crimes. "It's a world that has no soul, and I, my father's only son, have always wanted to make music. He built the studio for me when I was fifteen, thinking I'd get it out of my system."

"But you didn't." Sy played the keyboard, but it was his genius on the mixing board, the back dubbing and balancing, that made the band's tracks sharp and cutting edge.

"Not even close. So he gave me until my twenty-fifth birthday to either make it with music or get over it. Like I could ever get over music."

Sy was twenty-four now, so Sloan realized how much he had riding on the band's success. "So he's betting you're going to fail?"

"He's never lifted a finger to help me with connections. He could've opened doors anytime." He grimaced. "But now with this band, I have a shot at making it—we all do—which will really piss him off when we score."

"It's all we've ever wanted too—Jarred and the guys. And me." *Especially me.*

Tonight as Sloan went up the stairs, she understood that all of them had a lot riding on the upcoming announcement Jarred was going to make.

"What do you mean you'll be spending nights at this guy's house?"

The sharpness of Ben's voice on her cell phone made Lani's

stomach clench. "It's an emergency, Ben. Gabe's grandfather underwent triple bypass surgery this morning and is in the ICU. Dawson wants to be with his father through the crisis. I need to stay with Gabe. What's so hard to understand?" She hadn't told him about the first night she had slept over at the Berkes' that allowed Dawson to stay the night at the hospital, and now the irritation in Ben's voice reminded her why she'd held back. But early that morning Franklin Berke had gone into surgery and Dawson had asked her to stay more nights. She had quickly agreed.

"Where will you be sleeping?" Ben asked, in a tone she didn't like.

Lani was sitting in her car in front of the Berkes' house, having already explained what was happening to Melody while she packed a small suitcase. Inside the house Dawson and Gabe waited for her, Dawson anxious, Gabe excited Lani was staying another night. She wanted to scream at Ben, but she held back. "I'll be sleeping in Gabe's room. Dawson put a twin mattress on the floor for me so I'll be there when he wakes up. And we'll keep to his normal routine. He's not yet three, Ben. He doesn't really understand what's going on. It's not easy for him." She wanted to say, "*Or for any of us,*" but didn't.

"A lot to ask from a babysitter," Ben said, his displeasure flowing through the cell phone.

She gritted her teeth. "On top of everything, Gabe has a chest cold and I've had to administer his quick-acting inhaler several times. I need to be close by." She didn't explain that she had to put him on his nebulizer three times a day but that his breath tests on his peak flow meter still weren't where they should be, because Ben didn't get the dangers of asthma. Ben had no idea the serious condition could actually kill a child.

"Dawson doesn't need his father and his son in the hospital at the same time."

Ben went silent, then mumbled, "Call me tomorrow, okay? Let me know what's going on. And if you'll be seeing me like we planned this weekend. I expect that."

His last words were a dig, but she let them pass. "I will." *No promises, though.* She cut the connection and sat brooding in the car, remembering not Ben's words but Melody's warning just before Lani had dashed out the door.

"Don't get too attached."

"To what? Helping a child?"

"To *this* job, and *this* child, and his family. Getting emotionally involved was one of the things they warned us about in law classes. It's easy to get caught up in a case. And with a client. So we were counseled to keep our emotional distance. I'm sure they teach you that in nursing classes too."

Lani bristled, jerking open the front door. "Thanks for the warning, but I know how to behave like a professional." Yet even as she said the words, Lani knew she was involved up to her eyeballs. She loved Gabe. It was his father, Dawson, and her feelings for him that she fought to keep at a distance.

Sloan made her way to Jarred's side. He wrapped his arm around her waist and hiked the heel of his boot on the bottom rung of the pipe rail. "Big announcement time, babe. You ready?"

"Been ready for a long time, and you know that."

He turned to Bobby, Hal, and Sy, who took places along the rail on either side of him and Sloan. "Whistle 'em in, bro."

Hal placed two fingers on either side of his lips and let go with an ear-piercing whistle. People looked up. Jarred held up his hands. "Cut the music! Loose Change has an announcement to make!"

The music stopped midstream. "Hurry," a voice from below yelled. "I got to take a leak."

"Well leak this," Jarred shouted. "You know our summer tour starts in a few weeks. The Big Blue Beast is gassed and ready to roll." Cheers went up. "Some of you may even be coming on a ride-along."

"I'll keep you warm, Hal," a girl called.

"Promises are cheap, sweet thing!" Hal returned.

Jarred held up his hands to again quiet the crowd. "I know all of you can't come on the road with us, but on June seventeenth, I expect all of you to show up." He paused for dramatic effect. "At Bonnaroo!"

The news electrified the crowd. The Bonnaroo Music Festival was one of the South's premier summer events. Held on a seven-hundred-acre farm off I-24 in Manchester, Tennessee, music giants and immortals played Bonnaroo. Up-and-coming groups got noticed. Careers were launched. Thousands of music lovers—the Roo community—came from all over the world, camped in tents, RVs, cars, even slept on bare ground during the four-day celebration, where the music never stopped.

In April, Jarred had sent their demo CD to Sonicbids, an online contest that would choose two bands from a slush pile and earn each a spot on the upcoming Bonnaroo venue, along with a thousand bucks. Loose Change had been selected. This was their big break . . . a long time coming. Sloan snuggled closer to Jarred, looked down at the throng, and told herself all the waiting and hard work had been worth it.

Bobby whooped, pumping his fist into the air. "Bonnaroo! World class, man."

Shouts rose for the band to come down to mingle and celebrate. Jarred nuzzled Sloan's ear. "Guess we shouldn't let them down, should we?"

Sloan linked hands with the others, and the five of them made their way down the staircase and into the sea of fans below.

⁓

Lani heard Dawson come home when daylight was barely creeping under the window shade of Gabriel's room. She rose quickly, tugged a lightweight sweatshirt on over her nightshirt, and tiptoed from the room. In the kitchen, Dawson was splashing water on his face from the kitchen sink faucet. She asked, "How's your dad?"

He grabbed a paper towel, rubbed his face dry, and turned. Seeing her in his kitchen barefoot, hair mussed, eyes blinking off sleep, wearing a sweatshirt saying TRUST ME, I'M A NURSE AND I CALL THE SHOTS, made his pulse quicken. "I didn't mean to wake you."

"You didn't. Gabe is having a good night. He slept straight through with no coughing."

Hearing that Gabe was doing better was a relief. "Dad came through the surgery fine and he's back in his room, asleep."

"Wonderful." She reached to touch Dawson's arm, caught herself, and drew back quickly. *Hands off . . . too personal.* She offered a smile instead. "You must be wiped out. I know it's hard to rest in one of those hospital sleeper chairs."

He had watched her hand fly away from his arm and

regretted her pull back, because he wanted her to touch him and give himself an excuse to touch her. Impulsively, he tucked a wayward tendril of hair behind her ear, letting his fingers graze the soft skin of her cheek.

She realized she must look a fright and stepped away.

When she moved back, he wondered if he'd offended her, covering the awkward moment by glancing at the kitchen clock. "Got to be at work in an hour."

"Can't you take the day off?"

"Boss needs a full crew this week. A little coffee and a shower and I'll be good to go."

She walked toward the coffeemaker on the far side of the room. "I'll get the coffee going."

"Appreciate it," he said, regaining equilibrium and leaving the kitchen.

Lani busied her hands, still trembling from her close physical encounter with Dawson. She had wanted nothing more than to have him hold her, just once, but also knowing that "just once" would not be enough.

CHAPTER 27

"So this is Bonnaroo. What a crush." Hal was looking out the windshield of the Big Blue Beast at an overarching entrance sign leading to the field reserved for RVs and campers. Traffic had been crawling ever since they'd left Nashville and headed east, and what should have been an hour's drive to Manchester had been a four-hour trip clogged with vehicles.

Sy held up his cell phone. "They're reporting it's worse on the back roads."

The parking field was maddeningly close. Hal rode the brakes to keep from bumping the red and gold luxury RV they'd been tailing. The Beast groaned. "Hope this hunk of metal doesn't die on us."

Jarred, fiddling with his phone, never looked up. "Once we park, Beastie won't have to move until Sunday afternoon. According to the newest stats, the festival expects upward of ninety thou this year. Takes time to shovel them in."

"And out again," Sy added sagely.

All Sloan heard was that ninety thousand people were coming—and she'd have the chance to sing for many of them.

She was stretched out on the bus seat, her head in Jarred's lap, her bare feet propped on a side window. This festival was her Nirvana, a journey begun when she was eight and an old man in the next trailer felt sorry for her, a lonely little girl sitting outside singing to herself and drawing in the dirt. The man, who'd told her to call him Gramps, had told Sloan her voice was pretty, that he'd once taught music to children, so he should know. And he'd brought a guitar to her, said it had a beautiful tone and needed to be played, and she shyly told him she didn't know how.

So he taught her. First how to hold the too-big instrument, then basic chords, and over time how to position her fingers on the fret, strum the steel strings that eventually made calluses on her fingertips, and how to use picks that changed the timbre. He taught her how to take care of the guitar, how to restring it, clean it, and gave her an old battered case to protect it, and said the instrument belonged to her now. When Sloan was twelve, and after many lessons, Gramps had died alone in his trailer, but the guitar was still hers, and no matter how rich she became, she'd never part with it. Her voice and her guitar, now appearing at Bonnaroo. Gramps would be pleased.

The Beast was halted at the entrance, and a team of men searched the bus for contraband—drugs and booze in glass containers (the booze wasn't the problem, only the glass) and anything that looked like a weapon. They got wristbands and were sent into the field to find parking. Hal maneuvered the bus along the bumpy ground of the cow pasture and wedged the Beast between two older campers far less flamboyant than the Beast. "Home, sweet home . . . at least for the next few days."

They cheered, piling out of the air-conditioned bus and into heat and humidity that felt like a smothering blanket. Sloan shielded her eyes and skimmed the area, saw they were pretty close to the POD, where the porta potties, showers, and fresh drinking water were stationed. In another field, tents looked like blooming mushrooms.

Bobby stretched, turned to Sy. "Going to be a hot one. You got the beer locked down?"

"Do I look forgetful to you?"

"Let's fire up the generator." Bobby had insisted on buying the unit that ran on propane gas with a chunk of the performance fee they'd received. He'd insisted it was a good investment, and now in the suffocating summer heat the others agreed. The guys set to work and soon the AC was humming. "Beer break," Bobby said when they were finished.

Jarred grabbed Sloan's hand. "Going to check out the stages. Recon for my band. Won't be gone long. Save us a cold one." Jarred studied the map of the Bonnaroo grounds he'd pulled up on his phone. "Centeroo is that way."

The concert field, Centeroo, held the performance stages, vendors, and giant tents set up for the masses. Sloan was wearing a halter top and shorts, but without a breeze, Centeroo, already thick with people, felt like a furnace. Jarred led her to the clearly marked VIP tent, set up for people willing to pay the higher fees for higher comforts. Wristbands were being checked at the door. Sloan balked. "Hey, this isn't our tent. I don't think we're allowed in there."

"Don't you believe it." Jarred held up two bands of another color, clearly marked VIP, and tugged them onto his and Sloan's wrists.

"Where did you get—"

"I made some connections."

"Jarred—" He interrupted her with a hard kiss.

"You'll thank me later."

She followed him inside the enormous air-conditioned tent where she saw a lounge area, a fully stocked bar, and waitresses taking drink orders. People sat on comfy sofas and chairs. Two guys were playing a game of table tennis. Hard to believe this oasis existed away from the human mash outside. The place was amazing, but Sloan was suspicious because VIP wristbands cost hundreds of additional dollars. The band was supposed to vote on major expenses, and they sure hadn't voted on VIP wristbands! "What kind of connections?"

"The leader of the band kind." He grinned. "Trust me, babe. This is for the greater good."

"Why only two bracelets? What about our guys?"

"Deal only included two. We can share these with them, or not. Keep it our little secret."

What kind of deal? she wanted to ask. She didn't like Jarred's evasiveness. She started to light into him when a skinny guy with wild red hair, a row of earrings down one ear, and eyebrows riveted with hoops and studs walked up and held out his hand. "I'm Mick. You Jarred? With Loose Change?"

Sloan shot Jarred a look. *Who—*

"And this is Sloan," Jarred said before she could react.

"Jarred said he'd be with the best-looking woman at the festival. He didn't lie." Mick had an accent, maybe British, and roamed her body with his gaze.

She offered a stiff smile, recognizing sleazy when she met it. "Funny, he hasn't mentioned you to me."

"Well I've heard your CD, luv, and your voice is a total turn-on. And so are you."

Jarred took Sloan's elbow. "Hey, babe, why don't you get us

a table by the bar and order something. Mick and I'll be right over."

Sloan bristled over being dismissed like a child and started to object, but the look in Jarred's eyes warned her away. She had no idea what was going on, but she didn't like it. She leaned into Jarred, rubbed against him seductively, pressed her lips to his ear, and kept her voice low and steely. "This is our big chance. We're all counting on you, so don't blow it for us." She felt him flinch; then she backed off, smiled, and kissed him playfully and cooed, "Don't be too long, now, darlin'. You know how impatient I can be."

⁓

"Dad's getting better because he's getting cranky. A sure sign." Dawson and Lani were sitting in lawn chairs on the back patio watching Gabe ride his Big Wheel across the expanse of concrete. "Your bringing Gabe for a visit this morning helped his mood considerably, but I'm sure the nurses will be happy when he's released."

"Doctors don't always make the best patients," Lani said with a smile. "Gabe didn't want to leave when it was time to go. He's really missed his Pops." Lani moved her feet as Gabe barreled past, his legs pumping hard.

"Slow down, buddy," Dawson called. "Yeah. The visit was good medicine for both of them. Good for me too." He stared pensively into the glass of lemonade he held. "Until this happened, I never saw Dad as mortal. When I was a kid, he came and went a lot, but he was always there for me. And Mom too."

He rarely spoke of his mother, but she understood how much she had meant to him. Lani liked it when Dawson trusted her with parts of himself, while at the same time telling herself to shut that door. Privacy meant guarding her emotions, keeping her feelings at arm's length. It was hard.

"I'm looking into a school and day-care place for the fall. He turns three in August and the private school Dad recommended says they have space for him."

The news came out of the blue and startled Lani. "What about his asthma?"

"They specialize in kids with issues. Already have a girl with diabetes and another kid with a peanut allergy enrolled." It would be a big step for Gabe, for himself too, but it was necessary. Once summer passed, Lani would certainly move on, return to college and the hospital program. Dawson had to find another way to care for his son. Gabe would miss her. So would he.

She warred with feelings about the upcoming change, kept her disappointment to herself. They watched twilight creep across the sky, changing from red to indigo blue. Sounds of a lawn mower from down the street ceased. Lani eyed Gabe, making sure he was breathing normally. "When your dad comes home—"

"He'll have home health care nurses checking on him, so don't worry, he won't be your patient. You'll still only have one kid to take care of."

She smiled at his joke, still struggling over the idea of losing Gabe. And Dawson. She tried to remain upbeat, said, "Knowing Dr. Berke, he won't be homebound for long. Maybe he can walk around the park with me and Gabe." She knew Dr. Berke would be on an exercise program, like all recovering heart patients.

"Dad's already making noise about returning to work." A

frown creased Dawson's forehead. "Not sure Lopez is totally on board with it, though."

In the gathering darkness, Lani saw a firefly glow, then another and another. "Oh look!" She jumped up and snatched a glass jar off the patio table. "Gabe! Come on . . . let's catch some lightning bugs."

The toddler climbed off his trike and, squealing, ran out onto the lawn. Dawson watched as Lani twirled and scooped the jar through the air. Gabe jumped up and down. "I see, Lani! Let Gabe see!" She clapped her hand over the jar's top and bent to huddle with the boy. Like twinkling captured stars, the glowing jar illuminated their faces, and for the first time in a long time, Dawson felt like the raw edges of his life had softened. His dad was recovering; his son was happy.

He wondered why he'd never noticed her in high school. Sloan. He'd never looked beyond Sloan Quentin, and he should have. Now he did. And what he saw was the brown-eyed girl with the thousand-watt smile who had stepped into his world and lit it up.

CHAPTER 28

Bonnaroo's main stages, the What and the Which, featured headliners and superstars. Smaller acts, the less well known and the newbies, played at This Tent, That Tent, and the Other Tent. Loose Change was scheduled to perform at two in the afternoon on Friday on the Other Tent stage and again at one a.m. Saturday—actually Sunday, when Sloan thought about it—at This Tent. She neither cared where or when they performed, just as long as they performed. She knew they were ready. Years' worth of work came down to a single purpose—to make a splash, to stand out amid the one hundred and thirty acts booked at the festival. Huge feat, Sloan knew, but so long as she had a stage and an audience, she planned to light a musical fire with her voice listeners could not forget.

Friday morning dragged. The summer heat built, baking the ground, sweltering the crowds, and despite the availability of daily showers, people began to smell like farm animals. Hats, sunscreen, stripped-down clothing, and gallons of drinking water did little to stem the scorch of the sun. Those not hydrating enough passed out and were carried to the medical tents and treated. Beer flowed in steady streams, and the aroma of marijuana permeated the air. So much for the ban on drugs. No one gave a damn. People were there to celebrate music and to party.

Because of the heat, Sloan traded her leather look for hip-hugging micro-mini red shorts and a silk scarf folded to make a halter top that cradled her generous breasts. She glued a bright red fake diamond in her belly button that glittered with every sensuous twist and turn of her body. "Smokin'," Jarred said, fingering the scarf's knot at the nape of her neck. She swatted his hand. "Don't even think about it."

Jarred took the stage in jeans and biker boots, his upper body bare, his massive biceps and forearms glistening with suntan oil and sweat. The long line of arrowheads aligned from his neck to his wrist stood out in dark relief. Bobby, Hal, and Sy were content to wear long shorts and black wife-beater tees. They started their set with hot guitar licks pouring from their amps. At the top of a crescendo, Jarred stepped forward, struck a screaming riff, and Sloan strutted onto the stage. The crowd erupted.

The show was to last an hour. It went twenty minutes longer. The band tore through their playlist, and Sloan held nothing back. She rocked from piece to piece, pacing the music to the mood, hot and sexual for one song, sultry and soft for a ballad with Jarred. He played to her strengths, leaned into her, locked gazes, brushed his lips across hers. The crowd went crazy.

And when their set was finished, they took bows to hoots and whistles and screams of adoration. Bobby reminded the crowd of their Saturday-night performance, shouted for people to bring friends. Then Sloan stepped forward, dug the red jewel

173

off her body, and pitched it. They learned later that two guys suffered broken fingers in the scramble to retrieve it.

───────⚡───────

Sloan walked hand in hand with Jarred through jam-packed Centeroo, sidestepping a crush of gawkers and long lines of people waiting to go into the tents. "Hard to come down," Sloan said, still stoked from the high-octane performance of their one a.m. show. If anything, it had been better than the first, certainly more crowded. Word had spread that Loose Change was a bright light among this year's newbie bands.

"No reason to come back to earth. We killed tonight. We'll be headliners here someday." Jarred dodged a staggering drunk man.

"I'd rather be an icon like the guy we saw last night. Twenty-five years and the fans still flock to hear him. That's what I want. Don't want to flame out early."

"You mean you want to be The Stones."

"What's wrong with that?"

He tugged her to him. "Not a damn thing." He was wearing a Western-style hat with two long black feathers stuck in the hatband, jeans, boots, and a seventies-style fringed vest over his bare upper body.

"Where'd you find the threads?"

"Same place you probably bought your dress—the sixties hippie vendor." He flashed a smile. "A dress that looks very hot on you."

She returned his smile, stroked the fabric of the psychedelic print. "I think it's cool. A little keepsake to remember tonight forever."

"What you wearing under it?" He ran his hands down her sides and across her belly.

Shivers shot through her. She caught his hand, pressed it to her breast. "Nothing."

His grin went lascivious. "That an invitation?"

She teased him with her tongue. "Let's go back to the bus. Bobby, Sy, and Hal are doing the all-nighter thing with three girls they picked up. We'll have the Beast all to ourselves."

His brow furrowed. "I've got an appointment."

"With who?" When he shrugged, she pushed. "That Mick guy?" Again he was silent. "I don't like him, Jarred. Who is he, anyway?"

"An agent."

"You're kidding. He doesn't look—"

"LA style. We're talking about a deal for the band, out there."

Her interest piqued. "Shouldn't all of us meet him together? The band should have a say in any deal."

"Let me open the door with him, make sure he's serious. I'll give a full report tomorrow." He began to back away, turned, kissed the air in her direction. "I'll meet you back at the Beast later. To remove the dress."

Before she could react, he melted into the crowd and disappeared. She wanted to follow him but felt a tap on her shoulder and turned to see a long-haired girl shyly staring at her. "Um . . . 'scuse me, but are you the singer with that Change band?"

Sloan nodded. The girl's eyes grew even wider. She spun and yelled, "OMG . . . It's her! I told you it was her!"

A small group of people quickly separated out of the masses. "I'm Allison!" Then as the others surrounded them, Allison grabbed Sloan's hand. "You were wonderful! Fabulous! I love your voice."

A chorus of voices chimed in. "Effin' great" and "I bought your band's CD" and "Where you touring next?" and "Posted one song from your show on my Facebook page and got a ton of likes." A girl in the back asked, "Where's your hunky guitarist?"

Her irritation with Jarred evaporated. These people were *fans* and were acting as if they knew her. She couldn't turn them away. "Glad you liked our music." She smiled, let their adoration wash over her and soak in.

"Where you going?" one of the group asked. "Can we buy you a beer?" A big guy with dreadlocks pushed forward, offering a smile and a hand. "Stuart. Serious about the beer. I'm buying."

The others hooted. "He *never* buys. Make him pay for all of us."

The experience was heady, lifting Sloan ever higher. Face to face with fans, a community of people in love with music, and now saying they loved her too. How could she say no? She hooked her arm with Stuart's. "Where should we go?"

Cheers went up. The General Admissions tent was a seething zoo of humanity. "In a few hours we all go home, go back to our real lives. No one wants it to end, though," Allison shouted above the din.

Sloan understood. She wasn't ready to return to Nashville and pull things together for the tour of tiny lounges, noisy bars, and in-and-out county fairs. She wanted *this*, festivals and fans who knew her and wanted to be around her.

"Hey," Stuart called, "no use hanging in this crowd. I got a beer stash at our tent. Come on, or we'll all be sober before we get service here."

The walk to the tent area was long, but Allison chattered about how she and Stu had hooked up online as fellow travelers from Florida in order to save money. Once they'd set up their tent, they made friends with others all around them. Five guys were there from Indiana, two girls from Wyoming, and an older couple had driven up from Arizona. "Been coming for four years," one of them said. "Save for it all year. And I have the best time of my life."

"I'm coming until I'm an old fart," said a guy named Tim.

"Honey, you're fifty. We *are* old farts," said the woman with him, making everyone laugh.

Once at Stu's camper site, he handed Sloan a beer. She took a big gulp and stretched out on a blanket someone had spread. Staring up at stars sprinkled like jewels on black velvet, she thought about Jarred's appointment but couldn't help wondering if the story about Mick was a cover so that he could bed some other girl . . . the way girls looked at him with invitations written on their faces. Sloan knew better than to expect him to be faithful to her. Not Jarred's style. She held their relationship together with music and sex. But he was faithful to the band, and that's what mattered most. She took another swig of beer, welcomed the numbing rush of alcohol to her brain.

Someone in the group lit a joint and passed it around. When it got to Sloan, she sucked in the potent smoke, as much to be a part of the group as to feel the buzz. Music from the festival drifted on the night air. She felt as if she belonged.

"Hey, look!" one of the group called. "Fireflies!"

Allison let out a giggle. "I want one."

"Your wish . . . my command." Stuart staggered up and grabbed for one in cupped hands. Soon all were standing, lurching around the site, chasing fireflies, stumbling, laughing, and capturing only air.

As a child, Sloan had chased fireflies because she believed they were fairies, bright winged beings who came at night for all to see, especially lonely little girls in trailer parks. Now she was all grown up. She was *somebody*! She felt her eyelids growing heavy, and when no one was paying attention, Sloan slipped away, heading toward the Blue Beast. Tomorrow back to reality, but tonight was magical. How she longed to stuff it in a jar and keep it close to her forever.

⁓

Someone was shaking her shoulder, forcing Sloan awake. She shoved at the offending hands. "F off . . ."

"Wake up, Sloan. It's important."

She forced her eyes open. Sunlight bounced through the bus's windows. She squinted through layers of interrupted sleep. "Bobby? I just barely got in bed. Leave me alone."

"Can't. You got to get up, Sloan. I have to tell you something."

She groaned but scooted upward in the cramped bed created from two bus seats and a thin foam mattress. "Okay. I'm up. What the hell's so important?"

"Cops are outside. They want to talk to us."

Still groggy, she pushed a hand through her hair, lifting it out of her eyes and saw that Bobby's face was bone white. He had her attention. "Why?"

"It's about Jarred."

She went cold all over. "What about Jarred?"

"They found him this morning. He OD'd last night. He *died*, Sloan. Jarred's dead."

CHAPTER 29

D eath is messy. Death by an overdose of illegal drugs at a music festival and with police involvement was messier. While RVs, campers, vans, buses, and cars exited the Manchester farm fields, Sloan, Bobby, Hal, and Sy faced the police. Their bus and all their belongings were carefully searched and they were questioned. For a long time. Sloan was numb, hardly able to function. Didn't the cops get it that one of their own had died?

In the police tent, filled with equipment and with the AC pumped high enough to make Sloan's teeth chatter, the band faced the head detective, Carter. He was big and broad-shouldered and looked very weary, with bags under his eyes. "When you kids going to learn that drugs kill?"

The four of them were over twenty-one, not exactly "kids," but who was going to correct the man?

Other cops stood around, a few who truly looked to be in their teens. They weren't. They were undercover narcs, both male and female, who cruised the festival to confiscate drugs. *They had missed Jarred's buy*, Sloan thought, because the search hadn't turned up any illegal drugs in the Beast. He'd bought his drugs on-site, and after he'd left her standing alone in the middle of the crowds. *Damn you.* She started shaking and Bobby put his arm around her.

"My friend's in shock—" Bobby started, but the big cop ignored him.

"We've had four OD deaths this year, and about thirty who had to be treated so they wouldn't die. All the deaths included 'dabs,' this year's bad boy of the drug world. Also called 'wax' and 'shatter.'"

"I . . . I . . . we don't know about dabs. Never heard of it." That was Bobby. He looked to the others, and they shrugged. "We're not users. We came to perform."

"Any of you willing to pee in a cup to test the truth of that statement?"

No one volunteered. Sloan realized the few hits she'd taken last night with her fans would show up. Maybe the others had also smoked, but even at Sy's house, at the all-night parties, they were careful about drugs. They had jobs and some of their employers drug tested.

"Didn't think so." Carter continued with his lecture. "For the record, dabs is super-potent concentrated oil—THC—pulled from high-grade weed. Gives a super-high."

"People smoke it in water pipes," another cop said.

"*Your* pal used it in an electronic cigarette."

"And it killed him?" Sloan blurted the question.

Carter nailed her with a look. "He mixed it with crack. That's what killed him. And stupidity. As if there's not enough of this drug shit out there, now we got to track dabs." He jammed his hands into the pockets of his khaki pants, skewering each of them with a cold stare. "You can go for now, but don't leave the site just yet."

"How long we have to stay?" Sy asked.

"Till I say you can leave."

Sy's jaw worked as if he wanted to speak, but he kept quiet.

The three got to the front of the tent before Carter called out, "Any of you know how to get hold of his family? A mother and father have lost a son. They should be notified."

Lani found Dawson sitting out on the patio with a beer and quickly realized that something was chewing at him. She came closer. "Gabe finally zonked out, after I read him three books. I think he's taking longer to go to sleep because it's still daylight at his bedtime."

"Summer turns around next week. The year's half over."

Time was flying, but Lani wanted to stretch out the days as long as possible. The summer would be over and she'd have to leave the job. And Gabe. And Dawson.

Dawson shoved a patio chair toward her with his foot. "Join me."

She sat, staring out on the backyard and a sky stretching rosy pink with a setting sun.

"How's it been having my dad around for the past few weeks?"

Lani propped her feet on a nearby railing. "Fine. He mostly stays in his upstairs office. Comes down for lunch with Gabe. They share notes." She leaned forward. "Gabe shows him his coloring book and your dad usually gives Gabe some pictures to color he's downloaded from the Internet. Dinosaurs, of course. Oh, and if Gabe and I are doing a project"—she pointed to a row of paper cups on a nearby ledge—"well, Dr. Berke makes a big deal over it. He's a great granddad."

Dawson stared at the cups. Gabe had told him, "Daddy, I prant widdle seeds" the week before. Now tiny green shoots were poking through the dark dirt. He wished he'd taken better notice. Lani went on to tell Dawson that Franklin took two walks a day and accompanied her and Gabe to the park if they went. Dawson nodded, but thought back to what his father had told him the night before. When Lani said, "I'm surprised he hasn't returned to work yet," he interrupted her.

"That's not going to happen, Lani."

"It isn't?"

"Not if he wants to go on living."

Lani blinked. Dr. Berke wasn't a hundred percent—that was for sure. Since the surgery and his release from the hospital and rehab, he'd lost weight and tired easily. Not the total recovery she'd expected. "What do you mean?"

"Lopez said his heart isn't up to the stress and pressure of the hospital job. He made it very clear to Dad that the surgery and his medications made corrections but couldn't fix the underlying problem—stress. His heart's permanently damaged and he's got to make lifestyle changes."

"H-he's quitting?"

"Dad's only fifty-two. He can't and won't quit." Although Dawson was aware of the financial hit such a change would make, it was the hit to his father's psyche and emotions that would damage him the most. Franklin Berke was a doctor. The job was absorbed into him like water into a sponge. Dawson also knew that Franklin held on to the house for Dawson's and Gabe's sakes. He had told his dad last night he'd move, find a better job, drop fall classes, but Franklin would hear none of it.

"What's he going to do? He's an icon at the hospital."

"He's taking a job at the University of Chicago Medical Center. An old friend on staff there called and offered it months ago, before his heart attack." Dawson flicked a mosquito from his arm. "He said no at the time but has now agreed. He's moving up next week to find a place and prepare for classes. It seems the Med Center is very interested in his Step-Prep program."

"It's a fantastic program, but how's that going to be less pressure on him?"

"He's only designing the program, won't have to implement it like he did here. He'll have a staff up there, and he'll also be teaching a few courses to med students. He says he's looking forward to the change, but I'm not sure I believe him. It'll be a huge difference for him. For all of us."

Lani's heart did a stutter step. "Chicago. What about you and Gabe?"

"He says we're welcome to move up too. I can look for another job, take classes at the University of Chicago. The city's only an hour by air from Nashville. Hope to go up for Christmas, look around."

Relocate. Lani felt a lump in her throat, swallowed it down. She reminded herself that her time with Gabe would be over by the holidays anyway. She struggled to keep her voice cheerful. "Chicago has snow. Gabe will love snow."

Chicago weather would be so different. Dawson hadn't thought of Chicago since . . . He couldn't remember. He took a long swig from his beer bottle. He had wanted freedom to live his own life, but now that it was staring him in the face . . . Maybe if he and Gabe had been the ones leaving. Maybe if Franklin was in great health. Maybe if— He gave Lani a side-long glance. Her profile was etched in a sidelight from inside the house. Maybe if she had never come into his life. Dawson stood abruptly. "I'm keeping you from going home, aren't I?"

"I don't mind." A part of her felt as if she were at home.

"No. Your day's over. Go do something fun. I'll see you in the morning."

Fun. What she had to look forward to was a flurry of texts from Ben about him feeling neglected. She stood, forcing a smile. "See you tomorrow." She walked through the house, through the front door, and out onto the driveway to her parked car, where she began counting the brevity of all the tomorrows she had remaining with Gabe. And Dawson Berke.

———

"Did you know he was using, Bobby? Did you know and not tell us? Did you?" The four of them were standing outside the bus. Sloan peppered Bobby with questions.

"I didn't know. Swear to God!" He looked to Hal and Sy to rescue him from Sloan's fury. "Did you guys know?"

Sloan spun to face the others. *"Did you?"*

The others shook their heads. "I never saw him use," Sy said.

"*You* were sleeping with him," Hal sniped. "If you didn't know, how could we?"

Sloan rushed toward Hal, but Sy caught her before she could rake her nails down his face. "Shhh. Calm down. This isn't helping. None of us knew, Sloan. My guess is he just did it on the fly. He hooked up with some dealer and bought himself some junk and paid for it with his life. Shit happens."

She couldn't hold back the sobs fighting to get out. Sy folded her in his arms, let her cry herself out. After the storm of tears, she pulled away, saw how the others had tears of their own. The loss of Jarred was sinking in and they were all unraveled. Heat radiated from the outside of the bus, the metal hot enough to burn bare skin. Sloan blew out a lungful of air, struggling to regain control. "Sorry, Bobby. I shouldn't have—"

"Not a problem. We're all wrecked."

The sun beat down without mercy.

"What now?" Hal asked.

"Soon as the cops say we can leave, we'll go back to my place . . . regroup." This from Sy. "For now let's get back on the bus. Hot as hell out here."

Hal cranked up the generator to get the AC going. Sloan took a seat, leaning her forehead against the warm glass of a side window. She gazed at the flat fields, the trampled brown grass, empty of Bonnaroo fans but spotted with crews of maintenance people cleaning up the site, where soon, like her dreams, all debris would be hauled away to the trash.

185

CHAPTER 30

"Pops go bye in plane?" Gabe asked, looking bewildered.

Standing in the Nashville airport, near the TSA line where only ticketed travelers were allowed to pass through, Dawson held Gabe for a last look at his grandfather. Minutes before, Franklin had told his son and Lani goodbye, kissed Gabe, waved from the far side of the security checkpoint, and disappeared into the flow of passengers. Gabe had seen no airplane, so Dawson understood why he was confused. "Yeah, little man. Pops is going on the airplane."

"No plane! Gabe want Pops."

Dawson watched Gabe's face begin to crumble into a good cry.

Lani, standing next to him, came to his rescue. "Hey, Gabe. How would you like a special treat?" She pointed to the place selling miscellaneous goodies to departing travelers.

Gabe's face lit up. Dawson lowered Gabe and Lani took his hand, and together they walked into the grab-and-go, where Gabe selected a bag of gummy bears.

"Thanks for the save," Dawson said as they walked toward the escalator. "He was about to have a meltdown."

"Distraction. A potent weapon."

Dawson nodded, but deep down he was as disconcerted as Gabe over saying goodbye to his father. The last week had been a whirlwind of packing up boxes of books, papers, clothing, memorabilia, and keepsakes that would be shipped to Chicago from both Franklin's home and Windemere hospital offices. Franklin had rented a place to live, arranged by a Chicago broker and seen only through photos online. The loft he'd chosen was a modern spacious two-bedroom near the Medical Center. A new way of life for all of them.

Once in the parking garage, Dawson asked, "What do you say we go find some dinner? I mean, since we're in the big city. That okay with you, Lani?"

"Love to. I'm starving." With last-minute details, the rush to get Gabe up from his nap—which left him cranky—and the fifty-plus-mile drive to the Nashville airport, Lani hadn't taken time to eat since breakfast. Once they'd piled into the SUV, she'd sat in the backseat with Gabe strapped in his car seat and read to him during the trip.

"Eat!" Gabe yelled. "Chicken nuggets."

Dawson rolled his eyes. "Don't want to go any place where we have to read a menu off a wall. Your thoughts, Lani?"

"Let's just drive until we see a place that we like."

Dawson opened the sunroof, remembering how Franklin had handed him the keys and said, "Don't need it in Chicago." The year before, Dawson had traded in his old car for a pickup, and although Gabe's car seat fit snugly in the truck's rear seat, the SUV was far more comfortable. Another gift from Franklin he couldn't repay.

Dawson turned out of the airport and headed into the sprawling city. A plane taking off roared above the SUV. Gabe, looking up, waved. "Bye-bye, Pops!"

They settled on a Western-styled restaurant chain known to be kid friendly and took a booth by a window with a view of the evening sky. Gabe sat in a booster chair, enthralled watching his dad shell peanuts from a bucket on the table and drop the shells on the floor.

Lani shelled a few nuts and gave the husks to Gabe, who tossed them downward and leaned over to see where his shells landed. "Must be a guy thing."

"Hope he doesn't carry the habit home." Dawson flashed her a grin.

They ordered and when the waitress dressed in a blue T-shirt, jeans, and cowboy boots, brought their food and set down the plates, she smiled and said, "Y'all have the cutest little boy."

"Oh. I—" Lani started to correct her.

Dawson shrugged it off and said, "Thank you." The waitress hurried away. To Lani he said, "Why explain? We do have a cute kid with us."

Lani busied herself with cutting up the restaurant's version of chicken nuggets for Gabe, enjoying the simple pleasure of the three of them.

Dawson thought she wore contentment like some girls wore new clothes.

She felt Dawson's eyes on her. Wondering if she had food caught between her teeth, she glanced at him self-consciously.

Gabe grabbed a french fry, brandishing it in the air like a sword. Dawson parked his fork on his plate of barbeque ribs. "Lani, there's going to be some upheaval in the house for a while."

She looked up, wary, wondering what "upheaval" meant for her.

"I'm trading in that shoe box–size bedroom on the other side of Gabe's room for the bedroom Dad was using." When he had turned his high school basement bedroom into Gabe's playroom, Dawson had moved into the third upstairs bedroom, a space barely big enough for a bed and dresser. The middle room, the former guest room, was Gabe's, his crib replaced by a toddler bed shaped like a train engine and with side guards so he wouldn't roll off but that he could easily exit. Gabe loved it.

The basement now held a sleeper sofa, a craft table and chairs, and walls lined with cubbies for toys, puzzles, and books. Riding toys were scattered for play on rainy or high pollen days. "I'd like to paint the room before I move in, but I'm wondering about the best way to deal with the smell and how it will affect Gabe."

"Don't worry . . . we'll figure it out." Lani was relieved that the upheaval was something simple and only involved sweat equity. Her job would remain the same.

The child looked up. "I paint too, Daddy."

Dawson tousled Gabe's hair. "Probably not this time, buddy."

By the time they were finishing their meals, Gabe was nodding off. Dawson put the boy in his car seat and drove to Windemere, trading a mix of music from his and Lani's phones on the SUV's audio system. At the house, Dawson carried Gabe upstairs, settled him in his bed, and turned on the bedroom's night-light and air purifier.

When he came downstairs and onto the porch, Lani rose from a wicker chair. "Did he wake up?"

"Never blinked." Sounds of tree frogs and crickets filled a night scented by summer jasmine. "I kept you too late."

"No way. I wanted to come with you. Your dad helped me go after my dream of becoming a nurse, and I'll always be grateful to him. I hope he'll be happy in Chicago." Now that they were alone and she was to leave, she thought of the waitress thinking she was Gabe's mother. She had to accept that she was Gabe's caregiver, nothing more.

Dawson couldn't shake a feeling of loss. His father was gone, just him and Gabe now. He stared down at Lani. And this girl . . . this tenderhearted girl who had come into his and Gabe's lives and made both their lives better. Somehow, over the months, his feelings toward Lani had changed. He wanted to take her in his arms, touch her skin, kiss her mouth. He wanted to feel her body pressed to his. He *wanted* . . . He stepped closer.

Lani's heartbeat quickened. She wanted him to kiss her. From down the street came the sound of a car door slamming, and with it the return of reality. Life had boundaries. She was a caregiver. She could not afford to alter her commitment to the child no matter how much she wanted Dawson Berke. She took a step backward.

Dawson saw her move away, and it stopped him cold. If he touched her, if he kissed her the way he wanted to, everything would change. Gabe needed Lani more than Dawson, and for much longer than this moment, this single night. In the final equation, Gabe was what mattered. Dawson sucked in his breath, stepped aside, and jammed his hands into the pockets of his jeans. He cleared his throat, hoped his voice held steady. "See you in the morning?"

"Seven sharp." Trembling with what had almost happened between them, she hurried down the porch steps and jumped into her car. She backed out, glancing at her cell phone, dumped earlier on the front seat, and saw that she had a text from Ben sent hours before.

Where are u? When I came to pick you up tonight
Mel said you went to airport. Why didn't you tell me?
What's going on?

Lani groaned. She had totally forgotten her movie date with Ben. Feelings of guilt and self-recrimination flooded through her. She was an awful girlfriend! Ben deserved better. Her feelings for Dawson had resurfaced, taken root. How could she stay with Ben when her heart longed for another?

⟿

Sy had called a meeting of the band's remnants in the house's great room, not poolside, so the three of them knew it was important, different from other meetings. Three weeks gone since Bonnaroo, since Loose Change had knocked it out of the park, twenty-one days since . . . since . . . As soon as they had returned to Nashville, the guys packed up boxes of Jarred's stuff to send home to his family. Sloan had not helped. She simply couldn't touch his things, couldn't stir up new pain. She moved out of the room they'd shared, taken one at the far end of the hall, listened to Bobby, Hal, and Sy work, with every zip of the packing tape sounding like nails across a chalkboard, making her flinch each time she heard it that long afternoon.

Today they trickled into the massive great room with its soaring ceilings and oversized furniture. Sun blazed through spotless windows, cleaned just that morning, inside and out, by a janitorial service. Glass-topped tables sparkled, objects d'art rested on surfaces of expensive built-ins, and paintings worth large sums of money stared down from stark white walls. Sloan scarcely saw the room's beauty as she settled in a club chair, part of a set centered in front of a massive glass and iron coffee table. Hal and Bobby took the sofa and Sy the other club chair. Without preamble, Sy said, "My old man called yesterday. He heard about what happened at Bonnaroo and he was"—Sy searched for words—"angry. Worse than angry. He's talked with his attorneys about liabilities, blah blah blah, and he's demanding I come to New York, then to Europe for the rest of the summer. He's shutting down this house and cutting off my money. Sorry, guys, but I gotta go."

Sloan wasn't surprised. Sy had spent days backing them out of the summer tour, making calls, giving regrets. No contracts had been signed, so dumping out had only proved embarrassing. There was no more band. Their brief shining moment was over. The day before while driving to the grocery store, Sloan had heard the ballad she and Jarred once had written and sung together on the car radio. The DJ had called it a tribute to lost talent. She'd turned it off mid-song.

"So we're being tossed?" Hal asked.

"We're all out."

"Do you have to go to New York? Do what he says?" Sloan

asked, because she knew how much music meant to Sy and how little his father's world meant to him.

"Only if I want to come into my trust fund from Granddad when I'm thirty." Sy looked grim and sad at the same time. "And when I get my hands on it, my old man will never be able to tell me what to do again. So, yeah, I gotta walk the line. For now."

A weird five-year prison sentence he couldn't escape, Sloan thought.

"How long before we have to leave?" Bobby asked.

"Two days." Sy took a deep breath. "It was all the time I could buy. The old man's ballistic. Doesn't want me sullying his glorious name. Hurts business, you know."

Sloan felt sorry for Sy. He'd carved out a unique sound for their band. And they'd come so close to grabbing the brass ring.

"What about the money in the bank for our tour?" Hal again.

"Yeah. That's part two of this meeting. I went to the bank yesterday to close out the account since I was a cosigner." Sy made eye contact with each of them. Sloan felt as if a rock had settled in the pit of her stomach because she knew exactly what was coming. "There is no money, folks. Jarred spent it all."

CHAPTER 31

"What the hell!" Hal shot off the sofa.

"All of it?" Bobby's voice cracked.

Sy calmly reached to the floor beside his chair and brought up several pieces of paper and a packet. "See for yourselves." He tossed the paper onto the glass-topped table and Hal snatched it, stared at it, then he handed it to Bobby, who scanned it and looked up, incredulous. Sloan stayed seated, didn't even bother to look.

"You closed it out with just five hundred bucks in it? There was supposed to be several thousand in it! We've been putting in cash every week since our tour ended last summer. Plus there was the Bonnaroo money."

"Five hundred eight dollars and forty-one cents." Sy held up the packet, then tossed it onto the table too. "It's for you three to split."

Hal jerked the statement from Bobby's hand, stared hard at it, leaped up, and paced the floor. "The money's been leaking out for months. What the hell did he do with it?"

Sy shrugged. "I blame myself for not checking the account more often. Sorry. If I'd been watching carefully—"

"Not your fault," Sloan spoke for the first time. "None of us blame you, Sy." She glared at Hal and Bobby, daring either to contradict her.

Hal growled, wadded the papers, and threw the ball across the room. "What did he do with it? With our money!"

"How much did he take to Bonnaroo?" Sloan's numbness was wearing off, replaced by cold anger.

Bobby crossed the floor, retrieved the paper ball, un-wadded it, smoothed the crinkles with his palm, and looked for the date of the last withdrawal. "Fifteen hundred. Two days before the festival. But he'd been spending it all along without us knowing."

Hal swore. "So he must have been planning the drug buy."

Sy shrugged. "We'll never know for sure. What we do know is that whatever price he paid it wasn't worth it."

They went silent. Sloan's gaze darted around the room, at the tableau of friends now fractured, swimming in sunlight from the vast glass wall, of plans now changed, and of hopes shattered. Betrayed by one of their own. She hated Jarred, even in her grief over losing him.

Sy stood. "Cold beer in the fridge, guys. One final pool party just for us. How 'bout it?"

They left the room, but Sloan didn't. There was only one thought in her head, running on a loop, a refrain from an old song written long after the death of three rockers in a plane crash: *"The day the music died . . ."*

Dawson was wrapping up his day, washing drywall mud off his arms from a hose at the construction site when his boss, Frank Younce, called him into the management trailer. He went inside from the heat of the afternoon to the welcome of the blast of cool air. Younce motioned to a chair and Dawson took it. Often such visits were called before a firing. He couldn't think what he might have done to warrant a pink slip, though. "Yes, sir." He wanted to ask, *Am I in trouble?* but didn't.

Younce was a good-sized man with a barrel chest and massive arms. His face looked like tanned leather from twenty-five years of working outdoors. Dawson considered him a good boss, tough, but fair. His boss said, "Windemere's a small town." Dawson nodded in agreement. "I'm just saying because people know each other's business." The words sounded ominous, but Dawson held his tongue. "I know your father is a doctor. Good one too, people say."

"True." For the life of him, Dawson couldn't figure where the foreman was going with his questions.

"You want to be a doctor like your dad?"

Dawson shook his head. "Never wanted that. Taking some classes at MTSU in business. More to my liking."

"How about your job? You like construction work?"

"Sure. Hard work, but good work."

Younce gave a satisfied nod, as if he approved of Dawson's words. "Been watching you on the job for months. You ever think of moving up in this kind of work?"

"Move how? To what?"

"Construction manager. Hastings Construction offers paid sponsorships to people who show promise at becoming managers for the company. Headquarters asks for recommendations every so often, and I thought of you. You're a good worker, you've done a turn at almost every job on a site, and people like you. You'll make more money and you'll get more responsibility when you're a manager, and it also means you can move up within Hastings."

The words surprised Dawson. He'd never thought about making a career with Hastings Construction. "I'm interested. What do I have to do?"

"It's good you're getting college credits, because there's a lot of construction specialties to consider . . . you know, directions you can go. But what's key for the job is personal skills, being able to solve problems and get along with others—not always easy with some of these guys."

Dawson knew it was true. Some of the men walked off the job without warning, showed up drunk, and got into arguments over anything.

The foreman studied him, said, "You already have two years of construction experience, and you appear to have the people skills. You might want to consider going for a sponsorship." Younce tossed a spiral-bound booklet on his desk, where it landed in front of Dawson. "Take this home, look it over, see where you might fit and might want to explore, then get back to me. This is a good opportunity, Berke. I think you have the stuff to make a good manager." Younce stood, gave a nod. "See you in the morning."

Dawson rose quickly, his head spinning over the offer. Sometimes life took a new direction when least expected.

⎯⎯⎯

The band members divided the money, Hal and Bobby taking $169 each and giving Sloan $170. They threw the forty-one cents into the pool. Sloan also took Jarred's car, and the guys settled on the Beast. At the last minute, standing in the circular drive in front of Sy's house, Bobby said, "You can come with us, Sloan. We can find new people, rebuild the band."

She shook her head. "I'm over the band."

"What will you do? Your voice shouldn't be wasted." Bobby's eyes begged her to come with him and Hal to Atlanta, where Hal's aunt had said they could stay with her for a "spell."

"Don't know yet. I'll figure out something."

"You'll keep in touch?"

"Sure." She said it but knew she probably wouldn't.

"Where will you go?" Sy asked.

"Not sure. Someplace where I can get a job." Of course, she knew where she was going; she just couldn't bring herself to say it out loud.

They stood there awkwardly, listening to the fountain in the center of the semicircular driveway gurgle under the hot sunshine. Hal reached for Sloan, hugged her, and climbed into the bus. Sy hugged her next. "You have a great voice," he said into her ear. "Never give up."

"And you don't let your dad kill your heart for music."

Bobby came last, holding her close and a little too long. "Love you, Sloan."

"Ditto." She told Bobby what he needed to hear but eased away, got into the hot car, started the engine, turned on the air, exited the driveway, and headed toward I-24, knowing she'd turn onto the ramp going east and take the exit for the Tennessee state road that would take her back to Windemere. She was out of options, had no money, no job, and nowhere else to go.

Sloan drove to the trailer park, turned in, and crunched slowly down the rutted road toward everything she'd run away from. She hadn't seen the place in almost three years, and yet it looked the same. No . . . if anything, it looked dingier and more run-down than when she'd left. Her stomach was tied in knots, her nerves hair-trigger taut over facing her mother. LaDonna would let loose with one of her tirades. She'd gloat, shovel out venom in spades. Sloan knew she'd have to stand there and take it and say what needed to be said in order to move into the trailer again. "I can do this," she told herself. Survival. Whatever it took.

When she stopped in front of the trailer and turned off the engine, she saw two small children playing in the dirt. Sloan climbed out of the car, pasting on a cheerful smile. "Hi. I'm Sloan. Who are you?" The kids shrank against the side of the trailer. She saw her child-self in the girl's frightened eyes. "I won't hurt you." She walked closer.

The boy, who looked to be the younger of the two, started to cry. The trailer door flew open, startling Sloan, causing her to jump backward. A woman rushed out babbling in another language, grabbing the kids by their arms and dragging them to the trailer door.

"Wait! Does LaDonna Quentin still live here?" Sloan started forward, but in a panic the woman stuffed the kids inside and slammed the door hard, leaving Sloan standing in the dust under a hot sun.

Sloan stared at the ugly green hulk of metal that had been her home once. LaDonna was *gone*? Where? When? She could ask the manager in the front trailer but discarded the thought. If her mother was gone, she'd probably left owing money. La-Donna's style. As the reality washed over her, Sloan got into the car and sat in the heat, hands clutching the steering wheel. *Now what?* She tasted fear. What was she going to do? Call Bobby and Hal? Try to catch up to them? Yet she rejected that idea as soon as it formed in her head. No, she couldn't walk it back. Never. Too much pain. Tears welled in her eyes. She backed the car away from the trailer, left the park, and headed toward the only other place she could think to go for asylum.

Lani was wiping down the counters from lunch when she heard the doorbell. *Yikes!* Couldn't people read? She'd hung the DO NOT RING sign above the doorbell every day during Gabe's nap time, yet now someone was dinging it anyway. Before it could chime a third time, she tossed down the wet paper towel she'd been using and rushed to the foyer and the front door, flinging it open and saying, "Please don't ring—"

Her words stopped cold. The woman on the porch was blond, pretty, and totally recognizable. Lani was looking into the face of Sloan Quentin.

CHAPTER 32

S loan stared through the open door at the girl standing in
the foyer. "I—I'm looking for Dr. Berke and . . . and his
son." She glanced toward the mailbox street side. "They, um,
used to live here."

Lani's mouth was cotton dry and her heart thumped like a
drum. "They . . . he . . . Dawson still does."

"Oh." A potential truth hit Sloan. Maybe Dawson had
married. Three years gone, anything could have happened.
"Are you his wife?" She ventured a guess, her mind sucking on
the idea like quicksand.

Lani squared her shoulders. "I'm a caregiver. To Dawson's
son." She attempted to keep her voice neutral, calm, matter-of-
fact. Professional. But her insides were in turmoil.

My and Dawson's son. Sloan's brain pushed against the
memory. The baby she had blocked from thinking about for so
long. Gabriel was alive. She found her voice. "Is . . . is Dawson
here?"

"He's working." Lani was holding the doorknob so tightly
that her hand had gone numb.

"That makes sense . . . I mean, if you're the babysitter."

More than a sitter. Lani didn't correct Sloan, still trying to regain emotional equilibrium.

"Um . . . I'm a friend of Dawson's. We went to high school together. My name's Sloan."

Still Lani said nothing. She saw Sloan's car, an older black Mustang in the driveway in need of a wash. Hadn't it once belonged to Sloan's boyfriend, Jarred?

Sloan studied the girl in the doorway, who was barring her entrance and withholding information Sloan needed and wanted. The girl wore an air of familiarity, something Sloan couldn't place yet tickled her memory. She gave up on placing the brown-eyed girl, too frazzled to care just now. She was going to have to pull information from this sitter, because nothing was being volunteered. "When will he be home?"

"Usually around five." Lani held herself rigid, prayed that Gabe would stay asleep. She wanted to shut the door, push away the flesh-and-blood apparition in front of her. "Maybe you could come back then."

"Can I wait for him here on the porch?"

What could she say? "It's just two o'clock. Three hours until—"

"I know it's a long wait, but I don't care. I need to talk to Dawson." Growing impatient, Sloan heard her voice pitch higher. "What about his father, Dr. Berke?" Sloan recalled that Franklin had always been nice to her. Maybe he had an ounce of goodwill left for her.

"He isn't here either." Silence.

Seething at the sitter, Sloan stepped to the side, walked over, and parked herself in a wicker chair. "I'll wait."

Lani swiftly closed the door, leaned against a wall, and

flexed her stiff fingers. Her body shook and she felt out of breath as if she'd run a race. And lost. Why was Sloan here? Lani retreated to the kitchen, found her cell phone on the counter, and sent Dawson a text. He shouldn't be blindsided.

A return text came quickly:

Do not let her in the house. Do not let Gabe see her.
Coming ASAP.

Lani decided she would keep Gabe distracted in his playroom after his nap. She'd feed him a snack there too, tell him it was a picnic for just the two of them. Already the effort to protect him had begun.

～♪～

Dawson drove home from the job site in his pickup as fast as he dared. After he had brought Gabe home as a newborn, he'd wondered if this day would come. Now it had. After Sloan left Windemere, he'd created scenarios in his head about her begging to return. For months he'd written and rewritten what he'd say and do. He'd reject her, refuse to let her see their son. Then he'd think of Gabe growing up without a mother, and he'd change the scenario and relent. After the first six months of Gabe's life, once Dawson mastered the skill set of tending to a baby's basic needs, and with Paulie's grandmother's help, he overcame his fear of raising this baby on his own. That was also when he'd shoved vengeful thoughts of Sloan into the far corners of his mind. Her choice to leave. Her loss. So why in the hell was she back? What did she want?

He turned into his driveway, pulled alongside the black

Mustang. Jarred's car. It cleared up the mystery as to how she'd disappeared. He checked the car to make sure Jarred wasn't sitting in it because if that a-hole got near him or Gabe . . . Sloan rose from the chair. He took his time exiting the truck and going onto the porch, all the while measuring her with his eyes, balancing his anger and his fears. Her hair was shorter, she was thinner, her cheekbones more angular. A small stud embedded on the side of her nose caught a spark of sunlight. She looked wary and worn out but held his gaze. "Hello, Dawson." Her voice, barely a whisper.

In the few years since she'd seen him, Dawson's body had filled out. He was tanned and well muscled, his black hair shaggy, his dark eyes as cold as black ice.

"Why are you here, Sloan?"

He stood like a stone wall and she shrank against the force of him. Her lips quivered, but she gave him her honest answer. "I need help."

He glanced to the black car. "Boyfriend dump you?"

She winced, knowing there was too much to explain just now. "Long story." She realized she must first reassure him. "I haven't come to cause trouble for you. I swear. I tried to go back to the trailer, but it seems my mother no longer lives there."

He grunted. "Good thing. She put us through hell after Gabe came home from the hospital."

Sloan's heart seized. "What did she do?"

"Long story." He tossed her words back to her. "And now's not the time to tell it."

Sloan closed her eyes and felt her body weave, and she realized she hadn't eaten all day, not even breakfast at Sy's. "Can we sit?"

She sat again. He did not. She looked pale, but he refused to feel sorry for her. She'd made her choices.

Dawson's body language screamed obscenities at her. Maybe she deserved it. Resigned, she prepared to scale the wall that separated them and shifted in the chair. "How's Gabriel?"

"I'm surprised you remember his name."

She bristled, went hard inside. "F you. I thought of him every day, Dawson, until I couldn't think about him anymore and not go crazy."

"As proof from all the times you called to check on him." *And me*, he thought, but didn't say.

"I knew he'd be all right with you and Franklin. I knew he wouldn't be all right with me. Not because I didn't care, but because I didn't know how to be his mother."

"I didn't know much about being a parent either. He didn't come with instructions."

"You had Franklin. I had LaDonna. You've already told me she caused trouble." She fired back a volley that stopped him cold. "And he has you. He has a home, a babysitter—"

"She's his caregiver. Lani's a third-year nursing student and works at the hospital."

The message was ominous. "He's sick? He isn't well?"

"Well enough."

Maddingly enigmatic. She wouldn't beg for details. Not yet.

"Since you're not here to cause trouble, and you're not interested in being Gabe's mother, what do you want from me, Sloan?"

Her nerves were so frayed she wasn't sure she could continue. Why had she thought he would ever forgive her? "Mercy" was all she managed to say.

Dawson lowered himself into the chair across from hers, leaned forward, rested his forearms on his thighs. The day of hard work was nothing to the emotional exhaustion he felt. The air was hot, stagnant, and he longed to be inside the house drinking a big glass of sweet tea and listening to Lani talk about Gabe's day and watching Gabe playing with his race cars on the kitchen floor. He glanced up, studied Sloan's face. She looked truly frightened. Something bad had happened to her, something that had driven her back to a place she hated and to him because there was nowhere else she could go, no one else she could turn to. He'd been so intent on making her pay for her past, her desertion of him and Gabe, he hadn't heard her out. He felt no satisfaction in the way he'd been treating her and blew out a breath. "Tell me what you need."

His voice was gentler this time, so Sloan began her story about their years apart, about the band, the career that almost was and now wasn't. And she told him about Jarred, breaking down when she told of him dying. She wiped her nose with the back of her hand, ashamed of not holding up. "I . . . I just need a place to stay until I get on my feet. I'll get a job, save up money until I can afford to move out on my own. I won't be in your way. I'll do whatever you say. Will you . . . help me? *Please*, Dawson."

The news about Jarred was jarring, but Dawson had no way to comfort her. He couldn't be vindictive. He couldn't dismiss her. Sloan—a girl he once wanted and loved. Gabe's mother. "I . . . I need a little time. Give me some time to think this through."

"Okay." She rose, legs unsteady, anxious to retreat from this emotional firestorm inside her. "Will a couple of hours be long enough? I'll go get something to eat." At the edge of the porch, without turning, she asked, "Should I just call you?"

"I'll call you. What's your number?" He took out his cell, waited for her answer.

She shrugged. "The same as when we were in high school. I should have changed it while I lived in Nashville, but I never did."

Somehow her admission undid him. She had *always* been a phone call away, but because he'd been nursing his own anger and hurt, he had never once attempted to reach her. Once she drove off, Dawson sat in a wicker chair, brooding. What would his father do? No-brainer. Franklin was a doctor who lived by the credo *First do no harm.* But he wasn't his father. He wanted to protect Gabe, but he couldn't ignore Sloan's plea for help. Could he trust Sloan to keep her word? He straightened, realized that he had an ally inside the house. Lani. She was dedicated to Gabe, and extremely fond of him. She could be his safety net . . . *if* he could urge her to stay on until Sloan moved out. Making up his mind about what to do, Dawson rose and went into the house.

CHAPTER 33

Dawson found Lani and Gabe in the basement putting puzzles together. Seeing his dad, Gabe's face lit up. "Daddy!"

"Hey, buddy." He picked Gabe up, tossed him in the air, and caught him while Gabe squealed with delight. "Is there a TV show he can watch now?" This to Lani.

"I'll find one." She located the remote.

"I'm going upstairs with Lani, Gabe. Yell if you need us."

Gabe grabbed a baggie full of goldfish snack crackers and scampered to his beanbag in front of the television.

Lani followed Dawson upstairs and into the den. He took Franklin's old recliner and she took the sofa. She easily saw the strain of his meeting with Sloan on his face.

"Sloan's bottomed out and needs a place to stay until she can get back on her feet."

Lani felt as if she'd been punched in the stomach.

Since he'd started at the finish line of the story, he now backtracked. *Just the facts, none of my emotional baggage.* He saw Lani flinch when he recounted Jarred's death. Of course. They'd all been in the same senior class. Everyone knew

208

everyone else in Windemere, or at least something *about* everyone else.

In her mind's eye, Lani pictured Jarred with his long hair and cocky attitude onstage with his band, Sloan at his side. "I'm sorry about Jarred. He and Sloan were a couple . . . for a time," she amended.

"Did you ever hang with them in school?"

"No. We ran in different circles."

"I only spent a year at WHS, so I didn't pay much attention to who was who, and what mattered or didn't matter. All I wanted was to graduate and get out of there." He shook his head. "Then homecoming happened."

Lani saw how the memories of those days still haunted him, so she jumped to the present. Her mouth felt dry as cotton as she asked, "Now that she's returned, do you know what you're going to do?"

"Much as I'd like to, Lani, I can't turn her out. Her mother's disappeared, left no forwarding address, and she has no place else to go."

Lani's heart nosedived. He wasn't going to send Sloan away. Lani wanted to crawl into a shell and pull it around her for safety. Shells were hard and strong and protective. "What can I do to help?" A safe question, and the only one she thought she should ask.

"I want you to take care of Gabe, like always. If that's still okay with Sloan staying here." He wanted to ask her to remain throughout Sloan's stay but quickly decided to not overload Lani, so he saved that part for another time.

"I won't leave Gabe." *Or you.*

He slid her a smile. "And you don't have to put up with any crap from her either. I'll make that clear. She can sleep in

Gabe's playroom on the pull-out sofa. Maybe she can land a job quickly and leave quickly."

"Gabe's not going to know what to think when she moves into his playroom."

"I'll come up with a story for him. I'm supposed to call her to come back, and I'd like you here when she does. I want Gabe to meet her with you here. Do you mind?"

Dawson was establishing a hierarchy and Lani quickly understood her order in it—Dawson, Lani, Sloan—and felt giddy about it. "I don't mind. It's all about Gabe. He's number one."

Dawson nodded. "For you and me, yes. But it's a message I want to make sure she gets loud and clear."

Sloan returned to the house with Dawson's words on the phone rattling in her head. Two things, set in stone. One, she must not tell Gabe she was his mother. She didn't mind. Perhaps one day he would learn it, but she sure didn't want him to know it now. Too many things to explain, to confess, when he was too young to understand. Two, whenever Dawson wasn't home, Lani was in charge. Sloan didn't like that as much, the thought of maybe this Lani ordering her around, but she agreed to it.

Dawson was alone on the porch waiting when Sloan returned, where he restated his ground rules. Once she agreed to his face, he called to Lani, who stepped out the front door holding the hand of a small dark-haired boy, his head down, reluctant and shy about meeting this stranger. Sloan's heart banged in her chest.

"Gabe, this is a friend of mine and Lani's from when we were in school. Sloan is going to be staying in your playroom for a while. She'll be spending nights there." Dawson took Gabe's other hand. "Can you say hi to Sloan?"

Sloan's eyes grew moist remembering the dark-haired baby with IV lines and an oxygen mask, a baby that at the time she didn't think would survive. The child said nothing, refused to look up. Sloan didn't know what to say, how to act. Her gaze flew to Dawson's. Lani dropped to her knees, lifted Gabe's chin, and looked him in the eyes. "Gabe, remember your manners. It's polite to say hello."

The child shyly raised his head. Sloan felt her breath catch, and she blurted, "He . . . he has blue eyes like . . . I . . . I mean . . . I thought—"

"That his eyes would be dark," Dawson finished for her, a cautionary note in his voice. "DNA's funny that way. Never know where it's going to show up."

Gabe glanced at his dad, confused, but did say, "Hi, Daddy's friend."

"Hi." Sloan couldn't stop looking at him, a blend of her and Dawson, melded to create a most beautiful child. Words stuck in her throat.

The awkwardness of the moment spurred Lani to action. "We should go inside, get Gabe into the air-conditioning."

"Your things in the car?" Dawson's question zapped Sloan into the moment.

"In the trunk. It's not locked."

Sloan followed Lani and Gabe inside and Dawson went to retrieve her few belongings, while another day echoed in his memory of her coming into this house with the child, yet unseen.

"Are you crying, Lani?" Melody came through the front door of their apartment to the sight of Lani on the sofa and a pile of tissues on the coffee table.

Lani quickly wiped her eyes. Once she'd left Dawson's and come home, she'd crashed onto the sofa. "Just throwing myself a pity party." No use trying to hide the reason for her crying jag from her sister. Mel could wring truth out of the most accomplished liar.

"Why? What's going on?"

"Maybe later."

"Maybe now." Melody was firm. "I'll fix us some tea."

"Don't want tea," Lani called to her sister's back. Resigned, Lani pulled another tissue from the box in her lap and blew her nose. The rays of the setting sun slanting through the windows gave the room a warm glow that couldn't reach inside her heart.

Melody returned, forced a glass of tea into Lani's hand, and settled in a cushy chair beside the couch. "Please tell me." Her voice sounded gentler, less demanding. "You look so sad."

"Sloan Quentin showed up at Dawson's house today. She's Gabe's mother."

Melody's forehead furrowed. "Ouch. The mother who deserted him? What does she want?"

"Refuge." Lani detailed what was going to happen, what was expected of Lani. "Seems her life's falling apart and she needs a place to live for a time. Dawson . . . he told her she could crash in the basement. That's Gabe's playroom."

"I don't think running interference between these two adults is fair to you. Is that what Dawson expects of you?"

"He's asking me to do my job, to protect Gabe and keep watch over him."

"Protect him? From his own mother? Why would he even let the woman into his home after what she did? Do you think she's expecting to waltz in and start fresh?"

The same questions had buzzed Lani's brain. She had no answers. "Please, Mel. I don't know! Dawson thinks he should help her, but only until she can get on her feet."

Melody shook her head. "Bogus. Maybe he wants to get back together with her, have her take up the slack and step into her mommy role." Lani flinched, and seeing it, Melody stopped her angry speculation. "I'm sorry, Sis. I didn't mean to fall into lawyer mode. It's just that you're hurting. I hate seeing you hurt."

"It isn't the only hard thing that happened today." She sucked in a breath while Melody stayed quiet and waited for Lani's other news. "Ben and I broke up. He . . . um . . . he sent me a text—"

"He *texted* a breakup message? The coward! He couldn't tell you to your face?"

Lani motioned for her sister to calm down. "I won't say it's unexpected. Some of my friends from school . . . nursing students, have let me know that he's been flirty with a couple of the girls who come around the pool when he's on duty. That's how I met him. Remember?" She glanced at Melody, saw her dark expression. "It's all right, Mel. I . . . I haven't felt like we were a couple for . . . well, for a while now."

"Because your job comes first." Mel's voice was flat but loaded with implications.

"Gabe means a lot to me. I can't help it. Every time he wheezes, I know how to help him breathe. Can Sloan do that? *Will* she do it?"

The sun had set and shadows had crept across the carpet

and up the far wall. Neither of them reached to turn on the lamp. Melody set her glass on the floor and took her sister's hands in hers. "Look at me." Lani raised her eyes. "This isn't just about the little boy, is it? It's about the father too. Ben's just been a distraction. Correct?"

"Yes." Lani's voice was barely audible.

"Losing Ben isn't the tragedy here. The tragedy would be losing Gabriel and his father."

Her lawyer sister had made a perfect summation. Lani turned pleading eyes on Melody. "What should I do? I can't quit. I can't leave Gabe. And I . . . I can't face Dawson and Sloan getting back together."

Melody steepled her fingers, leaned back, and asked, "Lani, do you know the difference between emergency workers and regular people?" Mel's voice came through her gloom with a question that felt so far out in left field that Lani simply stared at her. "*What?* What kind of question is that?"

Melody repeated it, adding, "Humor me. Tell me the difference and maybe you'll see the point I want to make."

"I don't *know*! Uniforms?"

"That's not the answer I'm thinking of."

"Well you'll have to tell me because I'm lost here."

Melody straightened up and looked into Lani's eyes. "Whenever there's a disaster, regular people run away from it while emergency workers run toward it."

"So?"

Melody stood up. "You're smart. . . . Figure it out, little sister. Which one are you?"

Feeling completely confused, Lani watched Melody turn on the lamp to chase the darkness as she left the room.

214

CHAPTER 34

S loan felt warm breath on her face, plus the smell of
Cheerios. She struggled through a layer of sleep, forced
open one eyelid, and saw blue eyes peering at her from the side
of the sleeper sofa. Both her eyelids snapped wide open. Gabe
was propped on elbows, leaning into her face, in a serious stare-
down. "Gabe!" She scooted back on her pillow, bringing him
into better focus. He wore Spider-Man pajamas and clutched
a stuffed toy dog under one arm. She had no idea what time
it was, only that it seemed like she'd just gone to bed. Still
she offered a smile, pushing away cobwebs in her brain. "Good
morning. You're up early."

He held out his dog, a dachshund made from smooth brown
leather. "Woof-Woof says hi."

She visually examined the floppy leather ears and black
button eyes and nose. *Cute.* "Good morning, Woof-Woof."

Seemingly satisfied with her greeting, Gabe trotted to where
her roller bag lay, its contents spilling onto the floor. Sloan
scrambled up. Dawson had been quite clear that she was to be
on constant guard against Gabe's curiosity. She had cigarettes

somewhere in the suitcase and didn't want Gabe finding the pack. "Gabe, that's my stuff . . . you shouldn't bother it."

He passed the bag and stopped at her guitar case. "What's dat?"

"My guitar."

He gave her a quizzical look. "Want to see."

"Maybe later," she said, still trying to shake out the cobwebs.

"Gabe? You down there?" Dawson's voice from the top of the stairs.

Gabe's eyes widened and he scampered back to the stairs. "I here, Daddy."

"I told you not to go down there and bother Sloan."

"It's all right!" Sloan called. "I'm up."

"Come here *now*, Gabe." Dawson sounded cross. His voice mellowed as he added, "Lani's here."

"Laaaani!" Gabe's face lit up and he hustled up the stair steps.

Sloan watched Gabe disappear up the steps that had been carpeted before— Well, *before*. She let out a breath, realizing that ready or not, her day had started, and she promised herself she'd go to bed much earlier from now on. She hurried to the bathroom to shower and get ready for a day of job hunting.

⟶ ⟵

Lani was loading the dishwasher and Gabe was sitting at the table with a pile of Play-Doh when Sloan came up into the kitchen. Lani offered a smile. "Morning." She felt completely at loose ends, unsure as to how to interact with Sloan, but knew she had to make this work out for Gabe's sake.

"Hey."

Gabe ignored them as he rolled up tiny dough balls and set them in a straight line on the tabletop.

"Dawson gone already?"

Lani looked at the clock. "Left twenty minutes ago. His job starts early." Lani busied herself, sidled Sloan a glance. "Breakfast? Eggs in fridge, cereal in upper cupboard—"

"I know where things are around here," Sloan cut her off testily.

Lani retreated into silence, realizing that Sloan knew every nook and cranny of this house, for she'd lived here before Lani was ever a hireling.

Sloan pulled open the refrigerator door, peered inside, shut the door. She wasn't a breakfast person. She went to the pantry, opened that door, and pulled out a box of Pop-Tarts. "This is fine. Any coffee?"

Lani motioned to the carafe on the other side of the kitchen. "I can make fresh."

"And I can drink this." Sloan had no desire to buddy up to this Lani. She went to the cabinet that held the coffee mugs and took one, filling it with what remained in the pot.

The tension in the room was palpable. Lani stiffened her back. Coexisting with Sloan wasn't going to be easy. "I'm taking Gabe to the park."

The word *park* galvanized Gabe. "Now, Lani? Go to park now?"

"Not in your pajamas."

Gabe looked down at himself, giggled. "I get clothes." He scooted off the banquette and ran for the upstairs.

"Does he run everywhere?"

"Mostly," Lani said.

217

Sloan drank her coffee, mentally weighing her day's options, and decided that job hunting could wait another twenty-four hours. "Can I go to the park with you and Gabe?"

Her request surprised Lani, and she couldn't come up with a reason to say no. "If you want."

"I don't want to impose." She made the word sound like an imposition. She locked eyes with Lani. "But I think we should talk."

Lani felt a chill skitter up her back. "I think we should too." She left Sloan in the kitchen and went upstairs to help Gabe dress.

—⁊—

Morning was a good time of day to take Gabe to the park he loved. Lani settled him and a black backpack into a shiny red Radio Flyer wagon for the five-block trip. Riding helped conserve his energy for the playground. Sunlight dappled the sidewalk from overhead trees, and the air held a just-washed smell of grass and freshly turned soil and summer flowers. Sloan followed behind the wagon, and Gabe pointed out *everything* that caught his interest along the way, which turned out to be everything. At the park he tumbled out of the wagon and ran to the slides, jungle gyms, and swings, all brilliantly painted in primary colors.

"Push me, Lani!" He threw himself across a sling-style swing, almost running over a toddler younger than himself.

Lani threw a visual *Sorry* to the boy's mother and settled Gabe on the hard rubber seat.

"Won't he fall off?" Sloan motioned to the nearby cage seats designed for safety.

"He's been practicing pumping his legs for weeks to surprise his father." Gabe grabbed the chains on either side, and Lani gently pulled the swing backward and let go. "All he needs is a little push." She and Sloan stood behind him, watching him struggle to go higher. Once he was swinging smoothly, Lani said, "You wanted to talk."

Women sat chatting on benches that surrounded the play area, abandoned strollers parked on the grass. Children ran and shouted. Sloan shrugged. "I guess this is as good a place as any." She kept her eyes on Gabe's back, on his short legs stretching toward the sky. "Dawson and I talked for a long time last night."

Lani trained her eyes on Gabe also, unwilling to look at Sloan.

"He told me about Gabe's asthma. I don't know anything about asthma."

Lani wondered if Sloan expected her to give her a brochure or something. She decided to say nothing, make Sloan ask for anything she wanted. *Don't volunteer.*

"Dawson told me about Franklin too, his heart attack and moving to Chicago. I was sorry about that. I like Franklin, and he was always good to me."

"His doctors say he'll be fine if he just watches his stress levels and takes his heart medications. We all miss him, but he Skypes us every week."

"Dawson told me Franklin handpicked you from his nursing program to take care of Gabe. He said he agreed to Franklin's choice."

Sloan made it sound as if Franklin had twisted Dawson's arm. Lani fought to keep her cool. "I'm qualified."

"Of course you are. Paid help should be capable."

Was that what Dawson had told Sloan? That Lani was only *paid help*? Lani thought back to the night on the porch, of Dawson taking a step closer to her, the look on his face. Or had she seen only what she wanted to see, longed to see? How she'd struggled not to fling herself into his arms! "Gabe's more than a *job* to me. I love caring for him. He's an amazing little boy, and he's an asthmatic, a special needs child." She set Sloan straight about her role with Gabe.

Sloan's gaze scraped over Lani. She felt it, sharp as a razor.

"You're not really a nurse, though, are you? You're just studying to *be* a nurse."

"I've been working in the hospital for three years, attending classes for two. My third, and final year, starts at the end of next month. Why the third degree?" Lani bristled at the way Sloan was putting her on the defensive, decided she needed to stand her ground. "Dawson talked to me too. This morning. He said that your stay at the house was temporary and that as soon as you earned enough money, you'd be moving out."

"Look at me, Lani! I flying."

Lani turned her attention to him, saw he was swinging higher than she liked. Lani caught the swing as it neared the ground and stopped it. "Whoa there, Spidey. Don't want you flying into outer space." She circled round the front, saw that his face was red with exertion, listened to his breathing, and thought it sounded labored. "Hey, it's time for a snack and a juice box." She lifted him from the swing and took him to an empty bench, telling Sloan, "Bring the wagon."

Sloan didn't hesitate, because even she heard the wheeze in Gabe's breath.

At the bench, Lani lifted the backpack, unzipped it, and brought out Gabe's rescue inhaler. "How about taking a puff for me, Spidey." He did, and laid his head on her shoulder while the vapor seeped into his bronchi. She held him close, soothing him until his breathing normalized. Once he perked up, she took out a juice box and a pack of cheese crackers, sat him beside her, and helped him peel away the paper. Minutes later Gabe seemed fine.

"Go play." Gabe pointed toward the slide, wanting to join the other children. Lani gave him permission.

Sloan had watched, fascinated. How quickly his breathing had deteriorated, how quickly Lani had picked up on it. "His asthma?"

"Yes. He can have an episode if he gets overheated. He has meds and does nebulizer treatments at home. He seems to understand that he's not like the other kids."

"But he's okay now?" The episode had shaken Sloan.

"He is, but we won't stay much longer. Heat and humidity aren't his friends." Again she felt Sloan's eyes on her. She turned her head, saw that Sloan's expression had shifted from concern for Gabe to disdain for Lani. "What is it?"

"After I went to bed last night, I had time to think about why you looked familiar to me when you answered the front door yesterday."

"Same senior class."

"True, but then something else came to me—Lani . . . Alana Kennedy, Kathy Madison, the cheerleaders, all of you. You were part of that clique of little bitches who hated me and called me trash, weren't you?"

CHAPTER 35

Lani recoiled from Sloan's verbal slap. Where had this come from? Lani's anger flashed, and she wanted to blast Sloan, yet she didn't because she knew the accusation wasn't exactly unwarranted. Plenty of girls had spread gossip about Sloan, all right, and Lani might not have joined the chorus, but she hadn't spoken up in the girl's defense either. The wounded look on Sloan's face hit Lani hard, and she saw not the now-grown woman, but the girl kids made fun of all through school. "I'm sorry, Sloan. Maybe that's too little, too late, but I still need to say it to you." Lani hoped her face reflected the sincerity she felt.

"And especially your best friend, Kathy. She was Bitch One." The rancor returned.

"Yeah. We were friends for a long time, but no more. She doesn't even live in Windemere now." When Lani thought back, the friendship had begun to unravel on homecoming night and tumbled downhill from there, when Kathy had started running with some of the Queen Bee senior girls. Kathy had dismissed Lani, no texts, no calls, no time for her.

Hurt at first, Lani finally gave up and jumped into being a hospital volunteer and her job at Bellmeade. Riding Oro had filled in many a lonely weekend. "Kathy was jealous of you, Sloan. She was fixated on Jarred. You had him. She didn't and never would."

The mention of Jarred made Sloan stiffen.

"And," Lani swiftly continued, "you have that voice. When you sing . . ." She ventured a smile. "The Anarchy band rocked, and you looked rocker-girl perfect onstage. Every guy who saw you perform wanted you." *Dawson Berke included.* "And the bitch clique hated that because no matter what they said about you, nothing could stop the way an audience went nuts when you were onstage."

Surprised, taken aback by Lani's unexpected evaluation, Sloan bit hard on her bottom lip. Moisture blurred her vision. "Jarred's dying stopped it." She hadn't sung in weeks. Except in the shower. She blinked hard, not wanting Lani to see her tears.

"And I'm sorry about Jarred too, about what happened to him. And the band." A bee buzzed around them, searching for a flower with nectar. Children's laughter floated up from the playground. Was Jarred Tester the first of their graduating class to die? If so . . . a terrible tragedy and a dark distinction.

"Did you know him? He knew so many of the girls."

The tone of Sloan's voice gave Lani to understand his death wasn't all that ached within Sloan about Jarred. He must have caused her pain in other ways too.

"I knew him only from a distance, from watching him perform with his band."

From another bench, a mother's voice called to her kids that it was time to go home. Time to think about lunch and naps and afternoon television cartoons. Lani called to Gabe, and he hustled over, caked with sand and grime and looking happy. "What do you want for lunch? Grilled cheese or hot dog?" She smoothed his forehead, brushing back the matted thatch of black hair, and settled him in the wagon.

"SpaghettiOs!" he counteroffered.

Sloan waited while Lani fussed over Gabe, dragged back into the reality of time and place, memories of Jarred and performances long over fading into the summer day. The memories had been sobering, upsetting, but necessary. It was time for her to start over.

They walked back toward the house in single file, Lani, Gabe in the wagon, Sloan. No chatter from Gabe this time, worn out from play. Lani concentrated on the clacking of the wagon's wheels hitting sidewalk cracks, thinking Mel would be proud of her because she'd figured out what Mel had tried to tell her the night before. Today she'd run toward a disaster, not away from one. She and Sloan had found a place to meet, first inside the past and then into the present. She and Sloan Quentin would never be best friends. But they didn't have to be enemies either.

⁓

When the band had been together in Nashville, Sloan had taken on an assortment of jobs mostly in restaurants and lounges where tips were good, and since jobs were simply to support their music, the work didn't matter much. She showed up, worked, and she quit whenever the band faced a tour or a not-to-be-missed gig. Nashville was a big city with a lot of hourly wage options. Not so much in Windemere.

After a week of searching and filling out applications, she took a waitress position in a major chain eatery by the interstate, near the mall. She had to settle for the lunchtime slot because dinner hours were prime time and already fully staffed. Dinner shift was where the best money was, with its higher volume of diners and their tips. Lunch hours were low volume and slow, but it got her foot in the door. Based on experience, Sloan was sure that after Labor Day, many of the waitstaff would move on, return to school, take other jobs, leaving her in a good position to take better and longer hours. She also let it be known that she'd sub for a server whenever anyone needed time off. Her midday hours were steady, the other hours sporadic, but all earned her money.

She came and went from Dawson's freely and counted herself lucky. She had a place to live and a small (very small) income, most of which she saved because she was determined to keep her promise of moving out of the Berke house. She had free time, and she had the rapt attention of a small boy whenever she took her guitar from its case and played. His favorite song was "You Are My Sunshine," and to amuse him, she performed it in every genre she could think of—country, jazz, classical, rock. He loved every one and took to calling her Sing Lady. The name stuck, defining her for him. And one day, once he was older, and if he ever asked about his mother, Dawson could say, "Remember Sing Lady?"

"Well . . . they're not exactly . . . beautiful." Melody stared down at the large platter of cupcakes smeared with red and blue frosting. "In need of triage, I think."

"Please, don't spare *my* feelings," Lani grumbled, standing beside her sister on Dawson's patio in front of the dessert and gifts table. "I've never baked and decorated forty-eight Spider-Man cupcakes before. It took me four hours. Have a little respect for the effort."

Melody kept eyeing the gooey mess, made worse by the afternoon heat. "Okay . . . the black squiggles sort of look like spiderwebs . . . I see that now." Behind them, the backyard bloomed with the squeals and laughter of children invited for Gabe's third birthday party, all wanting to take a turn on Gabe's new swing set. "Good thing I brought brownies for us grown-ups."

Lani crossed her arms and scowled.

Dawson walked over from his place behind the grill to listen to the two sisters' banter and grinned. "You should see the kitchen. How'd you get frosting on the wall on the other side of the room, anyway?"

"A slight miscalculation when I forgot to turn off the mixer before lifting the beaters out of the bowl. I'll clean it up."

He threw back his head and laughed. "And the ceiling too?"

"There's frosting on the ceiling?" Melody rolled her eyes.

"A smidgen."

Dawson reached around Lani's shoulders and gave her a hug. "That's what tall guys are for."

"Don't burn the burgers," Lani mumbled, feeling the hug travel down the length of her. What she wouldn't give to have it last and last.

Dawson returned to his grill, where several neighborhood men had gathered to address his grilling techniques. He flipped the burgers, rotated the hot dogs. "Supper in ten," he announced.

He owed this party to Lani, for she'd organized every detail . . . handing out invites to the children Gabe knew from the playground; decorating the patio with "Happy Birthday" banners; setting up tables with Spider-Man plates, napkins, and balloons; and baking the sad-looking cupcakes. As for himself, he and a couple of neighbors had assembled Gabe's oversized swing set in the backyard—a difficult job too, especially when he had two long screws left over. But the expression on Gabe's face when he saw the shiny apparatus glowing in the sunlight had been worth every scraped knuckle and cut finger.

Smiling, he watched Gabe chase two little boys, his red Spidey cape flying behind him. Never mind that Spider-Man doesn't wear a cape. Dawson could have never imagined three years ago that he'd be in this place—a suburban dad, hosting a barbeque for children and neighbors. Not at all the life he'd planned. He saw Sloan in a far corner of the yard, sitting under an oak tree, apart and alone. What was going through her head? What did she see when she looked at their son? He poked the glowing briquettes with his spatula. To her credit, she had kept her word, gotten a job, and stayed out of his and Gabe's way. Nor did Lani have any complaints about Sloan's presence in the house. *Still . . .* he wondered.

He gathered up the burgers and hot dogs, set the tray on a food table covered with bowls of salads, beans, chips, and cut up fruit, and called everyone in. Later, when the sun was below the horizon and darkness spreading across the sky, Lani handed out the gooey cupcakes, placing one with three sparklers in front of Gabe.

But before she could light the sparklers, Gabe shouted, "Sing Lady! Git-tar. Sing song!"

Sloan, sitting back in the shadows on the outer fringe of the group, looked as if she wanted to bolt, and for a moment Dawson thought she might. He tensed. Gabe wouldn't stop begging, so with a cast of his gaze, Dawson gave Sloan permission. "How about it, Sing Lady? Want to lead us in 'Happy Birthday'?"

She scrambled to retrieve her guitar from the house. When Sloan returned, Lani, her fingers trembling, lit the sparklers. Sloan strummed the strings, and Gabe's smile broke open. Others joined in singing the words, but all Dawson heard was the clear, distinct sound of Sloan Quentin's voice rising like smoke into the night sky.

CHAPTER 36

"You sure you can handle all this?" were the first words out of Melody's mouth after Lani outlined her fall schedule. They were dining downtown in Mel's favorite restaurant, talking and nibbling on a bowl of crunchy rice noodles while they waited for their food.

"Of course I'm sure. I'm in the classroom during the mornings Gabe's in school. I'll pick him up at noon, study while he naps, and leave when Dawson comes home. He wants me to stay on the job, and there's no way I won't." He'd asked the day after Gabe's birthday party, and she'd quickly agreed. She would also have to fit in her hospital work toward Step-Prep credits whenever she could, but she didn't mention it to her sister.

"And two nights a week, you'll stay late so Dawson can take a course that his company's paying for. Plus, you'll keep working weekends at Bellmeade." Lani had already told this to Melody. "What about sleeping? Set aside any time for that and any social life?"

Lani drummed her fingers on the tablecloth. "It isn't a problem, Mel. Just back off."

"But the real reason you're twisting your life into a pretzel is so that you can continue to care for Gabe. Wasn't this supposed to be only a *summer* job?"

"You know how I feel about Gabe; plus, starting preschool will be an adjustment. He needs continuity."

"What about his mother? Isn't she still at the house? Why can't she pick up some of the slack?"

Lani glanced around for their waitress, hoping she'd rescue her from Melody's third degree. Giving up, she pushed back into the booth. "Sloan works too, and I've told you, Dawson doesn't want Sloan left alone with Gabe."

"I met her at the party, Lani. She hardly seems like a monster. In fact, Gabe acted as if he *likes* her."

Mel's evaluation didn't brighten Lani's mood. Truth was, Gabe did run down to the playroom if he heard the strum of the Sing Lady's guitar. Lani began to think of Sloan as the Pied Piper of Strings. "It goes to history. Dawson doesn't totally trust her."

"Is he afraid she'll run off with their son?"

Lani sidestepped the question with "Just last week, Sloan played with a kitten in the park, and when Gabe got around the kitten's hair *on her clothes,* he started wheezing and coughing. I had to use his rescue inhaler. Sloan panicked. She shouldn't be left alone and in charge of Gabe. We never know when he'll run into a trigger. His bedroom is full of little stuffed animals he's been given from the time he was a baby by well-meaning people and before his asthma was diagnosed. They're all stored on high shelves in plastic bags so he can see them, but he can't play with them, because stuffed toys get dusty and Gabe reacts to dust. His favorite 'stuffed' toy is a dog made out of leather his grandfather gave him. Doesn't hold dust. I wipe it clean."

Melody rested her elbows on the table, her chin on fingers woven together to make a bridge, and Lani continued. "I've tried to explain to you that asthma is a very serious condition. I'm Gabe's nurse. He's only three, and I can't walk away from him just now. Don't you see?"

"My apologies, Lani. I forget that nursing is your career and something you're passionate about. It's as important to you as law is to me. If you ever need help, call me."

Lani relaxed, believing that her sister finally "got it," got her. However complicated her feelings were about Dawson, Lani was Gabe's first line of defense with his asthma when Dawson wasn't around.

Melody cleared her throat. "Except I won't mess with that horse. I draw the line at mucking stalls and hugging your horse."

Lani laughed, was still laughing when the petite server appeared, balancing plates of food and bowls of rice and placing them on the table. The aromas of sesame-soy beef, oyster sauce, and tangy sweet and sour chicken made Lani's mouth water. "Deal!" she said, and dug into her food.

⁓

Sloan sat on the patio drinking beer and gazing up at the stars spread like pinpricks of cold light on a black canvas. The moon was waxing, on its way to becoming full and bright. September was gone, October half gone, and autumn coolness had crowded out summer heat. She felt restless tonight, restless and lonely, and even though she'd pulled a double shift that afternoon at the restaurant today, she wasn't a bit sleepy.

She worked six nights a week now, four at the restaurant,

two in a sports bar, where the tips were better. Life at the house had fallen into a rhythm, with Gabe the main event, Lani and Dawson the supporting cast, and herself a walk-on player. Any extra time, Sloan spent writing music and sometimes entertaining Gabe. She tried never to think of Gabe as half hers. He wasn't. The boy belonged totally to Dawson and partly to Lani. Sloan struggled against her growing attachment to him, told herself she had no stake in him, and her promise to move on as soon as she could was one she planned to keep.

She missed the band, the singing, the all-nighters of arranging songs and jamming, and wondered what Bobby and Hal were doing, hoped that Sy was faring well under his father's financial tyranny. She didn't want to spend the rest of her life waiting tables and squirreling away tip money but didn't want to connect with them again either. They were in her past, along with the crazy plans she'd had of becoming a singing star.

"Sloan? You all right?"

Dawson's voice startled her from the doorway. She glanced over her shoulder. "Boss didn't need me tonight." Usually he was gone when she got up in the morning and she was gone when he came home. Their paths rarely crossed. "You're getting in late."

"I went to the library to study after class. If I come straight home, I'll fall into bed and *not* study."

"Want a beer? I'm on my third, but I have more." She held up a longneck.

He had sent Lani home when he walked through the front door. She'd given him a quick rundown of the day, then rushed out because she had a paper to write. He didn't know how she stuck to her schedule but was grateful she'd come up with the plan for staying on the job with Gabe. She was indispensable to him. Lani . . . he missed having any time alone with her. The beer Sloan held up was tempting. The long day had caught up to him. He stepped out on the patio, placing Gabe's monitor on a small side table so that he could watch the black-and-white image of his sleeping son.

He dragged a chair next to Sloan's. "How are you doing?"

"Okay."

He recognized her dejected mood. "I, um, hope Gabe isn't too noisy in the mornings when you're trying to sleep in." Over the time she'd lived there, he had mellowed toward her because she'd kept her word about staying clear of Gabe. Except when she practiced the guitar.

"He loves to listen to her play and sing," Lani had told Dawson. "No harm."

"I never hear a thing in the mornings. You remember how hard I sleep—" She stopped because she hadn't meant to bring up their shared past. To cover her slip, she took a long drink from her beer, stared up at the stars. The night was lovely, cool and crisp. Sloan didn't want to be alone. "So how about telling me about my mother, how she made your life miserable. I know she made *mine* miserable."

He recalled telling her it was a long story, and since she'd asked, he figured this was as good a time as any. "You sure?" She nodded. "Gabe was home from the hospital for about a week when LaDonna showed up looking for you. I told her you'd split, but she wouldn't believe me, wanted to search the house. Course I told her no."

"Imagine that, LaDonna thinking I was hiding from her." The words dripped with sarcasm. "Did she ask to see the baby?"

"Eventually. Franklin let her sit on the porch and hold

Gabe while we sat with her." Dawson remembered how La-Donna had held the blue wrapped bundle away from her body, as if it were a foreign object. "Gabe slept through the whole visit."

"Did she ask for money?" The question was blunt, but Sloan understood what motivated the woman, and it was rarely anything altruistic.

"Not at first. But a few weeks later she showed up demanding we respect her rights as Gabe's grandmother. She'd been drinking and was wobbly. Said she hired a lawyer to 'get what was hers.' That's when she asked for money." He recalled her standing on the front porch spewing a tirade about them trying to take away her natural rights and that it would cost them for her to sign Gabe over completely. "Dad hired a lawyer too, and it turns out that in Tennessee, grandparents don't have many rights when there's a stable biological parent involved. We offered her supervised visitation rights."

"She didn't take the deal, did she?"

"No. After she hit our front lawn on a couple of nights, screaming and yelling and waking up the neighbors, we had to get a restraining order. After a while she stopped coming. I drove out to the trailer park once just to check, and she was gone."

Sloan raised her beer in a toast. "Good riddance."

Dawson hurt for Sloan, for the damage to her childhood from the alcoholic mother who had all but left her to grow up on her own. Sloan couldn't help who she'd come from. "You aren't like her, Sloan. You got away from her, and you made it out of that bad place where she tried to keep you." He wasn't talking about the trailer park, but about LaDonna's life spiral.

"Have I? Sometimes I'm not so sure." Her head spun as she

pushed against emotions she didn't want, a past she couldn't change, and music she had lost. She stood abruptly, and so did he. "Time for bed." She stepped forward and stumbled. Dawson caught her, and when he did, she burrowed into him, flung her arms around his neck, and buried her mouth into his.

Shock, like from an electrical wire, shot through him, and then fire, a backdraft of oxygen-starved flames. He reeled from her heat. Her mouth was hot, her tongue cold from the beer. They were both breathing hard when she broke the kiss. "Stay with me tonight." Her voice a cracked whisper. Her hands secure around his neck. "I remember how things used to be . . . in the beginning . . ."

He remembered too. Every cell in his body remembered. It would be easy, so very easy, like falling backward into deep familiar water. In his mind's eye, he saw Gabe's face, and from other shadows, the incandescent smile of a brown-eyed girl who mattered to him. He gulped air, reached up, and untangled Sloan's arms, catching her wrists but keeping her close. "No."

His refusal rocked her. Desperation to escape loneliness drove her to try again. "Just for a little while. I need you. It . . . doesn't have to *mean* anything."

Still holding her wrists, he dipped his forehead down to touch hers. "And that's the point, isn't it? It *should* mean something." He released her gently and stepped away.

Sloan watched him pick up the monitor, step through the doorway, and recede into the dark.

CHAPTER 37

The next morning, Dawson stared bleary-eyed into his shaving mirror. He hadn't slept much. Even the needle-fine cold water spray of the shower had done little to clear his mind of the fiery moments he'd spent with Sloan on the patio the night before. It wasn't as if he hadn't wanted to take her to bed. His body had wanted her, and there had been a time in his life when he'd never have walked away. But in the deciding moment, the images that popped into his mind had stopped him. *Gabe. Lani.* Two people who mattered more than sex with Sloan.

"Way to go, Berke," he grumbled to his reflection. He swept the razor down his cheek, along his jaw, and over his chin. "You have two women around you day and night and you can't touch either one." The razor nicked and blood appeared. *Great,* he groused. He snatched a square of toilet paper from the roll and stuck it on the cut.

A glance at the digital clock on the bathroom counter showed that he was running late. Where was Gabe? Typically the boy was sitting on the side of the tub watching Dawson's shaving ritual, but not this morning. "Gabe! Are you up?"

No answer. Dawson shook his razor under running water, wiped the remaining lather off his face, and went down the hall to Gabe's room, where he found his son sitting on the floor, playing with his collection of dinosaurs. "What are you doing, buddy? Get dressed. You're going to be late for school."

Gabe ignored him. "No want school. Gabe stay home."

His uncharacteristic reluctance surprised Dawson. After the first few days of adjustment, Gabe eagerly went into the classroom. He talked constantly about his teacher, the other kids, the games, and endless art projects. Wearily, Dawson crouched in front of his son. "You like school. Pick out a shirt and get dressed."

Gabe continued fiddling with the plastic animals. Dawson stood, went to the bureau, and pulled out a long-sleeved Titans football jersey, one of Gabe's favorites, and a pair of pull-on jeans, and tossed them into the boy's lap. "How about wearing this?"

Gabe wadded up the shirt and threw it across the room. "No like."

Patience ran out. Dawson lifted his son and set him on his feet. "Get dressed now, son." Gabe stuck out his lip. "What's your problem? Get. Dressed. Now."

Gabe refused to look at his dad, but he shimmed out of his pj's and retrieved his shirt, all the while acting like a rebellious prisoner with a hateful warden. Baffled, Dawson shook his head. He'd thought the "terrible twos" were behind them. With a sigh, he held out a peace offering. "How about we go through the drive-through and get you a special breakfast before school?"

Gabe shrugged halfheartedly, but he continued to dress.

Sloan hustled around the playroom gathering up clothes for a load of laundry, her mind full of what had happened last night between her and Dawson. Or more accurately, what hadn't happened. What had she been *thinking*? What had gotten into her? The beer. Obviously. But more than that—harsh memories of growing up, of her now total dependence on Dawson's generosity, of a little boy she was becoming far too attached to, of her in-the-toilet life so removed from dreams of a singing career she couldn't recover—all had turned into a perfect storm, and she'd tripped and fallen into its vortex. She had screwed up. Dawson hadn't wanted her. He could throw her out. She wouldn't be surprised if he did.

She slammed down the lid of the washer, turned the dial, and heard the machine hum into service. She didn't have to be at work until four, but she knew she couldn't hang around the house until then. The walls were closing in. She needed to get out and wanted to leave before Lani showed up with Gabe from school.

Sloan showered and dressed quickly, considered her options. The holidays were coming. Maybe she could use today to apply for a third job. Stores hired extra employees for the holidays and the extra money could put her over the top and toward locating her own place sooner. She pulled up her phone calendar, entered a reminder for December: *Must move before Christmas.*

Once upstairs, she saw that it was raining. A perfect match for her mood. She scrambled for an umbrella, looking around the quiet kitchen, knowing that Gabe would come bounding through the front door with Lani soon. She needed to leave before the imagined noise of smothering normalcy drowned her, and hurriedly jogged to the car parked in the driveway.

"How you doing, Gabe?" Lani asked cheerfully. The boy was in a weird mood, withdrawn and quiet, not at all his usual self. He'd hardly said a word on the drive home and only picked at his lunch.

"Okay."

"How was school today? What did you do?"

She saw his shoulders rise and fall in a shrug.

She went to the kitchen banquette, where he rested on his knees, hunched over the tabletop, coloring. "I didn't know Spidey wore black. When did he start wearing black?"

Gabe ignored her question, kept a heavy hand on his black crayon. Maybe Gabe was getting sick. The thought galvanized her. "How about we do a check on your peak flow meter." She hurried to grab the unit that measured airflow in his lungs. He did the test three times and each time his flow registered well. He returned to coloring, his mood unimproved. She put the meter away, went to the fridge and cupboards, and started pulling out baking supplies. "How about we make a batch of chocolate chip cookies? I'll get the batter mixed up and you can dump in the chips." The ritual was familiar, one Gabe loved. Today he only shrugged.

Totally baffled by his lack of interest, Lani started the process.

"I see Daddy kissing Sing Lady," Gabe said.

Lani froze. She slid Gabe a look. He was bent over the coloring book, his black crayon moving over another page. "When?" She hated herself for asking.

"Last nighttime."

"You mean you saw them in a dream." Her heart was hammering now.

"No dream. I wake up. Can't find Woof-Woof. I say, 'Daddy. Daaaddy!' But Daddy not come." Gabe looked at Lani, his blue eyes wide and serious. "I go look for Woof-Woof."

She pictured him padding down the stairs, thinking that if Dawson had been in his bedroom down the hall from Gabe's, he would have heard Gabe calling. "Did you find Woof-Woof?"

"I find him by cars." He smiled finally, pleased with his successful hunt.

Lani realized that if he'd found the dog in the living room, he would have passed the patio doors on his journey. Is that where Sloan and Dawson had been together? She felt her knees go weak with images of them holding each other and kissing. Gabe couldn't have made it up. "Does your dad know you got up to look for your doggie?"

Gabe shook his head furiously. "Gabe very quiet. No one sees me and Woof-Woof."

Lani continued through the motions of preparing the cookies—turn on the oven, cream the butter and sugar, measure out flour and baking soda. She worked by rote, her mind numb. Last night a corner must have been turned between Dawson and Sloan. A corner Lani couldn't turn with them. Tears jammed the back of her throat.

From the table, Gabe started humming, as if telling his nighttime adventure to Lani had unburdened him. Which was the way it was with secrets, she told herself. Sometimes a person just *had* to share, and someone else *must* listen and hold on to the secret, no matter how bad it hurt the hearer's heart.

CHAPTER 38

The gloom of November settled over Windemere, and daylight ceded to dark and time tumbled toward the upcoming holidays. Dawson had finished a day's work and was in his pickup heading home when his cell chimed. His father's number popped up. "Dad! How you doing?"

"Rushing toward the end of the semester. How about you?"

"Same. Winding down classes and working. Good to hear your voice." Franklin usually called via video so he could speak to Gabe. "What's up?"

"I have a proposition for you."

"I'm listening." Dead leaves blew across the rural road he was driving into town and rattled against the windshield.

"I want you and Gabe to come up here for Christmas. I've been too long without a grandson fix. I'll send you plane tickets and meet you at O'Hare."

This Christmas was Franklin's first in Chicago, and except for the video calls, Dawson and Gabe hadn't seen Pops since June. "Can you petition your weatherman for snow? Gabe would love to play in it." Growing up, Dawson had seen a lot of snow, but

Tennessee didn't get much except in its mountains. A few inches from the winter before had made Gabe wide-eyed with wonder.

"Can't promise snow, but I can promise wind."

Dawson laughed. "Gabe will love flying. You putting up a tree?"

"What kind of a question is that? Of course there'll be a tree. And I'm told the city gets all duded up with lights and decorations."

It would be good to be together as a family for the holidays. "Send the tickets. We'll be there."

There was a space of dead air alerting Dawson that either the call had dropped or his father had more to say. "Dad?"

"Still here." His pause lengthened. "Um . . . when you come . . . there's someone I want you to meet."

Dawson slowed for a traffic light. This invitation went deeper than a family visit. Someone. A hint that Franklin had met a woman he cared about. For an instant, Dawson rewound time to when he was fourteen and Franklin had had a date with a nurse from an area hospital. Now, years later, Dawson couldn't recall her name and face but did remember how he'd reacted. He turned mean and hateful when Franklin asked his son to meet her, spewing anger about Franklin trying to replace his mother. He saw things through different eyes now. He knew how lonely life could be. He cleared his throat. "Looking forward to meeting her."

"*Her?* Did I say 'her'? I just said 'someone.'" He felt his dad's smile of relief come over the phone and through the distance between them.

"Does she have a name?"

"Connie Baylor, my age, divorced, two grown girls, and amazing, smart, and beautiful."

The vision of his mother's face faded. He was ready for another to take its place. "Well, for the price of two tickets, she must be worth it."

"She is."

"See you both next month." Dawson clicked off, dropped the phone onto the front seat, and turned into his driveway, where he sat thinking back to all the head-butting he once did with his father. Now all ancient history. The journey had been rough, unplanned in many ways, and both of them changed by it. He missed Franklin and looked forward to Chicago. He wouldn't tell Gabe until the last minute because the boy would be bouncing off walls when he heard.

With the heater off, the air inside the truck turned colder, and Dawson roused himself. Through the windshield, he saw that Sloan's car was gone, while Lani's waited. And inside the house Gabe waited too.

Lani drove Dawson's SUV on a round of errands, Gabe in his car seat singing off-key about the wheels on a bus going around. She glanced in the rearview mirror, saw his dark head bobbing, his hands busy shaping the limbs of a plastic action hero into impossible contortions. Gabe looked happy. Lani wished she owned some of the boy's contentment. The revelation about Dawson and Sloan still haunted her. Not only the image of them kissing, but also the implication. If Dawson was allowing Sloan into his and Gabe's life permanently, Lani couldn't stay. Leaving, moving on, would break her heart, but she would have to quit. She had no choice.

Her cell phone blared out her ring tone, snapping her from

243

her sad thoughts. She picked it up, saw that Jon Mercer, owner of the Bellmeade stables, was calling. *Why in the world . . . ?* "Jon?"

"Lani, where are you?" His voice sounded taut, serious.

"Not too far from the Berke house. Why?"

"Can you come to Bellmeade now?"

Fear ratcheted inside her. "What's wrong? What's happened?"

"Oro's been snake bit. Probably a cottonmouth . . . got him on his nose while he was grazing. The vet's on his way."

"No!" Not her horse. *Not Oro.* "I'm coming!" She turned the car around in a neighbor's drive, then pushed the pedal hard, sending the auto down the tree-lined street faster than any speed limit allowed.

Minutes later, Lani whipped into the Bellmeade grounds and braked at the main barn, where Ciana waved her down. Another car was parked to one side. Soldier, the Mercers' big German shepherd, came up wagging his tail, and Ciana sent him away. When Lani jumped out of the SUV, Ciana caught her by the shoulders. "Take it easy, Lani. The doc's with your horse. Jon actually saw it happen and got to Oro pretty quick. Jon got him calmed and into the barn, called the vet and then you."

Tears welled in Lani's eyes. She opened the back door, unbuckled Gabe. The boy was wide-eyed. "It's all right, Gabe. My horse is hurt, but he's with a doctor." She motioned to the barn.

"Gabe see horse?"

"Maybe later." She had shown Gabe photos of Oro on her cell phone, and Gabe had asked before to "go see horsey." At the moment, all Lani wanted to do was run inside the barn and check on Oro.

Ciana stepped up. "Gabe? I'm Ciana, Lani's friend. Would you like to walk over to the fence with me and look at the horses in the field?"

Gabe shrank against Lani's leg. She knew he wouldn't go with Ciana willingly and she didn't want him to have a melt-down. Lani picked him up. "Let's take a peek inside, okay? Then you wait with Ciana out here."

Gabe's lip trembled, but he nodded. She took him into the barn and Ciana followed. Oro was tethered in the center, his golden head drooping. Jon and another man were working on the animal, Jon soothing Oro with words and strokes, keeping the horse's head lowered.

"Not to spread the toxin," Ciana whispered to Lani.

Gabe pointed. "Horsey sad?"

Lani walked closer, holding Gabe, her heart in her throat. "How . . . how . . . ?" Her voice cracked.

The other man, crouched by Oro's head, looked up. "I'm Dr. Perry. You know the last time he had a tetanus vaccination?"

"Maybe a year. I'll have to look it up."

"I'll give him a booster."

Lani wanted to stroke Oro's withers, let him know she was there. The horse had been her salvation after Arie died, her constant companion for years. She couldn't lose him! She re-positioned Gabe from her hip to the front of her body so that she was looking directly into his face. "Gabe, sweetie . . . listen to me. You need to be a big boy now and go with Ciana." He wrapped his arms around her neck. "Please, honey. Just for a few minutes. I promise I won't stay long. Will you—"

A tear ran down her cheek and Gabe touched it. His chin quivered. "Okay, Lani."

She lowered him to the floor, and Ciana held out her hand. "Come on, cowboy. I'll let you sit on the fence and I'll tell you the names of all my horses."

Gabe took her hand and trailed out of the barn at her side.

Lani came over slowly, so as not to startle Oro. She stroked the thick winter coat on his golden neck. "Hey, Oro."

Her horse almost raised his head, but Jon interceded. Lani had been told that Jon was a horse whisperer with an uncanny ability to communicate with animals. When he spoke, Oro calmed instantly, and Lani saw how true it was. She knelt, saw Oro's muzzle, and felt sick. His nose area was fat and swollen and two fang marks could be clearly seen in the fleshy part of his muzzle.

Beside her, Dr. Perry said, "Jon swears it was a cottonmouth that got him, based on the fang marks and depths. A rattler would have given Oro a warning shake and it would have spooked him, not so a cottonmouth. Let's give Oro a dose of antivenin. He's big, and he's been well cared for, all in his favor for recovery," the doc offered. "We'll keep a close watch on him, treat the open wound for a couple of weeks."

"But he'll be all right?"

Perry offered an encouraging smile.

"I'm getting my rifle, and me and Soldier are going snake hunting." Jon's green eyes flashed when he spoke.

Just then the barn door opened and Ciana came in carrying Gabe. "Lani . . . he . . . he's acting funny. Can't catch his breath."

Lani shot to her feet, her heart in her throat. She grabbed Gabe, saw that his face looked chalky and his breath came out wheezy and labored. "Oh no! No! Gabe . . . !" The horses!

Was he reacting to the horses? Her eyes darted around the barn, and like stop-action photography her gaze fell on what she hadn't seen until now. *Hay.* Bales and stacks of alfalfa hay everywhere she looked. An asthmatic trigger as deadly as a snakebite.

CHAPTER 39

Lani reached for his rescue inhaler, then realized it was in her purse in the car. Holding Gabe upright, pressed against herself, she ran for the SUV. Ciana, who ran behind her, pulled open the door. "Inhaler in my purse! He has to stay vertical."

Gabe struggled, gagged, coughed, tried to speak and couldn't. Ciana dumped Lani's purse on the car's seat, found the inhaler, and gave it over. Lani thrust it between Gabe's blue-tinged lips and pushed the medication into his mouth. He kept struggling for air. She used it again, all the while talking to him. He momentarily rallied, tried to say her name, couldn't. Tears welled in his blue eyes.

Lani braced her leg on the inside of the doorjamb, sat him on her knee, and lifted his arms over his head keeping his air passages open. "Call an ambulance!"

Ciana reached for her phone, but Jon materialized beside Lani, his voice breaking through her panic. "Put him in my truck. An ambulance will never get here in time."

Clutching Gabe, she ran for Jon's truck and climbed inside while Gabe struggled for air. Lani felt the side of his neck. His erratic pulse raced much too fast. "Hurry." She was weeping now, unable to control herself. "Hold on, baby . . . hold on." His head lolled on her shoulder. She forced him to sit straight, saw that his eyes were rolled back and his lips bluer.

Minutes felt like hours, but Jon sped and screeched to a halt in front of the emergency room doors in record time. He jammed the truck into park, leaped out, ran to Lani's door, and threw it open. Lani's arms shook from the strain of holding Gabe upright. Jon took him from her, and together they raced into the ER. She yelled, "Asthma! He can't breathe!" And in moments, Gabe was in triage. A breathing tube was threaded down his throat and hooked to life-giving oxygen. Lani and Jon, shoved aside by the ER team, watched them put Gabe on IVs and a monitor. Gabe's color pinked. His abdomen, gone concave from oxygen deprivation, swelled into its natural shape. Lani saw the numbers measuring his heartbeat and blood pressure leap across the screen and edge toward normal as Gabe's condition stabilized.

Lani's knees buckled, and Jon caught her. "Come with me. You're as pale as a ghost."

She didn't want to leave, but the ER doctor barked, "Please! Go! I don't need two patients in here right now."

Jon guided her out into the waiting area, where brilliant sunlight streamed through floor-to-ceiling windows. A pacing Ciana quickly wrapped Lani in her arms. Lani buried her face into Ciana's shoulder while Jon gave his wife an update. Ciana stroked Lani's hair. "You got him here. I'm sure he'll be all right now." She pulled back, offering Lani a wad of tissues.

Just then, an admittance clerk came over holding a clipboard. Despite her many hours of working in the building, Lani didn't recognize the woman. The clerk said, "They want

to admit your child, so we need you to fill out some paperwork."
Still too shaken to clear her head, Lani stood mute. The clerk
asked, "Are you the child's mother?"

Lani shook her head. "His . . . his caregiver."

"Well, we need a parent or a legal guardian to admit him.
Can you reach one of his parents?"

Lani nodded but didn't move. Ciana, who had been holding Lani's purse, held out the bag. "I stuffed in everything from
the seat and drove your SUV here. Your phone's in the purse."
Lani couldn't control her shaking hands, so Ciana found the
phone. "Can I send a message for you? Make a call?" Ciana's
eyes brimmed with compassion.

Lani shivered. No nurse's training in the world had prepared her for sending the news to Dawson she must, but realizing her trembling fingers might be unable to hit letters on the
tiny phone screen with any accuracy, she said, "Please." She
blew her nose, wiped her eyes, and dictated:

Gabe in ER. Asthma. Hurry.

Ciana pushed Send.

—⸙—

"You understand that we have him sedated because of his intubation . . . just until I'm satisfied he's out of the woods."

Dawson, standing beside Gabe's hospital bed, heard the
doctor, yet was unable to take his eyes off Gabe lying so still
amid tubes and IVs and monitors. His beautiful son looked
like an inert mannequin. He placed his hand on Gabe's chest
simply to feel the rise and fall of it, to assure himself Gabe

lived. He wished with everything that his dad was the doctor in the room.

"We've got him on cortisteroids. His BP has normalized and we're pushing fluids." Dr. Nelson, Gabe's pediatrician, was a kind man trying to reassure Dawson. "He's had a terrible, dangerous allergic reaction, but I believe he'll be fine once the meds do their job. His caregiver's fast action of getting him here so quickly helped."

When Nelson left, Dawson turned to Lani, who had edged into the background while the doctor was in the room. Icy, mind-numbing fear had so consumed him when her message arrived that he couldn't remember driving to the hospital from his job site, where he'd been framing a house in a new subdivision. She had met him on the Pediatric level, at the fourth-floor elevator doors, the first words from her mouth, "I'm sorry . . . so, so sorry."

Now with her back braced against a wall, she looked ready to fall apart. He wanted to put his arms around her, comfort her, but she'd always kept him at arm's length, lately even more so. She was withdrawn around him, no more easy chats when he came home from work. She simply hugged Gabe and said goodbye. He hadn't been able to figure out why, what had happened to change things between them, but he missed her smile, her easy laugh. Right now, though, in spite of his fear for Gabe, he wanted to console her. He clenched his fists at his sides to resist reaching for her. "What happened today?"

His voice was soft, but she couldn't yet look him in the eye. She told him about her horse, the rush to get to Bellmeade and of taking Gabe into the barn without a single thought as to what might harm him. Her words were halting, heavy with recrimination and strangled tears. "My fault, Dawson. All of this." A tear escaped and tracked down her cheek. She wiped it furiously.

"Lani, I don't blame you. We're still figuring out his triggers, so there was no way for you to know that anything in that barn would hurt him."

She felt no consolation and shook her head. "I didn't think it out . . . animals, hay, mold everywhere! I should have—"

"Stop. You beating up on yourself won't help anything. It happened. Can't un-ring a bell. The good thing is you got him help. You saved his life, Lani."

Can a person be a villain and a savior at the same time? She wanted to believe him, but the wound was too fresh and raw. "Jon Mercer . . . he drove us. I'd never have made it on my own."

Dawson had a vague memory of the owner and storied horse trainer. "I'll thank him too. But right now, you look ready to drop. You don't have to stay."

She had left her books and laptop at his house because she'd planned to study while Gabe watched his favorite cartoon shows that afternoon. Yet she didn't know how she could leave the hospital now either. "I . . . I left stuff . . ."

"It's okay. I'm here. Right now, I'm going to call Dad, tell him what's going on. Go to the house, and I'll text you if anything changes."

She knew Dawson was right. She needed to collect herself, return later. Perhaps by then the breathing tube would be gone and Gabe upgraded to a respiratory cannula.

She was in the doorway when Dawson said, "If . . . if Sloan's there . . . not gone to work yet, will you tell her about Gabe? I don't really want to call or text her about it. But she should know."

Lani closed her eyes. *Sloan. Gabe's mother.* That truth reared up. Sloan held a card Lani never would. "I'll make sure she hears it from me."

Sloan didn't go to the hospital right away. She wanted to see Gabe with all her heart, but she couldn't face walking into the place again, even after all this time. When Lani first told her, Sloan assumed he'd come home quickly. But he didn't, so days later she gathered her courage and went to see him. She arrived early on a morning when Lani would be on the campus for classes and Dawson would be at work. She wanted to see Gabe without either Dawson or Lani around when she went into the room.

Just walking into the hospital made her stomach queasy. The antiseptic smells, the voices from intercoms paging one person or another, the sight of so many people in blue or green scrubs, caps, and dangling face masks—it all brought back memories she didn't want returned. When the elevator doors opened on the pediatric floor, she stepped out, glancing at the cheerful colors and cartoon animals painted on the walls, a world away from the neonatal ICU. On this floor, she felt a little less like an alien on a foreign planet. Lani had given her Gabe's room number. She stood at the door, her heart pounding. Taking a breath, she pushed through the doorway, then stopped because Dawson was standing beside Gabe's bed. He looked surprised at seeing her.

"I . . . I thought . . . ," she mumbled.

"Boss asked me to pick up something in town. Stopped here first to see him since it was on the way." His eyes seemed to penetrate her skin. "No change."

She stared at the bed where Gabe lay sedated, stepped closer.

"Your first time to visit?"

He knew it was, so his words were a rebuke. She ignored his barb, told herself she shouldn't have come. But she had. Because now things had changed . . . three-year-old Gabe had smiled at her, sat at her feet when she played and sang. He had called her "Sing Lady," breathed the scent of cereal on her face. Her chin trembled. She raised her gaze to meet Dawson's, squared her chin. "He's bigger now, but he's in a hospital, still has a tube down his throat, he isn't moving, and his eyes are shut tight. So no. Not much difference at all." Her eyes drove into his. "And not one single bit easier now than it was when he was born. It hurts just as bad."

CHAPTER 40

D awson quickly realized that he'd stepped out of bounds. What had happened in the past when Gabe had been born needed to stay there. "Sorry. Sarcasm uncalled for. I know how it hurts to see him like this. But his doctor says the steroids have had plenty of time to work, so he might pull the tube and start waking him up tomorrow."

The news cheered Sloan, and she traced her fingers along Gabe's cheek. His skin felt cool from the room's temperature, but soft as silk. She flipped a thatch of his dark hair from his brow.

"Lani does that too . . . the moving his hair thing."

"I haven't seen her since this happened. Probably no reason for her to come to the house unless Gabe's there." Sloan spoke the words as an observation, not a criticism.

"She comes here every day, soon as her classes are over. And because she works here in the nursing program, she's able to check on Gabe. She sends me regular texts. That way I can work and still know exactly what's going on with him."

"She's a gem."

Dawson gave Sloan a sharp look.

"She loves him." Sloan amended her comment. "He's not just a job to her."

Dawson felt his phone vibrate, reached in his pocket, saw the caller on the display, but didn't answer. "Boss is wondering why I'm taking so long on this errand, so I got to go." He shoved the phone back in his pocket. "But you don't have to go just because I do." He hoped she would remain because he disliked leaving Gabe alone even when the boy was sedated. "You can talk to him too. Lani says that the sense of hearing is ongoing. Coma patients wake up and tell of conversations overheard while they were"—he searched for a word—"out, under, whatever. Maybe Gabe hears our voices and knows we're here."

Sloan nodded. "All right."

He thought of something else. "Did you tell anyone at the nurses' desk that you were coming to his room? Because they want visitors to check in and wear a tag. It's one of the rules, to protect the kids."

She had no tag, of course.

Not wanting her to think she wasn't wanted, he added, "I'll stop at the desk and put you on the approved visitor list."

She watched him go and then returned to staring at Gabe. She touched him again. How beautiful he was. Perfectly formed. Part her, part Dawson, totally himself. Where did she fit in his life?

Lani rushed through the doorway. She was giving up her lunch break to spend the time with Gabe. When she saw Sloan, she halted. "Oh! Excuse me. I . . . I didn't know you—"

"Were coming?" Sloan finished. "Yes, I wanted to see him."

"I . . . I'll come back later."

"You don't have to run off." Sloan faced her. "Tell me again how this happened. From the beginning."

Lani hadn't seen Sloan for days, and facing her now, seeing her cool expression, was unnerving. When she'd rushed into the house days before, she'd been frantic, barely coherent when she told Sloan what had happened. "I . . . I did tell you. Hasn't Dawson explained further?"

Sloan saw no reason to admit she'd been avoiding Dawson at home and had only accidentally run into him minutes before. "I know how careful you are with Gabe, how you watch over him . . . and yet"—she motioned to the bed—"here he is."

Emotions crumbled Lani on the inside. Dawson had forgiven her, but apparently Sloan had not. Lani repeated what had happened at Bellmeade, leaving nothing out, nor offering any self-defense, adding the words, "It was my fault," to the story.

Sloan saw emotions of anger, fear, guilt, panic, tumble across Lani's face as she told the story, each one written in her eyes in large print. Lani didn't know how to slant the story in her favor; Sloan saw that instantly. Some people were born liars. Some weren't. Lani was an anomaly in Sloan's experience. Yet through the telling, the self-blame, recriminations, and guilt, Sloan saw emotions she never expected from Alana Kennedy. *Shame and humiliation.* She recognized the duo because she had worn both all her life like an itchy sweater. She was La-Donna's kid, the trailer-park girl whom other kids shunned. Lani seemed a "golden girl"—smart, capable, efficient, loved by a devoted sister—but this failure with Gabe had rocked her.

"I would give anything if I could go back and change that day." Lani's gaze went to Gabe, as if absorbing the image and the pain it brought would change things. It didn't. She still ached over her failure to protect him.

Ambient noise from the hallway, of food trays clattering on carts, the slow hiss of oxygen being delivered inside the room, the sound of an insect beating its wings on the window outside, filtered slowly into the moment, Sloan on one side of the hospital bed, Lani on the other, the beautiful child between them.

Then Lani heard Sloan say the oddest thing. "I should have never let Jarred walk away that night. I should have stopped him. I should have made him stay with me. Or followed him. Something. The next day when I was in the police tent, all the pieces fell into place, a perfect fit, of what he'd intended to do and why he didn't want me with him. I didn't see it at the time, and hours later, it was too late and he was dead." Lani could only surmise the complete story, but she certainly understood the pain and guilt attached to it. Sloan had allowed Lani a rare glimpse into a closed off part of herself, and Lani realized it was a gift of sorts . . . Sloan's way of offering leniency to Lani about Gabe. Guilt was the common denominator, the thing that put them on equal footing through events that neither could change.

Sloan glanced up, her eyes shimmering with unshed tears. Focusing on Lani, she came back to the present. "Serious mistakes have no do-overs."

"Please stop beating up on yourself, Lani. This could have happened to anyone taking care of Gabe. Even his father." This from Melody when Lani came home that evening. They were in the living room, the gas fireplace logs glowing, and mugs of hot chocolate and a tray of popcorn between them on the coffee table.

"But I'm the one who wants to be a nurse."

"And nurses never make mistakes?"

Lani sighed. After her conversation with Sloan, she was almost to a point of forgiving herself. Almost. "When Gabe's awake, I'll be better."

"How's your horse?"

"Doing good. Jon and Ciana keep me posted, but I haven't gone to check him myself." Lani swirled the few sips left in her cup, studied the muddy liquid. "I'm going to run out to the stables this weekend. Every free minute I have now I want to spend at the hospital."

"Mom and Dad want us to come for Christmas." Melody changed the subject.

The first thought Lani had was *What if Dawson and Gabe need me?* Then she remembered that Dawson was taking Gabe to Chicago, which meant they would be gone for the holidays. And thinking of Gabe out of the hospital and having fun with his dad and granddad lifted her mood. Besides, she missed her parents, so it would be good to see them, even though Kenai, Alaska, in December would be cold, dark, and deep in snow. She grabbed a handful of popcorn.

"If we go to Alaska, we won't have to put up a tree," Melody said.

"What! Not put up a Christmas tree? Of course we'll put up a tree."

Her sister burst out laughing. "I wish you could see your face. You'd think I suggested we drown a puppy."

"I want to bring Gabe here and show off our tree when

he's out of the hospital. We'll put a tree up at his house too. And his Pops will have another for him in Chicago. Sounds perfect." Lani launched the wad of popcorn and it rained down on Mel's head.

Melody ducked, grabbed her own fistful of the popcorn, and tossed it at Lani. In seconds, a popcorn war erupted and the two of them were laughing and dodging the bombardment of white puffy kernels. In no time the bowl was empty, and the room and dark green carpet were spotted with white.

Melody grinned. "It's good to hear you laugh."

Lani quickly sobered. "Felt good too. Thanks for the break." She glanced at the mess.

Mel said, "Tell you what, let's not throw it away. We'll put it into plastic bags and make popcorn and cranberry chains for the Christmas tree you want to decorate."

Lani offered a wistful smile, her mind returning to Gabe. "Can't have too much Christmas when you're three."

Lani came out of her morning classroom and headed for the parking lot in a cold gust of November wind. She reached in her purse for her phone, wanting to turn it off vibrate, and saw that she had a text message from Dawson. Heart thumping, she stopped in the flow of foot traffic, got bumped and barked at by the two guys who'd walked into her. The message read . . .

Doc pulled tube. Gabe awake.

CHAPTER 41

Lani couldn't get to the hospital fast enough. He was sitting up in the bed, still on oxygen through cannulas in his nose. Dawson, sitting in a chair next to the bed, stood and grinned. Gabe, all downcast, brightened, opening his arms as Lani rushed to hug him. "Lani." His voice was hoarse, whisper soft. "Take Gabe home."

She glanced at Dawson. "I've been trying to explain that Dr. Nelson decides when he can leave, not me."

Lani pulled away from Gabe, offered her hundred-watt smile. "Before lunch? We can't leave before lunch. I saw the food cart in the hall and peeked at the food. Macaroni and cheese and green Jell-O. Looks yummy." She knew he liked both dishes.

Gabe glanced to the door. "When?"

"I'll go get it for you." She zipped into the hall to the large service cart, found the shelf and tray with his bed number, and walked it to the nurses' station. "I have the tray for Gabriel Berke. Little guy's really hungry. His dad's with him, and I will be too."

The busy duty nurse nodded, and Lani carried the tray into the room where Dawson had positioned a wheeled service table across Gabe's bed. She lifted the cover while Gabe fumbled with the plastic wrapped spoon. He dug in, but after a couple of swallows, he dropped the spoon onto the plate. "Hurts."

The intubation had left his throat raw and sore. "It'll get better." She wedged herself beside him on the mattress, a hospital no-no, and kissed his temple.

Her tenderness touched Dawson, and he remembered Sloan saying, "She loves him." When Lani glanced at Dawson, he thanked her with his eyes.

She picked up the spoon. "Bet the Jell-O will feel better going down." She offered him a scoop of the wiggly gelatin, but he wouldn't try it.

He laid his head on her shoulder. "Home, please."

"Would you like to watch cartoons?" She picked up the remote and turned on the TV on the wall, toggling to one of his favorite programs. The colorful cartoon images caught Gabe's attention, but after a few minutes, the boy began to search his bed. "I want Woof-Woof. Where Woof-Woof, Daddy?"

"At home, buddy, in your room. I'll bring him later."

Gabe began to cry. "Want him now!"

Again Lani intervened. "I can go get him right now."

Gabe looked a little panicked. "Not go, Lani."

"I or your dad can go right now. Or . . . we can watch cartoons together and bring Woof-Woof later. You choose."

Dawson, impressed by Lani's negotiating skills, hid a smile. He watched Gabe's face, his expressions as he warred over the choices. "Cartoons," he decided. He returned his attention to the television and settled in the bed. Lani smoothed Gabe's hair and Dawson offered her a wink.

She winked back, then settled in to watch the screen, feeling for all the world like one of the family. In her case, a pseudo-member.

After her shift ended, Sloan checked her phone messages while she sat in her car, shivering and waiting for the heater to blow warm air through its vents. Gabe was awake! The text had come around six, not from Dawson, but from Lani, during the busiest time in the restaurant. Sloan checked the dashboard clock. After eleven. Too late to stop at the hospital tonight, but first thing in the morning . . .

She was there at ten a.m., picked up her visitor's pass, went to Gabe's room, and found him sitting up but tethered to the bed by oxygen tubing, his stuffed dog under one arm and the TV remote in his hand. "Hi, Gabe."

He looked at her, broke into a smile. "Hi, Sing Lady." He held up his dog. "Daddy bring Woof-Woof."

Sloan petted the dog's smooth leather snout. "I bet he's missed you, because I know I have." That much was true.

"You take Gabe home?"

His request tugged at her heart. "I can't, Gabe. But I can visit with you for a while."

He pouted. "You sing for Gabe?"

"Um . . . I don't have my guitar." He frowned, and she hastily added, "But I'll bring it next time I come. How's that?"

He turned his attention toward the television, and she

263

watched it with him until Lani showed up just before lunch. Gabe shouted hello, and Sloan rose from the chair, picking up her purse. "Don't go," Lani said.

"Something I have to do at the house, but I'll be back after lunch. I'll leave Big Bird's latest adventures to you and Gabe for now." Sloan waved goodbye and swept from the room.

⁓

She kept her word and returned with her battered guitar case just as the food trays were being cleared. Lani was gone. Gabe clapped when Sloan lifted out the well-worn instrument.

"Sing 'Sunshine'!"

She settled on a chair and strummed the steel strings, was into the song and the creative ways she'd invented to play it when a woman in scrubs and a stern expression marched into the room. "What's going on in here?"

"Just a little music for Gabe."

"Well, the noise is carrying down the hall and other children are supposed to be resting."

Noise! The woman was calling her music noise! Sloan bit back angry words.

"Sing Lady play for Gabe. I like," Gabe announced from the bed.

"It's rest time," the woman snapped, making Gabe cower.

Sloan came out of the chair.

"Hey! What's going on here?" Lani, in her red shirt uniform, jogged into the room, saw the look on Sloan's face.

"This young woman needs to leave. It's rest time."

Sloan looked ready to bash her guitar against the head nurse of the pediatric floor. Lani stepped between them. "Mrs.

Carville, this is Sloan Quentin, Windemere's own singing star. She's famous, has played in Nashville, plus a ton of other cities—she's really well known. She's just popped in to visit Gabe Berke and sing him a few of his favorite songs, on my request. She won't stay long, and it'll mean so much to Gabe."

"The other children are asking questions about the music. They won't settle down."

In a moment of inspiration, Lani said, "Why don't we take the kids who want to listen to her sing to the playroom for an impromptu concert? Fifteen minutes of lovely live music. How can it be a bad thing?"

"No one's authorized—"

"I can run down and get Mrs. Trammell's okay . . . but why bother her with this? Fifteen minutes. This will be a special treat."

By then, several other nurses had come into the room, and they began to voice their enthusiasm for Lani's idea. She saw Carville beginning to soften and asked the others, "It's extra work to bring the kids and take them back to their rooms, but would any of you mind?"

No one did. Mrs. Carville caved. "Fifteen minutes," she said.

The other nurses scurried to gather the "well" kids on the floor, those able to leave their rooms, and to get them into wheelchairs or walk with them pushing their IV poles to the playroom. Lani helped Gabe into a wheelchair, while he chattered and giggled.

"You do know some kid songs, don't you?" Lani asked Sloan out of the side of her mouth.

Sloan sidled her a look. "I've learned a few. But for Gabe! I've never sung for a bunch of kids."

"Sure you have. Just think of them as preshrunk high schoolers." She flashed Sloan a brilliant smile and pushed Gabe to the door.

Shaking her head, Sloan was bemused by Lani's staunch argument for a mini concert, of her calling her famous and a renowned homegirl when she wasn't. It was totally unexpected and had caught Sloan completely off guard. Sloan hugged her guitar to her side and, smiling, followed them down the hall. *A singing gig was a singing gig!*

<hr/>

The fever hit with amazing speed. After the concert, Gabe took a nap, and when he awoke and his vitals were checked, he was spiking a temperature of over a hundred one. When Dawson arrived after work, Gabe had been sedated and intubated again. Dr. Nelson met with Dawson in the hall to say, "Bacterial pneumonia. We've got him on IV antibiotics."

"How long?"

"It's a wait-and-see for right now."

Dawson's heart contracted. The look on the doctor's face, solemn and somber, told him more than any words. Gabe was gravely ill.

He called his father, catching Franklin in his office and between teaching sessions, told him what was happening, heard a long silence. "Talk to me, Dad. Tell me what's going on. Gabe's getting the strongest antibiotics available, but they're not working."

"Germs are more and more antibiotic resistant. Supergerms. Maybe you've heard of MRSA . . . a staph infection that can live almost anyplace, even in hospitals with excellent protocols. Medical science keeps looking for new drugs to fight them, but they're resilient, morphing into new strains in order to survive."

"But we were always so careful with him."

"Don't blame yourself, son. This infection was most likely caused by the original intubation. Ironic, but sometimes the case."

Dawson felt nauseated. "So his previous treatment is what's caused his pneumonia? But . . . but there was no other way!"

"I'm so damn sorry." The heaviness in Franklin's voice left Dawson unable to respond. His dad asked, "Do you want me to come? Because I'll drop everything and catch the next plane. If you want me to."

Somehow having Franklin come right now was like giving up hope. Dawson couldn't do that. Gabe had to recover. He *had* to! "Not yet. What . . . what should I do?"

"Pray the antibiotics work. Tell Gabe Pops loves him. And, son, I love you too."

They disconnected and Dawson stood like a statue listening to the hum of the floor, the opening of elevator doors, the ding of electronic devices, the quiet chatter of families coming to visit their children, the brush of nurses passing by him, the passing of ordinary lives. His was *Life Interrupted*. Dawson sent two text messages and returned to his son's bedside.

CHAPTER 42

Lani was brushing Oro's thick winter coat after a long ride when a message hit her phone. Assuming it was Melody asking when she'd be home for dinner, Lani ignored opening it until her horse was brushed, fed and watered, and tucked into his stall. She wasn't going to rush grooming her horse, especially when so much of her time lately had been absorbed by school, mandatory hospital work, and visiting Gabe every chance she got.

"He's looking good," Ciana said, coming into the stable from the November cold. Her cinnamon-colored hair was pulled back in a ponytail and tucked through the back strap of a ball cap stamped BELLMEADE RIDING & STABLES.

"He's always going to have the marks on his nose. The scar." Lani rubbed Oro's muzzle over the door of the stall where the fangs had penetrated.

"War wounds. He's a true veteran."

Lani smiled at Ciana. "Medal of Honor?"

"Extra oats."

"Thanks for all you did to take care of him."

"No problem. Jon marched the field with the dog off and on for two days, but the snake had crawled away on his reptile belly." She made a face. "The coward."

"Smart snake. Didn't want to face the wrath of Mercer."

Lani said good night and walked the lighted footpath from the back stables to her car, where it was parked on a newly poured bed of concrete beside the old barn. On the far side of the property, the huge new house, a stylized Victorian, glowed from up-lighting in dormant flowerbeds. Lani hustled inside her car, started the engine, and reached for her phone to tell Mel she was on her way. Except that when she pulled up the text, she saw it had come from Dawson. Her heart did a stutter step when she read it. She threw the car into reverse, spun the tires on the tree-lined gravel driveway, and wheeled onto the frontage road, speeding toward the hospital.

Sloan had read the text several times the night before, incredulous over the news. How could Gabe have become so sick so quickly? He'd been squirmy and talkative and giggly after the playroom concert and begging to go home. Now he was back in ICU. Sloan had arrived home very late, but she set her alarm early enough to run into Dawson upstairs.

He was brewing coffee when she came into the kitchen, and one look at him, red-eyed and unshaven, told her he hadn't slept much the night before. "Nothing new to report." He rolled his shoulders, shook out his arms, looking as tight as a compressed spring.

"You spent the night?"

"I couldn't leave him. Just came home to shower and change into fresh clothes."

"I want to see him."

"He looks the same as before he woke up . . . tubes and IVs."

Was this Dawson's way of warning her away? "I don't care."

She sounded defensive, and Dawson knew he wasn't being fair. Sloan had every right to be with Gabe. "I wasn't telling you not to go, just telling you how it is."

"Are you going straight back to the hospital?"

He shook his head. "I'm going in to work because I need to do something physical or go crazy. If something changes, the hospital will let me know and I can get there pretty quick."

"So can I. Don't have to go in to work until four."

"Lani says she'll be in and out of the unit all day too."

When Sloan arrived at the pediatric ICU, Lani was already in the waiting area and didn't look as if she'd slept much either. They acknowledged each other, then ventured into the unit together to stand over Gabe, looking as if he was merely asleep, as if his eyes would blink open and peer up at them. Sloan stared at the ever-present monitor, the squiggle lines and large blue numbers. Déjà vu. "What do the numbers mean?"

Dully Lani followed Sloan's gaze. "Erratic heartbeat, lower than normal blood pressure." She didn't elaborate, couldn't. She'd studied books, listened to lectures, taken written tests and scored high marks on tests, been a hands-on volunteer and an attentive student nurse, but none of it had prepared her for what was happening to Gabe. For what was happening to her watching Gabe struggle to survive.

The terse comment settled in Sloan's stomach like a heavy stone. She didn't ask another question.

—❦—

Gabe did not improve, instead spiraling downward, and forty-eight hours later he was moved into a private room and all restrictions on visitations were removed. His family could come at will, stay as long as they wanted. Nurses routinely checked Gabe, but the atmosphere had changed, gone softer, less frenetic . . . the monitor and respirator kept vigilance, the people were merely attendants. Sloan stayed during the day, and Dawson kept watch by night, folding his tall frame into a sleeping chair, waiting for his son to pass the crisis. Lani stole in and out of the room several times a day like a ghost, never speaking, simply sweeping the room with sad eyes, knowing what no one would yet say—Gabe was dying. Outside the hospital walls, rain came and went, temperatures fell, the sun vanished, but inside Gabe's room, time was in suspended animation.

Sloan told her bosses she had a "family emergency" and didn't know when she'd return to work. One boss told her he couldn't hold her job, that she needed to come in for her shift or quit, and she told him where he could stick the job.

On the morning of the third day of no change and after more testing, Dr. Nelson took Dawson and Sloan aside. Looking directly into Dawson's dark eyes, hollowed out by fear and exhaustion, he said, "You asked me to tell you when you should call your father. I believe it's time."

The words were like nails driven into Dawson's heart. "Not yet—"

"Gabe's put up a hell of a fight, but his kidneys are failing. His heart will too. Nothing left we can do."

Dawson made the call.

⁓

Sloan longed to run away from all that was happening in Gabe's hospital room, as if the very walls, the machines, the personnel, the ticking clock were responsible for leaching his life out of him. She blamed them all. This was a hospital. There were doctors here. They were supposed to fix people, not give up on them! She wanted to walk out the door, save herself from the pain of what was coming. She compared the excruciating wait to an accident she'd once seen on the interstate. Traffic at a standstill, backed up for miles, the slow crawl forward, telling herself to not look, but when her turn came to drive past the wreckage, she had looked, saw the carnage, two cars, their carriages crunched and crumpled like a wad of paper. From one car, with its door ripped away, hung a deflated air bag and a body half in, half out, only partially covered with a bright yellow blanket. She'd recoiled, shaken and angry at herself for looking, knowing that the images were going to be stuck in her brain. For all time. And so would these images of Gabe, his life slipping away like a vapor.

She couldn't leave Gabe, despite the realization that no one needed her to stay. Dawson was an island unto himself. Lani appeared, never made eye contact and never lingered. So Sloan hung on, steeling herself for the oncoming wreckage. And when Dawson told her Franklin was in the lobby of the building and that he was going down to meet him, Sloan knew it was time for her to say goodbye. Beside Gabe's bed, she stroked his arm, touched his soft dark hair, and smoothed his forehead. Leaning closer, she placed her cheek to his, pressed her mouth to his ear. "Something I want you to know, Gabe, something I want to say . . . before you go." Emotion clogged her throat. She fought to swallow and keep her composure. Dawson and Franklin would walk through the doorway any second. "A secret . . . just between us. I'm your mama, Gabe. Me. The lady who sings. And I love you with all my heart."

She straightened, hoping that Lani was right about a patient's sense of hearing, because now Gabe knew the truth, and he could take it with him when he left them all behind.

~♪~

When Lani heard Dr. Berke had arrived, she walked off her shift. Dr. Franklin Berke. Her mentor. A man who had believed in her, who had handpicked her to watch over his only grandchild. Her negligence had started the dominos falling, and she couldn't bear to face him. But she couldn't leave the hospital either. It was like watching a horror movie with a character opening a squeaky door and stepping into a dark room. She knew something scary and frightening waited in the room and wanted to yell, *"Stay away! Don't go inside!"* but like in the movie, the compulsion to sit and wait for the boogeyman to leap out was too strong. She felt immobilized, frozen in place.

Lani chose to remain in the staff locker room, sitting on a bench below her locker, longing for a miracle to save the child upstairs, knowing against long odds how unlikely a miracle would come. She waited, unmoving, through a shift change of personnel coming and going, laughing and sharing stories of their day. The room had no windows but she gauged the time to be after midnight simply by the foot traffic in and out of the room.

A voice from the internal PA system startled her with a Code Blue alert, summoning a crash cart and its team to the fourth floor. Her blood went cold, and she began to shake uncontrollably. She didn't have to be inside that room to know how the action was unfolding, because she'd watched it on a training video. Patient bagged . . . medication into an IV line . . . paddles placed on chest to jolt the heart . . . chest compressions between shocks from the paddles. The team would give the patient probably three rounds of shocks between compressions, a total of maybe twenty minutes, and if there was no response, the attending doctor would call time of death.

What was happening upstairs was no drill. Lani waited on the bench until she heard a few nurses come in, heard them talking about how sad it was to lose a child. Lani stood, turned, opened her locker, and swept its contents into a plastic sack. She removed her credentials from the lanyard around her neck, found a piece of paper, and scrawled a note. She rode an elevator up to the admin offices, now quiet and dimly lit, stopped in front of Mrs. Trammell's office, and stuck the note and credentials into the message box hanging on the wall beside the head nurse's door. She retreated briskly down the hall to the stairwell, pushed open the metal door, pounded downward to the echoes of escape, and ran coatless into the cold night and parking lot dusted by snow flurries, an inner voice chasing her like a banshee: My *fault, my fault . . . my fault.*

PART III

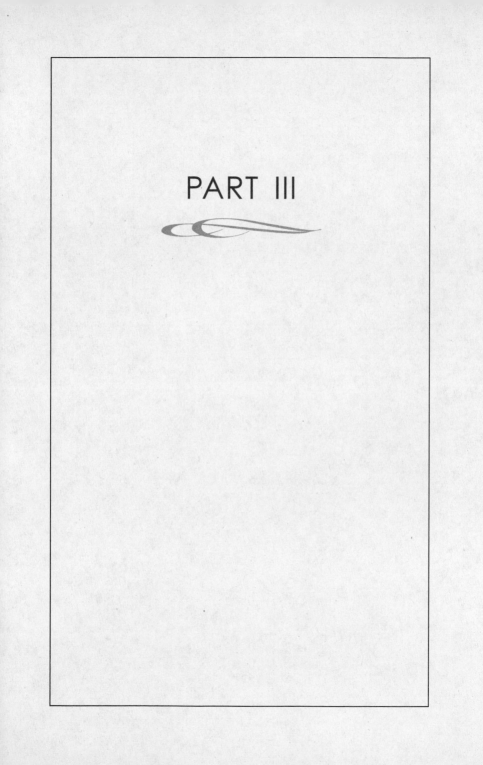

CHAPTER 43

Gabe was buried in the Windemere cemetery under a cold gray sky, the ground blanketed by brown grass and dotted with leafless barren trees. Dawson, hammered by grief, asked Franklin to handle the arrangements, for he'd been a kid when he attended his mother's funeral and the ritual of choosing a child-sized casket, flowers, the order of service wasn't anything Dawson could face. And yet, on that raw November day of the funeral, he realized that not much had changed through the years in this ritual of goodbye. As before, he stood with his father beside a casket and a hole in the ground covered by artificial grass and looked out on a sea of mourners he hardly knew, heard graveside words that he'd never remember.

This time, however, Sloan stood with him, clinging to his hand, sunglasses hiding red-rimmed eyes. He didn't know how to comfort her. How could he, when a chunk of his own heart would be buried with his dark-haired son? During the service, Dawson's gaze swept the mourners. He thought he saw Lani and her sister standing like stragglers on the far back fringes of the group, but when the service was over and he searched for them, they had vanished. He wondered if he'd really seen her at all.

For Sloan, if funerals meant closure, as she'd heard, this funeral failed to bring her such a thing. She didn't know how to let go of a child she'd come to love so late. She should never have returned to the hospital when she'd heard that Gabe had been struck with fever and put back on a ventilator. Yet she did return, and ultimately ended up standing in the room holding her breath, watching chest compressions, until a doctor said, "Calling time of death." So she felt no closure, and clinging to Dawson's hand was all that held her together throughout the service.

Franklin stayed four days after the funeral. On his final night at the house, they sat in the den, a warm fire glowing in the hearth, the woodsy aroma of a pillar candle lingering on the air. Dawson was thinking how normal his dad looked in the old club chair and then how freakishly different things really were. Time never stood still. Except for the dead.

"How you doing, Dad? Your heart." Dawson hadn't asked about Franklin's health for a long time, but after losing Gabe, he couldn't stand it if something happened to his father.

"Heart's good. No worries." After a few beats, Franklin said, "Please come to Chicago for Christmas like we planned."

"Christmas is for kids."

"You're my kid . . . always."

The words unraveled Dawson, and it took all his willpower not to break down.

Franklin cleared his throat. "And it's time you met Connie. She wanted to come with me, but I told her not for a funeral. No place to meet my son for the first time."

Dawson pressed the heels of his palms into his eyes,

considering his dad's request. "Sloan's still living here. I don't think it's right to ask her to leave just now." He didn't know what to do about Sloan. She had returned to her job at the sports bar lounge the day after the funeral, which he understood completely—keeping head and hands busy helped a person make it through the dark places of the soul. "And I need to work too."

Franklin nodded. "I get that. I worked day and night after Kathy died, but sooner or later, the frenzy stops. When you can think about the future, come to Chicago." He glanced at Dawson, cleared his throat again. "I thought I saw Lani, but she scooted away before I could speak to her."

Dawson heard harshness in his dad's voice. "She took Gabe's death hard too. Maybe she wasn't up to talking to us."

"She should take it hard. I trained her to know better than to take an asthmatic child into a barn, for God's sake."

"Dad, she—"

"Don't defend her to me. I'm glad I didn't have to face her at the funeral . . . wouldn't have been able to control my temper. Sorry I ever got you involved with her."

Dawson didn't know how to fend off Franklin's anger, was afraid to say how much Lani had meant to himself and Gabe. He missed her.

Once Franklin flew home, Dawson was adrift, unbearably sad. He slept in spurts, often waking with a start, listening for Gabe on the monitor still in place on Dawson's bedside table. And then he'd remember. He had yet to enter Gabe's room, unable to face the sight of his son's things or the scent of his little boy lost. He awoke one night to the sound of Sloan's guitar coming through the duct work from the basement, just mournful strumming. He listened until the notes stopped, but minutes later, he heard a rustling, sensed a presence by his bed. He turned, saw Sloan outlined by the night-light from the hallway. She was bundled in a thick robe, her arms hugging her body, and she was crying.

Without a word, Dawson lifted the corner of the down comforter, and she crawled in next to him, curling against him. He slid his arms around her, cocooning her, feeling the soft velour of her robe on his bare skin, cradling her while she wept quietly into the pillow. "I loved him, Dawson . . . swear to God. I didn't want to, didn't mean to, but I couldn't help it." Her voice floated on tears.

When they'd met, she had been a broken rebellious girl, him an angry frustrated boy. Now here they were mourning for a love neither had expected to share—for their child. He stroked her hair, whispered, "Gabe was the best parts of both of us. Remember that, Sloan." He held her until her sobs lessened, until he heard the quiet occasional catch of her breath that said she slept. In his arms, beneath the downy warmth of the comforter, they held off the dark together.

⟿

Lani attended Gabe's funeral with her sister to prop her up. She wanted to say goodbye to the child she loved, tell Dr. Berke how sorry she was. Standing at the far back of the mourners, many she knew well from her time at the hospital, feeling the cold wind hit her, and seeing the tableau of Dawson, his father, and Sloan beside Gabe's small blue casket, she changed her mind. She simply couldn't talk to any of them, not when she felt responsible for all that had happened. With her heart breaking, she quickly left with Melody, went home, crawled into bed, and retreated from life.

Three days later, Melody insisted Lani come to the kitchen to talk. Wrapped in an old quilt, Lani dragged herself to the table, where a bowl of soup waited and the old blue teakettle bubbled on the stove. Melody motioned to a chair and Lani dropped into the seat like a rock. The whistling kettle began to scream, and Lani clamped her hands over her ears. "Make it stop, Mel." Her plea went much deeper than silencing the kettle.

Melody lifted the wooden handle and poured boiling water into two mugs with tea bags. She walked them both over, set one in front of Lani, the other on the table at her place. "Lani, I'm worried about you. You've quit the nursing program, dropped out of school, won't take calls from people who are concerned about you. . . . Come on, you can't go on like this."

Lani hunched over, tucked her hands between her knees. "I don't want to be a nurse. That's why I quit. I see now that becoming an RN isn't for me." Gabe's passing made her realize there was no way she could ever separate her head from her heart, nor ever again endure losing a child she cared for and loved. All the light had gone out of her life. And at the funeral, the look of loss and grief on Dawson's face had broken her spirit.

Pity flooded Melody's eyes. "It's all you've ever wanted. Quitting won't change what happened, and it won't bring Gabe back."

Lani winced as the words struck her.

Melody grimaced. "I'm sorry. I don't mean to be so blunt, but I'm worried sick about you. So are Mom and Dad. We can't change what happened, Lani, and if you're still blaming your-self, please stop."

Lani dunked the bag listlessly, remembered Randy's voice through her phone from so far away. "Oh, sweet baby girl, wish we were there to hug you." She'd cried harder. "I guess buying you a horse won't fix it this time, will it?" *No, Daddy, not this time.*

Mel said, "Here's a travel update, Lani. We're not waiting until Christmas . . . we're flying to Alaska tomorrow. Tickets are bought. Mom and Dad will meet us in Anchorage. I'm tak-ing vacation time through Christmas, but you'll stay on for a while." Melody used her attorney voice, no room to quibble.

Lani looked up sharply, started to speak, when it hit her that without her job at Dawson's, without Gabe, without school, without the hospital, what else did she have to do? "Oro—"

"Is taken care of. I've spoken with Ciana, and she says she and Jon will look after your horse."

Lani wrung out her tea bag and plopped it on a napkin, too wounded to argue. Maybe it would be a good thing. Alaska was dark and snowy and wicked cold. Just like she felt inside.

CHAPTER 44

Dawson missed the familiar cadence of life with his son. Gabe's voice, the weight of the child's arms around his neck, his sleepy-eyed look at bedtime, the plea for one more drink of water before lights-out, the piles of abandoned clothes and toys, even his tantrums. Dawson missed every wiggle, every glimpse of the dark hair and blue eyes. How did he move forward from the void Gabe left behind?

And he missed Lani. He missed the way she swept into the kitchen, smiling and laughing, missed seeing Gabe run into her arms, fingers sticky with syrup or with milk running down his chin. She never cared how messy or sticky he came to her, just always kissed and hugged him until he squirmed to be let go. But Lani was MIA. His messages and phone calls to her went unanswered. Where was she? Why hadn't she gotten hold of him? Surely she was hurting too.

He thought he'd seen her at the cemetery, yet now he had doubts. Wishful thinking. Perhaps he'd imagined seeing her because he'd wanted her with him on that terrible day. He was puzzling about Lani's disappearance on the morning he came downstairs to the sight of Sloan's roller suitcase and guitar case standing in the foyer. He found her in the kitchen, making a sandwich. "Road food," she said, wiping the mayo knife across a piece of bread.

"Where are you going?"

"Back to Nashville. I have some money saved now, thanks to you. Nashville's a bigger city. A better job market." Her voice was crisp, her intentions settled.

"You don't have to go if you don't want to." Although he left early and worked all day, and she left before he was home and worked late into the night, just knowing someone else was in the house made coming home easier for him.

Sloan shook her head. "I have to go. Quit my second job last night. Pissed off another boss, but who cares?"

"And you're better than waiting tables and slinging drink orders."

She slipped the sandwich into a bag, zipped it closed. "I don't have many skill sets, Dawson. I do what I'm good at."

"You can sing. Find a band who needs a vocalist."

"Tried that before. A band is complicated, the personalities, the opinions, the in-fighting. It's different when you start on the ground floor, like . . . like we did in middle school." He hadn't been in her life then, so she decided to go no further with her explanation. That life was another hurt she couldn't fix. She jammed the sandwich and an apple into her oversize purse, headed to the foyer, not wanting to linger over goodbye. She'd experienced enough pain over the past months to last a lifetime.

"Wait," he said suddenly. "I want you to have something." He turned and took the stairs two at a time in his work boots, and a minute later, clumped back down. She watched as he opened his hand, calloused from work and chapped from cold weather. In his palm lay a tiny blue and white beaded bracelet. "Take it."

Her heart thumped as she picked up the circlet of beads. The white beads bore black block letters: BERKE BOY. Her gaze flew to Dawson's dark eyes. "This was Gabe's?"

"Yes."

"I . . . I remember a plastic band . . . ?" Emotion filled her voice.

"Hospital issue. This kind of bracelet is special. Dad told me a woman's group in some church makes them for the preemie babies. Sometimes . . . if things don't go right . . . well, it's all the parents have to bring home."

She cupped the thing, so small, in her palm. "And you want me to have it?"

He closed her hand with his. "Yes."

Her chin trembled. She stood still as a statue, looking at his knuckles, scraped and raw around her closed hand holding the almost weightless beads. In a faltering voice, she said, "I . . . I should tell you something. I broke my promise to you. When Gabe was on the machines, when you went down to meet your father in the hospital lobby, when I was alone in the room . . ." She paused. "I told him, Dawson. I told Gabe I was his mother."

A *thick cloak of silence*. Then Dawson lifted her chin, ran his thumb across her bottom lip, and said, "So did I."

She had no words, no way to thank him for his gift of forgiveness. She fisted the bracelet as she grabbed the handle of the suitcase. Dawson picked up her guitar case and opened the front door to a blast of cold air. He walked her to the car and loaded her things while she got in and started the engine. He retreated to the porch, watched her put the car in reverse, and drive out of his life.

—§—

Dawson dreamed. Gabe was riding his trike down the driveway, which appeared endless, murky in a swirling soupy fog. A thick metal chain was looped around the back of the trike, and Gabe was racing headlong into the fog, the chain rattling, bouncing, and scraping on the concrete surface, making a loud clinking noise. Dawson yelled, *Wait, Gabe!* The boy hurtled forward. In desperation, Dawson grabbed the chain in both hands, threw all his weight into stopping the trike and Gabe, but instead skidded stiff legged down the drive, the chain looped in his grasp, ripping the skin on his hands, setting them on fire like a burning rope. He couldn't hold on, and Gabe was being swallowed by the fog. *Gabe! Don't go!*

Dawson woke with a gasp, bolted upright in bed, his hands in tight fists and numb. He righted himself, returned to reality, took slow measured breaths to calm his racing heart. But the sound of rattling chains hadn't evaporated with the nightmare. He got out of bed and crossed to the window, raised the shade. Moonlight splashed across the backyard where he saw Gabe's swing set, the chains jangling in a perverse night wind. He remembered Gabe's birthday, the joy on his son's face when he first saw his very own swing set. Now the thing was an affront, an announcement that no small child would come to them again.

He dressed quickly, warmly, then went down, grabbed his tool chest, and marched through the yard, crunching the frosty grass under his boots. It took a long time to completely

286

take it apart, to dismantle the thing and pile it into stacks of metal and lumber on the cold hard ground. He sweated with the exertion, even as the cold bit into his skin. He couldn't feel his fingers. *Where were his damn work gloves?* He kicked the pile viciously. The beast was gone. No rattling chains in his yard again.

He stretched his back, looking up and through the branches of bare trees to the east, where he saw a pale pastel dawn struggling to scatter the night. To the side, the old house loomed dark, empty. Without Gabe, it was a prison, and Dawson was under lock and key. He couldn't remain in this house filled with memories one minute longer. He picked up his tool chest, went inside, and packed a suitcase.

CHAPTER 45

The drive to Chicago took Dawson ten hours, through weather systems of pelting sleet, spitting snow, and an occasional burst of sunshine. He went because he had no place else to run to. He called Franklin to say he was on the way, and when he arrived, his dad greeted him with a bear hug and led him into the loft he shared with Connie, the woman he loved.

"Nice place," Dawson said after Franklin had stashed the suitcase in the spare bedroom that was also a home office. The loft was in an industrial building from America's manufacturing era and had been refurbished into condos with high ceilings, tubular runs of overhead metal duct work, an inside brick wall, and a spacious interior that included two bedrooms, a kitchen, and a living room. Dawson said he liked the place a second time, so different from the house in Windemere.

"Connie's out making a food run. Weatherman says a storm's coming and she didn't want us to go hungry." He grinned, adding, "She's eager to meet you."

The loft was decorated for the holidays with fresh-cut greenery and fat pillar candles perched on the fireplace mantel and tabletops. A tree wrapped with white twinkle lights and shiny red and gold balls took up a corner. The ornaments looked new, uniform, and generic. A small pile of wrapped and tagged presents were gathered under the tree, a reminder that he'd come without any gifts. Dawson fingered the tree's needles, tried not to think about what was missing—gifts for Gabe. "Looks pretty . . . just different." Their family ornaments were still packed away in the attic of the Windemere house.

"Connie and I decided to make our own statement. She split her old decorations between her girls." Franklin sounded apologetic. "Anything of our old stuff you want to keep . . . or throw out . . . is all right with me."

At the moment Dawson couldn't think of a thing he wanted to keep, and starting over felt like a foreign concept. He walked to one of the sofas. "I know I came up earlier than we planned, so I hope it's all right. I couldn't stay in the house any longer."

"You've been through one of the hardest things life can throw at you, Daw, and I'm glad you wanted to come here. There's no expiration on your visit either. Stay as long as you want."

Dawson saw a film of moisture coat Franklin's eyes and had to turn his head before he too fell apart. In truth, he didn't know what he wanted to do. For now it was day by day, one foot in front of the other.

Minutes later, Franklin offered mugs of freshly brewed coffee and joined his son on the sofa. "Did Sloan leave?"

"No reason for her to stay."

"Things, um, okay between you and her?"

"We made our peace before she left."

"That's good, son." Franklin cleared his throat. "Do you

ever talk to Lani? I wouldn't blame you if you never spoke to her again."

Dawson still heard the edge in his dad's voice and realized he wanted Franklin to stop blaming Lani. "I haven't been able to connect with her. I've sent texts and called, but the calls went straight to voice mail, and she hasn't called or texted back, so, no, I haven't heard from her."

"Probably just as well."

"No, Dad, it isn't. I won't blame her for what happened, and neither should you." Dawson screwed up his courage, plunged ahead. "Let me ask you something . . . in your whole career as a doctor, did you ever make a mistake?" Dawson quickly saw he'd hit a nerve.

For a few minutes, Franklin kept silent, his fingers locked together in his lap. He stared through the floor-to-ceiling windows, finally edged Dawson a look, leaned back into the sofa, shut his eyes, and heaved a sigh. "Point taken. Yes, I've messed up. And to be honest, I don't blame Lani, and I'm sorry I said things to you I should never have said."

"She and I talked it out when Gabe was hospitalized and I thought she understood I didn't blame her either. . . . She *told* me she did. She came out of her funk when Gabe rallied, but when the infection set in and he was reintubated . . . well, she backed away, and now she's nowhere that I can reach her."

Franklin scrubbed his face with his hands, heaving a heartfelt sigh. "From the beginning, I saw she had a special aptitude for nursing and that it would never be just a job to her. It was a *calling*. . . . The work started in her heart, not her head."

Dawson nodded, figuring she had most likely moved into the lives of other kids who needed her care and love. Still, he wished he could talk to her again and make sure she was all right.

Franklin stood. "More coffee?"

Dawson handed Franklin his cup and sat brooding and watching banks of snow-laden clouds gathering in the sky through the loft's massive windows while Franklin headed toward the kitchen.

Just then, the loft's entry door opened from the inside hallway, and a woman balancing bags of groceries came in. Franklin hurried to help her. "Connie! Hey, hon." He relieved her of several sacks, then walked them across the room. "Dawson made it."

She kicked the door shut with her heel, came over, and beamed Dawson a smile. "So happy to meet you, and so glad you came."

Dawson returned her smile, said it was nice to meet her too. She was an attractive woman, small and slim, with stylishly cut brown hair, amber-colored eyes, and a dimple in her chin.

"Hungry?" she asked. "I've brought us a Chicago-style pizza for tonight and salad fixings. You like pizza? My girls love it." He nodded, and she hurried to the kitchen to busy herself with food prep.

Franklin returned with fresh cups of coffee. "You won't starve around here." He grinned, his fondness for Connie shining in his eyes. "And I know she isn't as big as a bug, but she eats like a trucker."

"I heard that!" she called.

Dawson raised his cup in tribute, while his dad went to help Connie, and soon the loft filled with the smell of hot cheesy pizza. He watched them huddle together, hip bumping and whispering to one another, which only magnified his sense of aloneness in the new world without his son.

⚬

Dawson bought gift cards for Connie and his dad from packed stores on Chicago's Magnificent Mile. They opened gifts on Christmas Eve, ate a simple dinner by candlelight, and walked through pristine new-fallen snow to a midnight church service. The wind had ceased and the night had grown quite still, holding a silent beauty that pushed Dawson's memory backward through time, before Gabe, before his mother's death, to when he was a boy and sorrow had not yet found him.

He made it through Christmas Day with beer, chicken wings, and football. Connie's girls called too. Justine was in Germany, where her husband was stationed, and Lily was a junior in college and spending the holiday with her father in Pennsylvania. "She was here for Thanksgiving," Connie explained, but he could see by the look on her face how much she missed both her daughters.

Dawson understood what it felt like to miss someone even in the midst of good company, and between games, he went out onto the condo's small balcony, into the bracing cold. Lani's number was on speed dial, just one button to push, yet when he did, he again was told her mailbox was full, so he knew she hadn't checked it. He said "Merry Christmas" anyway, even with no one to hear him but a crystal-white blanket of snow and a city gone silent.

⚬

Sloan moved into a multiunit apartment complex on the outskirts of Nashville, located just off the interstate and within walking distance from a strip mall with a grocery store, a bank, and a string of small businesses. She had a view of the sprawling blacktop parking lot from her small fourth-floor balcony and of the pool and tennis courts from her bedroom window.

She furnished the one-bedroom space with a bare minimum of functional furniture, bought from Goodwill and Salvation Army, all well used in previous lives. She kept to herself, a simple thing to do in the huge complex where moving trucks came and went frequently. She drove the interstate six nights a week to her job forty-five minutes away in a small bar called Slade's Saloon near Music Row. Foot traffic picked up on weekends to the Old West–themed bar, but mostly the place was frequented by die-hard music buffs who remembered the owners, Tom and Noreen, a country duo from the '80s. Sloan had to look them up on the Internet to hear their music, a country sound tinged with bluegrass. She downloaded two of their top singles to her phone.

She liked the couple as people too. They were kind and friendly and often turned their small stage area over to newbie musicians, giving newcomers the opportunity to sing for an audience. Sloan earned good money serving food and liquor, but when Noreen learned that Sloan could play and sing, she told her to bring her guitar and try out for a Saturday-night spot. "We're always looking for new talent."

"I'm not a soloist. I was with a band."

"Come on. Give it a try."

After Sloan performed in a private audition, Noreen studied her thoughtfully. "You have a great voice. And I can tell you're no beginner. What happened with the band?"

"It just didn't work out."

Noreen asked for no other details; she simply stood and said, "Band's loss. Plan on doing a few numbers next Saturday night. I know talent when I hear it."

On her days off, Sloan wrote music, sad ballads that sent ripples through her heart, still battered and bruised over memories of Gabe. Once, when she went to the grocery store, she bought a box of Cheerios, tore open the inner bag in her kitchen, and buried her nose in the scent of oats with a touch of honey, the fragrance of the breath of the child she'd loved and lost.

When the weather warmed, Sloan attended a street craft fair where she found a girl who made jewelry from wire, glass beads, and feathers. She paid the artisan to restring Gabe's baby bracelet onto stainless steel wire and add new beading to enlarge it and a sturdy safety clasp. The bracelet became the only jewelry she ever wore.

She thought too of Dawson, who was probably one of the best things that had ever happened to her, and her decision to walk away from him. Maybe one day, with enough time between them and what had happened, they'd meet again, and she wouldn't walk away.

Maybe.

CHAPTER 46

Lani remained in Alaska almost four months, fretted over by her worried parents while wrapped in a cocoon of warm blankets and endless nights. Melody returned to Windemere after Christmas but called every few days to chat. Mel had confiscated Lani's cell phone before they'd gone north, insisting that the device would just badger her with calls from well-meaning people drilling questions at her. Lani shuddered with the thought. Escape and regrouping meant leaving everything else behind, including Dawson. Especially Dawson. He was never out of her thoughts.

Lani returned in April. She missed home, and her long rides on Oro, which had helped heal her after Arie died. Perhaps riding would help heal her again.

"Because you missed your *horse*! What about me, Sister of the Year, who didn't rent out your room?" Melody teased as she drove Lani home from the Nashville airport.

"I missed you too!" Lani said with a laugh. "Make any changes in the apartment?"

"Took down the Christmas decorations."

"Progress, I reckon."

Melody reached over and took Lani's hand. "Welcome home."

A day later, Lani drove to Bellmeade, with a bounce in her spirit too long missing. Soldier, Bellmeade's longtime guard dog bounded up to her car, tail wagging. "Still remember me, boy?" She petted his thick white coat.

Ciana, dressed in jeans, a heavy barn coat, and work gloves, came out and greeted her with a hug. "You're home! Welcome back."

"How's Oro?"

"Fine. I ride him twice a week." Regular riding of saddle horses was good for a horse, and exercising others' horses had been one of Lani's jobs when she worked at Bellmeade. "Oro will be glad to see you," Ciana added.

"Thank you. I . . . I appreciate—"

Ciana waved her hand. "No need. You've been in a hard place. I truly understand." Of course Ciana understood. Arie had been Ciana's best friend, and the loss of her had upended Ciana for some time.

"How did you do it? Get over Arie's dying? I . . . I can't . . . Gabe . . . It hurts so much." Lani blinked against a swift rise of tears.

"I never 'got over it.' I miss her still, but good memories of her always sneak in to help me feel better. I still see her as she was in high school, her pretty smile, her love of life. Talking about her, our good times, also helps. Our friend Eden always calls on special days, like Arie's birthday or the day we lost her. No matter where she and Garret are in the world, Eden never forgets. We cry a little, laugh a little, then get on with our lives." Ciana's gaze swept the land, her land. "And sometimes when I ride, I feel like she's watching over me."

The day was bright with sunlight, and after the long nights of Alaska, the world looked fresh and new. *Perspective*, Lani told herself. Life needed perspective. "I owe you feed money for Oro. Let me work it off."

They had been meandering across the lawn. "Your sister paid his bills. You owe me nothing, but if you want your old job again . . ." Ciana stopped. "Wait. I forgot. You're in college."

Lani wasn't yet ready to talk about leaving the nursing program. "Still trying to figure things out, but for now, I'll take the job if you're serious about it. I've missed"—Dawson's image formed in her head, and she shook it away—"everything."

"The job's yours." Ciana's cell phone dinged with an incoming message. She read it and broke out in a smile. "How would you like to come with me and see something amazing happen?"

Lani welcomed the interruption. "What's going on?"

"Follow me."

They jogged down the path leading to the exercise track and the several new stables built since the tornado. Lani saw Jon's truck alongside another, parked next to a small freestanding enclosed unit that housed stalls designed for horse breeding. Nolte, the great black stallion rumored to have been a wedding gift to Ciana and Jon from a man in Italy, stuck his head over a corral fence and whinnied at Ciana. With a laugh, she called to the black stallion, "Your work's done, big guy. We're here for the main event." She quietly led Lani inside the building.

Jon and the vet who had saved Oro from the snakebite were

standing beside a stall, their forearms crossed on the upper railing. Jon turned. "Not much longer now." He acknowledged Lani with a welcoming nod, beckoned them both closer, and stepped aside.

Lani took his place, peeking over the top of the stall. A chestnut mare with a swollen belly. was breathing hard, her sides heaving. Lani caught her breath. "For *real?*"

"Not long now," Ciana said softly next to her.

Lani glanced at the vet. "Is she all right?"

"I'm just here as a precaution because it's her first."

The dark horse in the stall lay down on the fresh straw. Her legs stiffened, and Lani watched, awestruck, as a fully formed foal slid out of the mother's birth canal and onto the straw, wet from the womb and dark as night. The foal lay motionless.

"Breathe," Ciana urged, just as the animal's sides puffed outward and its front legs curved, seeking solid ground.

The foal struggled up onto all fours, wobbling and blinking with the light. His dam rose awkwardly and began to lick him, nudging him with her nose until he turned into her, nuzzling his way to her hindquarters and beginning to nurse. Jon, Ciana, and the vet broke into applause and broad smiles. "From what I can see, I think we have a boy," Jon announced, and lifted Ciana off the ground in a bear hug.

Lani couldn't take her eyes off the suckling foal, his long spindly legs already strong and ready to run had he been born in the wild. Life re-created. "He's beautiful."

"What would you call him?" Ciana asked in her ear. "Your first thought."

"Pure Magic," Lani answered without hesitation.

"Then that will be his name."

As twilight fell, Lani parked across the street from Dawson's house. She sat gazing longingly at wicker furniture never put away in the fall and front windows that should be aglow with lamplight but instead were dark and as blank as closed eyelids. The house was empty, lifeless. She took a shuddering breath. How she had loved the people in that house! Had it only been just over a year since she'd taken the job as Gabe's caregiver? It felt like a lifetime ago.

Lani picked at a rip in the car seat's upholstery. *Where are you, Dawson?* She missed him, but Melody had been right in urging Lani to leave her phone behind . . . so many calls and questions from friends, coworkers, admin at MTSU, human resources at the hospital, Mrs. Trammell, urging Lani to return. But it was Dawson's texts and voice mails that had made her regret the decision. Now that she was home, she wanted to reach out to him, let him know how sorry she was, how much she wanted . . . *what?* she asked herself as a sliver of silvery moon shone through her windshield. What could she give him except a speech about how sorry she was? And what of Sloan? Had they gone off together? Had Gabe brought the two of them together once more? She didn't know and was afraid of finding out.

Lani pressed against her eyes, brimming and burning with unshed tears. *Gone.* All was gone. She shivered, turned on the engine, and edged away from the curb, driving away from her dreams and all she'd once held so dear.

CHAPTER 47

Dawson remained in Chicago long after the holidays. "Not ready to go back," he told Franklin. He didn't think he ever wanted to see Windemere again. "Sorry about crashing on you and Connie. I'll get a job and promise to stay out of your way."

"Not a problem. Stay. We both work and are gone a lot." Franklin was returning to his classroom position and Connie to her job at Chicago's venerated Field Museum. "You'll never be in our way, Daw."

But it was Connie who offered a win-win solution for the three of them. "I own a condo over on Wells Street. My ex bought it for Justine when she attended the Art Institute. The place was big enough for her and roommates, so it more than paid for itself. Now that she's married and overseas, I was about to put it on the market. Why don't you use it until you sort things out in your life? It's fully furnished. You'll just have to pay utilities."

Dawson gratefully accepted and quickly found a job at a gym in the downtown area that he could walk to from the condo, so his car rarely left the parking garage. The gym catered to the young business crowd, city dwellers, many like himself in their twenties. He did grunt work, keeping the men's locker room clean, laundering wads of towels, and manning a small juice bar, where he prepared a menu of smoothies and protein shakes for members, mostly women in spandex after yoga and exercise classes. The women were attractive, fit and flirty, often dropping folded pieces of paper or business cards with their phone numbers into his tip jar. He couldn't say he wasn't tempted, because it had been a long time since he'd been with a woman, but he wasn't a one-night-stand kind of guy, nor was he interested in anything long-term.

A good thing about his gym job was that he had access to the machines, weights, boxing bag, and gloves. He grew a beard, kept it trimmed and neat, but with his dark shaggy hair and dark chocolate-colored eyes, he thought his mirror image reflected the darkness that lay inside of him. In the heart of winter, he took up running again, choosing a path along Lakeshore Drive where the wind whipped off the ice-edged water of Lake Michigan. When he ran, he wore a black ski mask, black gloves, and a couple layers of dark running clothes that wicked sweat off his hard, lean body. He ran in the bitter cold, his lungs on fire, with frost settling around the mouth and nose holes of the ski mask from his breath. He ran regardless of brutal weather—the harsher the better. He ran to forget.

April came, and with it a late snowstorm that laid down six inches of new snow. As soon as the streets and sidewalks were plowed, he went for a run in Grant Park and afterward ducked into a coffee shop. He was sipping hot coffee and staring out the shop's front window when a bus groaned past, a large poster anchored to its side. The sign was advertising a drug rehab center that posed a question:

Are YOU living in the valley of the shadow of death?

The words struck him as if he'd been slammed against a wall. Dawson Berke knew this valley well because it was where he was living every minute of every day since Gabe's funeral. *In the shadow of death.* The image of the brass plate that marked Gabe's grave flashed in his head. Name and dates . . . birth and death. Too brief a time line between the two numbers. And he asked himself, *Who will brush snow off Gabe's marker?* Or autumn leaves, or summer's mown grass? And then an answer: *Gabe's father should.* But Gabe's father had checked out. Gone away. And yet leaving Windemere had not stopped the pain of loss, merely transferred it to another city.

He stepped outside, breathing hard from the emotional body slam. He wanted out of the valley. The wind had stopped; the cold was numbing. He walked across the street to the park, where he eased his cell phone from his pocket. He tapped his photo icon and thumbed through the pictures—Gabe in his arms, swaddled in a blue baby blanket; Gabe at three months, and six months, nine months old. Dawson watched a video of his son at one year old, on his feet, lurching from one piece of furniture to another, babbling and saying "Dada," the first word Gabe ever said.

In every photo, Gabe grew, changed from baby to toddler to child, ever smiling, ever happy. He stopped thumbing the photos when he came to one from Gabe's third birthday party. Lani was holding Gabe, both of them laughing joyously into the camera lens. The image threw sunshine across the shadows of his heart.

He touched Lani's face on the screen with his thumb. Here in the quiet of the new-fallen snow, he thought of the times he'd wanted to hold her, kiss her—and had not. He thought of her day-to-day presence, the way she'd hurry through the doorway, all smiles, her brown eyes dancing. He missed how she covertly looked at him when she thought he didn't notice. He wanted to see her. The want was like an ache, a deep, unremitting need to be with her, and it triggered something in his spirit that whispered, *Home.* Windemere, the place he'd fled, the place he'd once hated. It had given him Sloan, Gabe . . . and Lani. He shoved the phone deep into the pocket of his ski jacket, then turned and began to jog with renewed purpose. Like a car stuck in a rut helplessly spinning its tires, sometimes you had to go backward in order to go forward.

Lani was mucking out stalls when her phone rang. She looked at the display screen and felt as though she'd been shot through the heart. Dawson calling. She answered with "Hello," and hoped her voice wasn't shaking as much as her hand.

"How are you?" His voice, deep and soft.

"I'm just fine." *Liar* . . . "How are you? *Where* are you?"

"At the house. Been in Chicago since December."

She wanted to weep from the simple pleasure of hearing his voice, of knowing he was nearby. "Good to hear from you."

A brief silence, then, "I'm calling to ask a favor."

Anything! "Of course. What can I do?"

"Dad wants to put the house on the market. He's asked me to clear it out . . . get rid of furniture and stuff." Her stomach twisted. He would leave again. "No heavy lifting," he added quickly. "I . . . um . . . I just need your help to clear Gabe's room." Long pause. "And . . . well, I'm not sure I can face it by myself."

She closed her eyes, rocked back on her heels, knowing that the task would hurt like crazy, but she could refuse him nothing. "What time?"

"Maybe two o'clock?"

It was now noon, so she'd have time to go to the apartment and clean up. "I'll be there."

"All right. And thanks, Lani." His voice had fallen to a whisper. He disconnected, and she pressed the phone to her breast, hoping she had the courage to lose Gabe and Dawson all over again.

CHAPTER 48

When Lani parked at the house, Dawson was leaning against the post at the top step of the porch, hands in his pockets. The sight of him caused her breath to catch and her heartbeat to quicken. He looked leaner, broader across his shoulders, and wore a dark well-trimmed beard. His eyes held shadows and sadness. Her heart went out to him.

She came up the steps wanting to throw her arms around him but couldn't because they'd never had that kind of relationship, and at the moment she couldn't recall why she'd ever insisted on keeping a professional distance between them.

He watched her come toward him while sunlight played on her long brown hair. He wanted to put his arms around her, but she had never granted him that privilege, and he thought it best not go there yet. But go there he would. After Gabe's room was behind them. He stepped back. "It's really good to see you again. How have you been?"

"Getting by," she said, and followed him into the kitchen, where cupboard doors stood open, emptied of their contents.

The once bright and cheerful room now looked forlorn. "How long have you been home?"

"A few days. It would have been sooner, but Dad remarried and wanted me as his best man."

"Married! That's wonderful."

The look on Lani's face lit up the kitchen. Dawson grinned. "Connie's pretty special. She has two daughters and one was in Germany, so it took a few weeks to pull it all together, but they did, so I'm just now getting back. I promised Dad I'd clear the house, so that's what I've been doing. The hardest part's upstairs." He shifted his eyes upward.

"What will you do with everything?" She gestured at boxes and once again felt the unbearable weight of Dawson moving away.

"I'm giving most of it to charity, but if there's anything you want . . ." She shook her head and he shrugged. "It's just stuff. Dad doesn't want it, and what do I need with a house full of furniture?"

"Where . . . where will you go?"

"Probably back to Chicago."

So far from Windemere. She struggled to offer a glad-for-you smile and failed.

"What about you, Lani?" He leaned an elbow on the granite countertop. "How have you been here since—" He stopped, then said, "All along?" She knew he meant "since the funeral."

"I went to Mom and Dad's in Alaska, didn't come home for three months."

"I left you messages. You never returned them." His tone was not accusatory, simply curious.

She told him about Melody confiscating her phone before leaving. "By the time I got home and read all my messages, well, so much time had passed. And . . . and I thought Sloan might still be here." That was the bottom line truth for Lani, one of the things she'd think about as she rode Oro, imagining Dawson and Sloan back together. "Is . . . uh . . ." She glanced around. "Where is Sloan?"

"In the wind." He offered no other explanation because he didn't want any part of Sloan standing between himself and Lani.

Her sense of relief was instantaneous.

"I went to the hospital looking for you. They told me you'd quit. Can I ask why?"

She felt her face flush, not wanting to talk about how she'd walked away the night Gabe died. "Let's just say I reconsidered my goal of becoming a nurse. I'm not sure I want that anymore."

"Please tell me you no longer think what happened to Gabe was your fault. He had an infection, Lani. He wasn't strong enough to fight it off. Treatment failed him, not you."

She stood mute, unable to voice the turmoil inside her, feeling that the distance between them was two feet wide and six feet deep. Knowing a truth in her head didn't make it bloom in her heart.

He saw her pain was still raw and unsettled and almost reached out to embrace her, but she had turned away. He quickly added, "For what it's worth, I think you'd make a great nurse, and so does my dad. He calls you a natural-born healer."

The words twisted in her heart. She looked up to the ceiling, not wanting him to see her eyes leaking tears. "Maybe we should get started. You know . . . with the room."

She'd clearly cut him off, so Dawson headed out of the kitchen and up the stairs, dreading what lay ahead. He'd stacked empty boxes in the hall already, so he scooped one up and said over his shoulder, "I'll use this box for special keepsakes. I've already set some of his toys aside for storage." He reached for the doorknob. "Ready?" He opened the door, and they went inside together.

⟋

The room was a time portal into the past, as disheveled and unkempt as it had been on the morning Gabe left with Lani to run errands. The air was stale but imprinted with Gabe's indelible child scent of freshly laundered shirts, jeans, and pajamas. Lani crossed the floor and threw open the window, allowing the cool air to pour inside. She swallowed down her sorrow, falling back on her student volunteer training from the hospital. When patients left the hospital, rooms had to be cleared and cleaned. She swiftly pulled off the bedding, the cartoon-emblazoned comforter and sheets still rumpled and twisted from where Gabe had lain. "I'll toss this in the hall and get it in the wash before I leave."

Dawson stood frozen near the doorway, but watching her sure and practiced moves pushed him deeper into the room. The room was merely a place where a little boy had once lived, one who had moved away without warning. This room, the whole house, was simply real estate that had to be sold. Time to move on. He dragged in boxes from the hall, plopped the biggest box on the floor under a shelf, and, reaching up, swept all the bagged and pristine stuffed animals into it. He folded the flaps. The stuffed animals were props in need of relocation.

"Where's Woof-Woof?" Lani asked.

308

"My room, on the dresser." Where he saw it every morning and night. He would put it into his special keepsake box later.

Lani found a black marker and wrote *stuffed animals* on the box. "I'll make sure this gets delivered to the peds ward, where they'll be loved on." Lani was moving on automatic now, diverting her ragged emotions into work energy.

They worked swiftly, Dawson going through the basket that held Gabe's art supplies, boxes of broken crayons, coloring books, papers, and glitter. He saved a short stack of Gabe's drawings in the box he'd set aside on the bedside table. Lani emptied dresser drawers and packed up the closet, holding out a few pieces for Dawson to consider keeping. Dawson stripped the walls of Spider-Man posters and a giant calendar where, before he was hospitalized, they'd begun to X out the days until Christmas. The room came apart, the boxes filled, the past butted into the present.

Once the room was stripped, Dawson got down on his knees, looked under the bed, and removed a rainbow-colored hardened lump of something. Standing, he asked, "What's this?"

Lani took the lump from his hand and turned the smeary colored mass over in her palm, held it up to the light, where it shimmered. Tears filled her eyes, but she also smiled. "Gummy bears, all melted together. He could have put them there and forgotten about them. Or maybe he thought they had turned into a jewel."

She and Dawson were on the same memory page—the day they'd taken Franklin to the airport to catch his Chicago flight. A good day. An *almost* day between the two of them.

He should have kissed her when he'd had the chance.

She should have gone into his arms when she'd wanted to so very much.

His voice husky, Dawson said, "I guess it was a special treasure to a three-year-old."

Lani handed the lump back to him and he laid it in the keepsake box because he didn't have the heart to throw it away.

Dawson lined the walls with the labeled boxes, tucking the one he planned to keep under his arm. The room had become an empty shell, a bird's egg cracked open, its fledgling flown. "It's done. Let's go."

He shut the window and Lani followed him down the stairs.

CHAPTER 49

Helping him clear the room had helped soothe the rawness of the pain Lani had been living with for the last five months. Closure. She'd heard the term used many times while on the job and in her classes, but now she knew what it felt like. The pain, so sharp before they began dismantling Gabe's room, had been dulled by tender memories and by touching everything the boy had owned. She'd seen his sweet face in every item of clothing, in every little toy his hands had held. She had loved him. That feeling would never go away. "He was a special little boy."

Dawson stood quietly staring out the kitchen window, his hands braced on the edge of the sink. Twilight was falling, and he heard every creak and groan of the old house. The afternoon had been painful but cathartic, cleansing him in ways that his running and gym work had not been able to do. Loving Gabe, losing Gabe. The highest highs and the lowest lows of the human heart. Dawson had known both in the few short years he'd had his son.

There was nothing left now except to move forward. To Lani, he said, "Thanks for helping me."

"Thanks for asking me."

He turned, saw her eyes shimmering in the dim light. She was draping a scarf around her neck, stepping to the door. He didn't want her to go. "How about some dinner? You have to be hungry. I am."

Her heart kicked up its pace. She didn't want to leave, wanted to stretch out every second she could with him. "Starving!"

"Pizza okay?"

She'd have eaten garden weeds if he'd offered. "I *love* pizza."

She flashed that smile that always lit up her face, and he smiled too. "I can have Pizza Shak deliver one."

"The best in Windemere." Another smile.

He grabbed his cell phone. "I know they're still in my contacts. Hold on." Concentrating on the screen, he thumbed through the list. "It's here somewhere . . . ah! Yes, I've got it." He poised his thumb over the number. "What do you want?"

The question stopped her cold, and she instantly saw two futures. A sharing of dinner, a few "wish-you-wells," her walking out the door. And he would move to Chicago without ever knowing how she felt . . . when what she wanted most was standing directly in front of her now. But to tell him so was a huge risk. Perhaps, as he'd told her earlier, he *had* forgiven her. But that didn't mean he could ever love her. Keeping her distance was the safe thing to do. Her heart thudded and her mouth went cotton dry as she trembled for seconds on the edge of indecision. And then she took a deep breath and spoke the one word that was in her head, the words too long lodged in her heart. She said, "You. I want you."

His gaze flew to hers, his dark eyes as piercing as arrows. She saw him drop his phone with a clatter onto the counter and cross the space between them in two long strides. And then she was in his arms, and his mouth was on hers, and she fell into him.

He broke the kiss, cupped her face between his hands, searched her warm brown eyes, and knew without reservation that he loved this girl. The kitchen had darkened with night shadows that softened all the edges. He scooped her up in his arms, cradling her against himself. She clung to him, and he walked with her into the den, a space not yet torn apart and put into boxes, and settled her on the sofa. He sat beside her, took her in his arms. "I've wanted to kiss you for a long, long time," he said, nuzzling her neck.

"And me, you." But for her, although he didn't know, the wait had been much longer. She drew back, rubbed his cheek, found his beard surprisingly soft, and flashed a mischievous smile. "It tickles."

"I'll shave it."

"Don't you dare."

He traced his thumb over her lips, still warm from his mouth. "So can we keep on kissing?"

She answered with another kiss, one that rose from deep inside her heart. And for now it was enough.

—⁂—

Sloan stomped into her apartment and flung her keys across the room so hard that the fob gouged the dry wall. Her car was certifiably DOA in the parking lot. Without it, she had no way to get to Slade's for work, and because it was Saturday night the place would be packed. She'd be missing her singing gig too. Over the months of Sloan's time onstage at Slade's, she'd earned a small following, an audience who said they came just to hear her. The group had helped her feel better about herself, but lately the old hunger, the old dreams to *become* someone had begun to haunt her.

Sloan paced the floor like a caged cat. If she called Noreen, Tom would be sent to pick her up. But a ride for one night wasn't going to solve Sloan's car problem. The mechanic who'd last serviced the old Mustang had told her it would cost more to fix it than it was worth. She'd said she couldn't afford another car, and he'd shaken his head and said, "Then think about selling it for parts."

So tonight, with a light November rain falling outside and her car ready for the junkyard, she was stranded. Sloan heaved herself onto the sofa, plucking at her bracelet, her talisman. Sure, she had a job, but in spite of a paycheck and good tips, what with rent, the car's upkeep, and monthly expenses, she had been unable to save much money. Her rent, due on Monday, had gone up by fifty dollars in July. She groaned, feeling as if fate were sucking her dry.

She remembered something that had happened just weeks before after the bar closed. She was cleaning tables while Noreen washed bar glasses and Tom swept floors, with the TV above the bar tuned to late-night news. Noreen said, "Hey, Sloan, listen to this." Sloan looked to the bright screen and saw a line of people and a perky blond reporter beaming into the camera. The smiling woman was saying, ". . . here in Atlanta, for *American Voice* tryouts, all hoping to audition and be selected for the star-maker show. Some hopefuls travel city to city chasing the dream. Last chance to wow the judges will be in L.A. in January."

Noreen had said, "I've seen some of those audition videos, and believe me, you'd be a shoo-in."

Now sitting in the semidarkness of her apartment, the memory surfaced, along with words from an old song from the sixties: *"I'd be safe and warm if I was in L.A. California dreaming on such a winter's day."*

Sloan sat upright. *L.A. Safe and warm. A shot at the brass ring.* In the year since Gabe's death, Sloan Quentin, the girl who'd once dreamed of being a star, had gone nowhere. She was restless, at loose ends, a runner with no finish line. *January.* Two months and a thousand miles to Los Angeles.

She stood, slowly looked around the room, at tired furniture and empty walls, and in that moment, Sloan Quentin knew exactly what she was going to do.

Sloan turned down three rides before she accepted one in the cab of a big rig with a woman driver. She climbed in and tossed her bag behind the seat, but kept her guitar case up front wedged between the passenger seat and the door.

"Mean night," the driver said. "Car break down?"

"Something like that."

The woman offered a toothy grin. "I don't usually pick up hitchers, but you looked pretty wet and it's late. Not good for a young woman on the side of the freeway on a night like this. Name's Rose Ann, but my friends call me Punky."

"I'm Sloan." She shook off her rain jacket and ran her

fingers through her hair, thoroughly damp despite the jacket's hood and a head scarf.

"Where you headed?"

"Los Angeles."

Punky gave a low whistle. "A far piece."

"I have some time to get there." Sloan had first walked to an ATM in the strip mall and cashed out her bank account, figuring that hitching was the cheapest way to get to L.A. She'd need every penny she had for living expenses once she was there. But if she won a spot on the show . . .

"I can get you to Oklahoma City; then I head north to Bismarck."

"Farther west than Nashville, so I'll take it." Sloan wasn't in the mood to talk and hoped the driver wasn't either. She leaned against the window glass, drying off in the heated air blowing from a vent, and watched the wipers slap rain from the windshield. The falling water sparkled like jewels with every pass of headlights from the eastbound traffic on the interstate. She was restless, scared, didn't want to dwell on the chance she was taking, leaving the settled world in the rearview mirror for the unknown. She plucked at her bracelet.

"You play that thing?" Punky gestured at the guitar case.

"I play."

Punky's face broke into a grin. "Long ride in front of us."

Sloan caught the hint. She snapped open the case and withdrew the battered guitar. The cab was cramped but she twisted to the side and held her instrument across her lap. Sloan strummed and a song long buried bubbled up and made her smile. She sang, *"You are my sunshine, my only sunshine . . . you make me happy when skies are gray . . ."* With each rendition in every musical genre, she saw Gabe's sweet face. And with it came an infusion of hope. She was the Sing Lady, and he was her heart.

When Sloan finished and rested her guitar, Punky whooped. "Wow, that was fine! You're gonna make this trip a whole lot shorter singing like that."

Sloan nodded, warmed by the praise from this perfect stranger. Maybe she had a chance in L.A. after all.

"So, tell me your name again. Just want to be able to tell people I gave you a lift when I hear you on the radio someday."

The sentiment made Sloan smile. "It's Sloan Quen—" She stopped as a truth struck her. She didn't have to be Sloan Quentin anymore. She could be anyone she wanted to be. Anyone. She touched her bracelet, cleared her throat. "My name's Sloan Gabriel."

Punky slid her a glance. "You mean like the angel?"

"Yes," Sloan said. "Like the angel."

ACKNOWLEDGMENTS

I am grateful to fellow writer Mark Parsons and his dear wife, Wendelin Van Draanen, for valuable input about the music business. Thanks, y'all! A big thank-you to Dr. Lee Perry of Chattanooga Allergy Clinic for his expertise about asthma and for answering my hundreds of questions during the writing of this book. Thanks, Doc! Also, I appreciate my personal trainer, Chris Marler, for his input. And a special thank you to Daniel Pippin, RN, for sharing his knowledge about the nursing profession.

ABOUT THE AUTHOR

LURLENE McDANIEL began writing inspirational novels about teenagers facing life-altering situations when her son was diagnosed with juvenile diabetes. "I saw firsthand how chronic illness affects every aspect of a person's life," she has said. "I want kids to know that while people don't get to choose what life gives to them, they do get to choose how they respond."

Lurlene McDaniel's novels are hard-hitting and realistic, but also leave readers with inspiration and hope. Her best-selling books have received acclaim from readers, teachers, parents, and reviewers.

Lurlene McDaniel lives in Chattanooga, Tennessee. Visit her online at LurleneMcDaniel.com and on Facebook, and follow @Lurlene_McD on Twitter.

Forever friendship and true love from

Lurlene McDaniel

*Discover how lives change
in heartbreaking, realistic fiction
that is sure to inspire.*

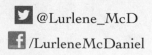

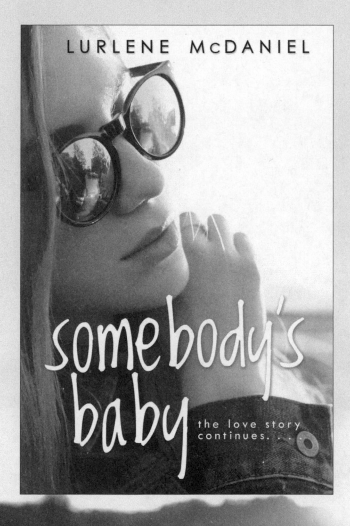